SCIENTIST IN THE DARK

a novel

KEVIN THOMAS MORGAN

Recently walking a trail, one I'd been running for over thirty years, I was surprised to see a member of my favorite plant division, the *bryophytes*. A healthy liverwort, the first I'd spotted here in three decades. It presented on the edge of the trail as a bright green display of *thalli*, the primitive leaves of these ancient plants. The liverworts preceded humans on Spaceship Earth by many millions of years. Crystal clear water was cascading over this ancient relic of the past. The spores had been sitting and waiting for damper times.

The climate is a'changing, coming ready or not!

Ecocide

Destruction of the natural environment by deliberate or negligent human action.

– Oxford Languages

INTRODUCTION

1962 - Rachel Carson published *Silent Spring*.

1969 - Cuyahoga River caught fire for the last time.

1970 - EPA created to protect our environment.

1972 - United States banned the use of DDT.

2017 - New President installed in the White House.

CHAPTER ONE

May 1st, 2017

The Global Ecosystem Protection Institute, GEPI, affectionately known as *Geppy*, was located on a quiet wooded lot, in the Greensboro Science Park, Greensboro, North Carolina. Dr. Jeb Newton, known to his friends as Fig, was just returning to the institute from a contemplative walk along one of the many trails provided in the park. He was wondering how to improve his mathematical model, EcoWorld, which predicted the effects of trophic cascades, or disruption, of the vast network of integrated food chains that span the surface of the planet.

Along with thirty other scientists, and nearly two hundred support staff, Fig had been working happily and successfully at GEPI for almost thirteen years. His research was designed to protect the Biosphere, that is all life on Earth, from the destructive effects of human activity.

On entering the building, on that fateful day, Fig found the place deserted. Even the front desk was abandoned. He then recalled that the newly appointed director, a Dr. Strickland, had scheduled an all staff meeting that morning, for nine o'clock, prompt. "Doesn't he know that working with scientists is like herding cats?" thought Fig. "And did prompt have be in bold?"

Fig headed for the main conference room in which the staff were packed with standing room only. In contrast to Strickland, Fig was a handsome guy in his early fifties, about five eleven, with wavy auburn hair and an open smile, rarely a frown, and what people would describe as a pleasant manner. Fig opened the door, to be met by a buzz of nervous anticipation from the packed crowd. He smiled at the new director, who was on a small stage at the front of the room. On Fig's entrance, Strickland said, "So glad you could find the time to honor us with your presence, Dr. Newton."

"The pleasure is all mine, Dr. Strickland," said Fig, creating a tittering laughter from his scientific colleagues, and a scowl from the new director. Fig found himself a place to stand at the back of the room, where he could watch the show.

Strickland was short with a bald head, in his sixties and reasonably fit. Fig noticed that he never stood still. Strickland was constantly pacing around in his expensive suit and shiny black shoes. He sure didn't look like any kind of scientist to Fig. The new GEPI Fuhrer went on to explain, in no uncertain terms, that it was time they stopped playing around and did some useful work for their sponsors.

Fig thought, "Doesn't he know there's an administrative firewall to protect our research programs from interference by the institute's sponsors?"

After a fifteen-minute harangue, laced with insults, Strickland proceeded to attack the work of six senior scientists by name, one by one. A clear threat was delivered in each case. Strickland had done his homework. The room became silent, as the staff realized that GEPI was about to change, and maybe not in a good way. The atmosphere in the room was so tense you could have cut it with a knife. Five of the six targeted senior staff, all excellent scientists, were gone within a few months. They left of their own volition as they were highly sought after environmental researchers who, in their words, "had no interest in working for a narcissistic jerk."

The sixth targeted staff member was Fig. Strickland made clear his dislike of Fig's work in network mathematics. This research was successfully revealing the clear dangers of many current industrial activities, when it came to the safety of animal and plant populations across the globe. Fig also received a subtle personal rebuke from this overbearing harbinger of change. Strickland made an oblique statement about Fig's "inadequate training in mathematics," whose degrees were in medicine and biomedical engineering.

Fig loved the institute and the remarkable vision of

the founders back in the 1980s. It was almost a second home to Fig. The research and training done there was the obvious solution to many long-term environmental challenges created by American corporations. Fig was well aware that industrial environmental safety regulation was a balancing act. Unnecessarily over-strict regulation caused US businesses to lose out to foreign competition, eliminating much-needed jobs. Under-regulation led to people or the environment being avoidably harmed. It required a careful benefit risk calculation, a matter often swept under the rug in deference to profits, and increasingly so in response to the edicts of the most recent occupant of the White House, President John D. Miller.

At the end of Strickland's rant, the staff wandered away in stunned silence. Strickland pulled Fig aside, saying, "I would like to meet with you in my office in fifteen minutes, Dr. Newton." Fig looked down on the guy's angry bald head, and said, "Sure thing, boss!" This meeting turned out to be nothing more than repetition of Strickland's displeasure concerning network mathematics, to which Fig said little as he didn't give a damn what the guy said. "This guy doesn't understand what my research is about," thought Fig.

Fig had developed an approach to the prediction of adverse environmental effects of industrial activity on a global scale, with special reference to chemical pollution. His method exploited the dynamics of interactions between large arrays of intersecting food chains, where a bad thing in one food chain can unbalance many food chains all over the planet, resulting in damage to entire populations of organisms, even leading to their extinction. Fig saw the Biosphere as a huge, integrated network.

Strickland's arrival at GEPI was followed by a series of senior staff resignations, and their replacement by third rate scientists loyal to both Strickland and President Miller. Fig would torment them from time to time by dropping a word or two about his admiration for his heroine, Rachel Louise Carson, the author of that prescient book, *Silent Spring*. Otherwise, he got on with his work.

CHAPTER TWO

From the arrival of Strickland, Fig was in a constant running battle with the guy. At every turn the new director attempted to interfere with Fig's work. Fig's defense was his reputation and intelligence. He could outfox the fox and did so regularly, but it was wearing on his nerves.

Fig continued to train students, and publish scientific articles on ecological damage done by industrial chemicals. Some of these articles Strickland endeavored to block, without success. Fig was well known as a scientist and as an effective reviewer of scientific articles in peer reviewed journals. He was also well known in climate change circles, even though that wasn't the main focus of his work. If his research was attacked publicly by Strickland this would be noticed. Being noticed was not part of Strickland's plan, but Fig had become a thorn in the flesh of more powerful people than Strickland.

As Rachel Carson laid out in *Silent Spring* industrial chemicals were everywhere, even in people's bodies. Many would remain in their bodies for their lifetime. The Biosphere, all life on the planet, is like a skin on the surface of the globe. It extends down from a population of bacteria floating high in the atmosphere, to some strange creatures living several kilometers deep in the oceans, and equally bizarre creatures living on the rocks on the surface. However, the Biosphere is a delicate paper thin membrane when compared to the mass of the planet.

In the same way that Rachel Carson had described an imaginary town in the heart of America, that went to hell because of DDT, Fig built an imaginary planet Earth, in the form of a mathematical model, EcoWorld. In the mathematics, Fig included energy from the sun, air including carbon dioxide levels, sea and fresh water, soil, rocks, plants, animals including insects, bacteria, fungi, viruses and archaea. He incorporated anything he was able to, mathematically, that would further his ability to predict ecological degradation. There was one critical biological variable not included in EcoWorld, the psychological motivation of humans. When asked about this, Fig said, "I never was that interested in primatology."

Most scientists thought Fig was wasting his time. "It can't be done," they would say with a sneer, "the world is too complicated to model mathematically." Fig would reply with the famous quote by British Statistician,

George E. P. Box, *all models are wrong, but some are useful*, adding, "I'm finding this one to be useful."

The output of Fig's model wasn't in the form of pictures of plants, with images of little animals running around. The output of EcoWorld was a massive dynamic spreadsheet of numbers and graphs. If Fig's model predicted a potential ecological disaster, he would collaborate with other scientists to venture out into the real world to find the evidence. He rarely failed to detect developing ecological nightmares. Naturally, many American industries were not so keen to have these events widely advertised.

Fig became public enemy number one in the minds of some powerful people.

CHAPTER THREE

Saturday, February 24th, 2018

The first sign of the institute's impending demise was elimination of the firewall between GEPI's basic research functions, and the short-term business and political interests of the sponsors. Fig had noticed increasing pressure by GEPI's management to downplay research findings that were unappreciated by the member companies.

One Saturday afternoon, Fig was working on his newest toy in the lab, an oscillating sphere micro-rheometer, when his office phone rang.

"Dr. Newton?"

"Yep!"

"Hi Fig, it's Jeff Nelson of Direct Chemical. How are you doing?"

Jeff was the head of product safety for one of the

largest financial contributors to the institute. He was a company man if ever there was one. He'd crossed swords with Fig several times in a fairly amicable way. Fig liked Jeff, but the guy was always looking for an angle that would make his bosses happy, rather than wanting to fully understand the science. That was Fig's only beef with Jeff.

"Fine," Fig replied, with suspicion evident in his voice, thinking to himself, "those business guys never call me anymore. They used to but now they go through Strickland. What the hell is this all about?"

"It's about that recent paper you published, concerning one of our commodity chemicals, chlorine. We would like you to write a paragraph for the US Chemical Safety Board, explaining how your findings in rats have no relevance to human health. It's obviously just a rat problem, wouldn't you agree?"

Fig said, "That's absolutely not the case, Jeff. As you well know we all use rats as surrogates for humans. Our observation is directly related to accidental chlorine exposure and the risk of developing asthma. Since that paper was published, I've received several letters from concerned parents."

There was spluttering on the end of the phone line and someone said, "There's no such thing as chlorine-induced asthma. What are you talking about, imaginary problems?"

Fig realized that other people were listening in. He asked what was going on and Jeff informed him that he'd invited three other people with an interest in Fig's work.

It was a prearranged conference call. Fig hadn't noticed the clicks as the others signed in. He was mentally still engrossed in his lab work, when he'd picked up the phone, and Jeff had arranged the conference call without asking for Fig's approval.

It was a set-up.

Fig asked to be introduced to the others and to know their affiliations. It turned out they weren't just any three other people. Two were also heads of product safety for two huge corporations, sponsors of the institute and extensive users of chlorine. The fourth person was introduced as Daryl Pickering, "One of my scientific advisors," said Jeff.

Fig said he had no intention of exonerating the risks of chlorine with respect to its potential to induce or exacerbate asthma attacks. Then Daryl said, with menace in his voice, "You do understand that these people pay your salary, Dr. Newton?"

Sure he knew, but Fig's Mum had drummed into his thick skull, "To thine own self be true," and "You can fight City Hall." These guys were much bigger than City Hall, representing as they did a significant share of the world's commodity chemical market to the tune of many billions of dollars.

Fig said, "Could you please explain the logical link between the source of my paycheck and the relevance of our research findings in rats to human health?"

They had a problem. Fig wasn't about to be bullied

into downplaying his data. After an extended silence and a muttered conversation on the other end of the phone line, Jeff said, "We'll be back in touch, Dr. Newton. Thanks for your time."

Click! Click! Click!

They'd threatened his job, his paycheck. A phone-call out of the blue that turned out to have been a prearranged conference call. Only one invitee was left in the dark, Fig. The heads of chemical safety for three of their largest sponsors, plus Jeff's scientific consultant, Daryl Pickering. "Who the hell was that guy?"

Fig's mind was racing, "No way I'm going to be blackmailed into downgrading the importance of our data to protect some damn company that only cares about shareholders' quarterly profits, whether they pay my not too generous salary or not. He ran his fingers through his mop of hair, went to the lab to power down his equipment, and returned to his office to finish a tedious job he'd been putting off for a while. Editing the galleys of a recent publication. "That phone call was clearly a setup. A direct request to downplay our data. Surely a better approach would be to work out what it really means and run a benefit risk assessment to address safety concerns accordingly."

Fig realized that the problem really lay in the urgent nature of business competition *versus* the plodding pace of basic research. Fig was surprised that this institute even existed. He knew it was a great idea, created by forward-looking scientists and businesspeople, but one that would discover human and environmental safety problems for big corporations.

While Fig was contemplating these things and considering returning to his crappy apartment, that phone call from Jeff Nelson about chlorine and the risk of asthma wasn't forgotten in the halls of power. Fig's refusal to comply, and his rejection of spreading a convenient lie, was noted.

These were challenging times in Fig's life, but science was what he did. It was his anchor, his port in the storm of his private life. He wasn't interested in fame or fortune! He just loved learning about living things. How they thrived and why they suffered. The study of chemical poisons that explained many of the mysteries of the chemistry of life had become Fig's passion, that and the power of trophic cascades, or ecological imbalances in food chains, to negatively influence life on Earth, even leading to species extinctions.

Fig had succeeded in multiple areas of science, finally ending up in applied mathematics, for which he thanked his lucky stars. Not that he considered there to be such a thing as luck, as he thought everything probably has a cause, in the past or the future. Yes, the future! Fig recently discovered that there had been a cover up by the physics community, to remove any suggestion of time moving backwards, the predicted effects of which were known as retro-causality.

"This could explain many of the secrets of life itself," thought Fig, which led him to the question, "When it comes to time, where the hell is now?"

In this particular now Fig's job was threatened. He had just put his finances back on track and his retirement savings were growing. His sons were finally out of college and into promising careers, and his ex-wife had a new boyfriend and appeared to be happy. He didn't need advanced math or a supercomputer to calculate the impact of losing his paycheck. But he had some savings, and he could always find another job, if things went south at the institute.

Even though it was getting late, Fig finished reviewing those galleys, a pre-print of an article before it finally goes to press. Pre-prints are provided by the publishers so authors can spot any lingering errors, and there always are errors lingering. Now Fig had to face going home to that stinky apartment, and it was probably dark outside.

He was about to turn off the light when his office phone rang, again.

CHAPTER FOUR

Homeland Security, St. Elizabeth's Campus, Washington, DC.

Fred Sassy, an almost bald and often nervously sweating, overweight, fifty-five-year-old mid-level administrator, in somewhat rumpled clothes, with a fine dusting of dandruff on the shoulders of his frayed jacket, was to be seen five days a week from 8:30 a.m. to 5:00 p.m., exactly, sitting at an old steel desk reclaimed from storage, where he waded through mounds of paperwork. His nondescript office was deep in the bowels of the forbidding red brick building of the Department of Homeland Security on the St. Elizabeth's Campus, 2703 Martin Luther Jr Ave SE, Washington, DC. To Fred it looked like a prison as he headed into the building each day.

Fred was low on all and any totem poles in this extremely political organization. Since President Miller arrived in the White House it seemed to be more about politics than anything else. Fred dealt with travel claims and had done so for many years. This work exposed him to all sorts of nefarious activities, if you read between the lines. Fred was known for discretion and commitment to his job, the government equivalent of a company man.

At 4:45 p.m., Fred was getting ready to close shop and walk to the Metro for his daily commute home. He had lived with five cats and half a bottle of wine each night, since his childless and largely joyless marriage went on the rocks several years previously. He liked it that way. Fred was accepting of his lot, but to deal with the loneliness he had a growing alcohol addiction.

There was a quiet knock on the door and who should walk in but Dr. James Turner. Always well turned out, Fred noticed, Turner was sporting an expensive tailored suit and tasseled loafers. "His government salary seems to be treating him well, suspiciously well," thought Fred.

Turner had recruited Fred to help him with his current project, containing a chronic irritant to the new president. He'd told Fred that he was creating a team of experts, like Fred, to stop "those tree-hugging enviro-pansies." Fred thought this a little extreme, but he liked the rare compliment, and accepted the job.

Turner said the work was of a covert nature, which made Fred a little nervous.

Turner had encountered Fred by chance, while looking for staff to build a database, for which an accountant would fit the bill perfectly. He approached Fred's boss, who said, "Sure you can use Fred for a few months, as our workload is low right now." Turner thought, "This is the perfect fall guy should things go south." He was well aware of the illegal nature of his current task. Why take any risks when underlings like Fred will see a golden opportunity. More likely an opportunity to end up in jail, not that Turner gave a damn.

Fred was quite familiar with secrecy because travel claims have been known to bring down powerful people. Even a few illegal phone calls to private lines on government phones can do that, if the person has attracted the right enemies. Fred had even fudged a few himself, with an extra meal or bottle of wine here and there during work trips.

Fred had been working on Turner's project for several months, compiling names and other public information on "tree-huggers." Fred was surprised to find out how many there were, when he first searched through publications on PubMed, institutional websites, newspapers and blogs.

Turner said, "Mr. Sassy, or may I call you Fred?"

"Of course, Fred, and I've enjoyed doing your work. It's made a nice change from travel claims, not that I'm complaining about that." He was a little scared of Turner, though he didn't know why. Unlike Fred, Turner wasn't even a Homeland Security employee.

"I've expanded our small team to exploit all the data you've collected," said Turner, "and as I said before, this work must be carried out in the utmost secrecy, which is why I chose you. Your boss told me that you are discreet, and you have shown nothing but discretion during your work with us. I would now like you to officially join our team. It could mean a small raise and some other benefits, if I can pull it off. No guarantees, but I promise to try. Are you game to join us? The president and I sure would appreciate it."

"Of course, sir"

"Just call me James. Not Jim, mind you, I hate that."

Fred was delighted at the prospect of a pay raise. His drinking was starting to stretch his budget.

The team in which Fred became embroiled was the Tree Hugger Containment Group, THCG. Its intended function was to find dirt on leaders and influencers amongst the environmental "troublemakers," and to use this information to hamstring their efforts. They did this by tracking down private indiscretions, finding errors in documentation, maligning them with public innuendo or publishing fake stories to seed doubt about their trustworthiness. Turner's team worked to contain or restrain their activities any which way they could, fairly or unfairly, legally or illegally.

After a few months of detective work Fred had created a database of over a thousand environmental scientists and activists, climate change enthusiasts, anti-coal, oil and gas pro-sustainable energy activists, and anyone who supported such efforts. The database included full names, family history, home and work addresses, even where they went on vacation, if he could find it in the public domain.

Turner said, "We've checked the accuracy of your work, Fred, and it is exemplary. You have exactly the

training and attitude we desire. By the way, your super-
visor said you could continue to be released to focus on
our work for as long as you are needed." This was the
result of a little pressure from Bill Hotchkiss, the
current head of the Department of Homeland Security,
DHS.

Turner realized that Fred was pretty naive and could
be easily manipulated. It also meant that Fred could be
manipulated by outside influencers, a fact he had not
considered. Turner was visiting Fred that day to spring a
trap - to get him locked in and culpable of any crimes
the group committed, whilst insulating himself from
such activities.

Turner said, "There are three people on our team,
you will be the fourth, Fred. We have a large conference
room nearby where we keep all our equipment, records
and the like, and we have a desk waiting for you. We
usually arrive around 8:30 a.m. It's in room 301, along the
hall. Can you meet me there tomorrow, at 8:30?"

———

Fred reported promptly the next day to room 301, where
he encountered a solid door with both electronic and
hardware locking systems. On the door was a large sign,
"High-Security Area," signed by the head of the DHS.
"Wasn't that guy replaced?" thought Fred. "They seem to
change on a regular basis." There was no response to
Fred's knock on the door, but a few minutes later Turner
arrived with a big smile.

"Prompt as ever, I see, Fred," said Turner, as he withdrew a key card from his wallet and then a metal key from his trouser pocket, that was attached to his belt by a thin chain. He turned the key in the lock, while activating the coded entry simultaneously. Fred thought, "What the hell have I gotten myself into?"

They entered a large square conference room, with a number of odd features. The windows had heavy metal screen barriers. All around the walls were large white boards, each with colored markers and erasers. About two-thirds of the boards were covered with lists of names. Fred realized they replicated his database, being divided into his three groups, Corporate, Academic and Miscellaneous, and Government.

In the center of the room was a square arrangement of four low-wall office workstations, each with a top-of-the-line computer. There were no printers or other accessories. At one end of the group of workstations was a coffee pot and a box of cream doughnuts. Each of the three cubicles was occupied by a young man between the ages of 25 and 35, who failed to turn and greet them. They were engrossed in their work, typing away.

Turner offered Fred a cup of coffee and a doughnut, and proceeded to welcome him to the THCG. He introduced the three other staff, who turned, grunted a reluctant "Hi!" and returned immediately to their screens.

Fred asked James, who had not taken a coffee and seemed in a hurry to leave, what exactly he should do, and Turner said, "Keep building your database. Here's your workstation Fred. It has extensive protections and is essentially invisible on the Internet. If you have any problems, Bruce can provide the help you need."

At the mention of his name, Bruce, a fit looking guy in a gray sweatshirt, with a shock of blonde hair, turned, smiled, apologized for being so distracted, and said, "Sorry to disabuse you sir, but nothing is invisible on the Internet if you know how to find your way around."

Bruce then said, "Nice to meet you, Fred, I guess you built the database. Good job! We have exacting work, have to take great care to do it correctly, so you'll find us poor company, I'm afraid." He then turned without another word and continued typing.

Meanwhile, Turner had quietly exited the room, thinking, "The less I'm linked to this the better."

Fred asked Bruce about his work, who replied that they were computer hackers and their job was to track down dirt on the people in Fred's database. He explained that they passed their findings along to another team he'd never met. Bruce did not divulge the nature of these issues. Fred thanked him for the information and returned to his new cubicle to enjoy his coffee and doughnut.

A while later, Fred got up for another doughnut, "Boy, they're good," and to refill his coffee. He wandered around the room looking at all the names lining the walls, many of which he remembered. He noticed that quite a few had a blue line through them.

If Fred had looked closely, he would have noticed that two of the crossed-out names were those of Drs. Nicholas Page and Jeb Newton.

CHAPTER FIVE

Fig answered his office phone, and soon regretted it.

"We need to talk, Dr. Newton. I've been discussing your recent work with a number of our patrons and I'm concerned about your attitude. Come by my office right away. We'll be waiting."

After wandering slowly to the front of the building, a journey he'd made a thousand times to go to the library, Fig knocked on Strickland's office door and entered without waiting for an answer. The director was sitting at his huge mahogany desk, probably worth half of Fig's research budget, with a smug smile on his face. Like the cat that got the cream. Next to him was the creepy company lawyer, Enrique Torres. They'd arrived as a matched pair. Torres was smooth in a dangerous kind of way.

Strickland handed Fig a letter on institute headed paper, with multiple signatures.

"I'm being fired!"

Fig started to protest that they had no grounds to fire him. If necessary, he would take them to court. The lawyer looked him directly in the eyes, and said, "As a matter of fact, Dr. Newton, we do have grounds for your dismissal. Dr. Strickland informed me a while ago that you seem to have poor social skills, especially when it comes to addressing our sponsors. The people who pay your salary and keep the lights on.

As a result of that concern," Torres continued, "I made a few phone calls and it turned out that a critical piece of information was missing from your original application for a staff position at the institute. You omitted to mention that you were diagnosed in high school with a mild form of Asperger's Syndrome, now known as part of the autism spectrum. When it comes to the delicate matter of the institute's interpretation of specific datasets, especially if member company reputations are on the line, lack of discretion on your part could be damaging."

Fig started to protest by saying sarcastically, "So the institute is a conscious entity that has opinions," which Torres ignored.

"Dr. Strickland informed me that he has received several complaints from member companies in this regard. Omitting information about your character that could negatively impact your interpersonal skills is most certainly grounds for dismissal. You can rest assured that I have thoroughly researched the legalities."

Fig stared at Torres, stunned by this long-forgotten personal revelation. Torres kept a poker face and Strickland smiled.

Fig reread the letter, which did not mention autism, said nothing, and left.

He headed back to his office in a daze, but his mind was working overtime. If he'd known what was coming next Fig might have made a few more preparations for his departure. He looked around his office-cum-sanctum with a sense of nostalgia. He wondered how much time he would have to finish up existing projects and set things in order for his two technicians, Beckie and Raymond. There was a two-week grace period in his contract, between official termination and physical removal from the building. It would take him all of two weeks to finish up, but right now he was exhausted so he headed home. Not an exciting prospect.

Due to a recent breakup, Fig had moved into a temporary, pay-by-the-week, insalubrious apartment. The threadbare carpet stank of tobacco smoke, and Fig had never smoked. Water leaked through the ceiling into his bathtub when the people upstairs took a shower. The apartment management couldn't see the problem. They said, "As the water lands in your bathtub and runs away, what's the problem, and what do you expect for $80 a week?"

After driving home in light traffic, Fig settled into his favorite armchair with a glass of wine and said to himself, "Damn, I've just been fired." Fig tended to look on the bright side of life, so he went through his usual list of things he had to be grateful for. It was an old stoic trick that helped him overcome life's challenges with equanimity.

He congratulated himself on being honest with Jeff about his chlorine research and escaping that insane girlfriend. It was time to end that relationship, for sure. He'd had enough emotional abuse in his life to know it when he saw it. It didn't matter how good she looked, how great in bed, their common interests. She was crazy, repeatedly attacking him based on false accusations of infidelity. When the hell he had time for that he had no idea, not that he had any interest in doing so.

Now in his early fifties, all Fig wanted was a quiet life with a good woman, to do his beloved research and exercise, and to know his kids and the cat, Sophie, were safe and well. He was going to miss his work at GEPI. It felt more like play than work, and it came with lots of fascinating toys. As a kid, Fig had always enjoyed biology. He loved going down to the bayou as a young teenager, to study the rich plant life, watch salamanders, frogs and snakes, and generally wallow in the joys of Nature. Plants and animals were all one thing to Fig.

The magic of life!

He took another sip of wine, and thought, "Most people seem to be having feelings all the damn time, many of which are destructive feelings, like anger and a desire for revenge, which lead to verbal abuse and outright hostility. That smile on Strickland's face was based on some weird feeling. Maybe he's jealous of my scientific ability, and by firing me he feels that he has won some kind of battle? Proved himself the better man?" Strickland reminded Fig of a sweat bee. Innocuous creatures that evolved to imitate something with a sting.

"Strickland is a pretend scientist," thought Fig, "and boy, this is good wine, but that's enough. It'll mess up my sleep. Better get some supper."

In spite of this horrible temporary apartment stinking up his nostrils, having no girlfriend and losing his job, Fig continued to cogitate. When conflicts arrived in Fig's life he would withdraw into a world of logical analysis. He'd wonder about the nature of life, time, the universe and everything in it, and whether the universe has an inside and outside!

Fig loved science. He never was too interested in people, unless they got in his way, "those incomprehensible capricious primates." Sometimes his naiveté got Fig into hot water, especially when it came to his choice of girlfriends. Then again, Fig always thought they did the choosing anyway.

Being widely read was Fig's most powerful weapon. He'd had a great career so far, and he knew enough about life to realize that change would come, whether he was ready or not, and here it was. What would his English Mum say, with her odd English expressions? No doubt it would be, "Jeb, go fight City Hall," and "be true to yourself."

Fig eventually realized these were wonderful guidelines for life.

CHAPTER SIX

After a surprisingly good night's sleep, Fig awoke on Sunday morning to no girlfriend, no job, a crappy apartment and a smile on his face. For some reason, Fig was glad to be shot of Strickland, while being concerned for the future of Beckie, Raymond and his collaborators at the institute, the Environmental Protection Agency, EPA, and elsewhere. It was nine o'clock in the morning. He'd slept late and the phone was ringing.

"Hi Fig, it's Dr. Strickland's secretary, Pam."

"Hi Pam, what's up?"

"He had me come into work this morning, on a Sunday of all days, to ask me to tell you that your entry pass has been deactivated and your personal effects will be delivered to your home in about an hour."

"That's what it's like working for a dick wad."

"Willie will be by your home to drop off your stuff

and to pick up your work computer and any institute documents in your possession."

Then Pam sighed and said, "I'm so sorry you decided to leave us."

"Thanks, Pam. Excuse my confusion, I only just woke up. I'll pull that stuff together," then he hung up the phone. "Shit! Strickland really is getting rid of me in a hurry." He booted up his work PC, only to find that the institute network no longer recognized his user ID.

"Damn and blast it."

Fig copied all of his data to a flash drive. While this was being done, he thought, "I doubt this has anything to do with chlorine. We make a simple observation, interpret its relevance to human health using the respective chemistry and immunology, propose a potential link between chlorine exposure and asthma, and my life goes to hell. That phone call from Jeff was a setup and I bet fucking Strickland was in the loop. It was probably a ploy to get rid of me."

He then phoned Beckie and Raymond to tell them he'd been fired. They were both dismayed and agreed to meet the next day for lunch, to talk it through.

Fig's first thought, after worrying about his staff, was his income. He was sure Strickland and Torres would do their best to minimize or eliminate any severance package. They clearly didn't like him. Fortunately, as someone who always planned ahead, Fig had plenty of savings. He'd paid off the divorce lawyer's bills and other court costs a while ago, and his sons were self-supporting in promising careers.

It crossed his mind to call his pension brokerage company on Monday, to see how best to use his retirement savings, if he needed them. He knew he would have to pay a penalty and taxes for any withdrawal, but he vaguely remembered someone telling him they'd used their retirement funds to buy a new car by borrowing from a rollover IRA, under some kind of self-loan arrangement.

Fig's brain was working overtime!

"Time for a run and calm down," thought Fig. Then there was scratching at the window. It was Sophie, his beloved tortoiseshell cat. She was very much an outdoor-indoor cat. Indoors for food, brief affection, and gone, unless it was raining or freezing cold. Fig had always been an animal lover. Their dog, a yellow lab, had remained with his ex-wife, but he'd kept Sophie, though he sure missed their lovely mutt.

He opened the window for Sophie, and of course she immediately demanded food. Her favorite was some milk and a little salmon, which were ready in the fridge. That problem solved. Fig got ready for a quick run. He'd been a runner much of his adult life, even competing in the Boston Marathon several times in his late forties. Now Fig confined his running to a local 5k loop. "Maybe I should pick up marathons again, as I'll have the time on my hands."

Fig knew someone was trying to suppress his work, but he needed to identify the source, which he was sure was not Jeff, Strickland or Torres. "I bet it's someone much more powerful because they have already emasculated the institute, and I guess I was the last real researcher left. But who? Someone gave Strickland orders to fire me, either directly or via that creepy lawyer, Torres. And how the hell did they find my old Asperger's high school report? That was over thirty years ago. I doubt I could find it myself."

He also couldn't ignore the conclusion that someone was trying to close the institute, and that that someone was probably pandering to the new disaster in the White House, President Miller. Realizing he might be up against a powerful enemy, Fig decided it was best, for now at least, to act as though he was interested in finding another job and was putting chlorine toxicity and global ecotoxicology behind him, but that idea didn't last long.

Later that day, after a small glass of Dutch courage, Fig got it into his head to create a new website, to keep his ideas alive, but there was more to it than that. He wanted to create a website that would act as bait, to draw out whomsoever wanted him out of commission. "They obviously hate my challenging the big money corporations and being pro-environment."

Fig said to himself, "You can fight City Hall, young man."

This made him smile as it brought back the sound of his Mum's voice ringing in his ears. He bought the domain *"the thoughtful eco-toxicologist"* and started to build a tempting website to fish for his enemy. He selected his most inflammatory ideas and ecological observations and populated the site with a wide range of solid research data. He also added his EcoWorld model predictions, much of it challenging certain industrial activities and their potentially disastrous environmental consequences.

Fig had no plans to abandon the memory of his idol and eco-heroine, Rachel Louise Carson. Instead his plan was to bait his hook to catch whoever had him fired.

CHAPTER SEVEN

The White House.

In the oval office were President John D. Miller, an overweight and overbearing man in his mid-sixties, who was in a conversation with two members of his cabinet, his chosen heads of the DHS and EPA, William (Bill) Hotchkiss and Alec Chariton, respectively.

"Well, Alec! Are you getting those damn tree-huggers under control? They're a real pain in the ass. I'm sick of protests about pipelines and the hoax of global warming. It sure isn't warm today."

"Yes, sir!" said Chariton. "We're making steady progress. I've replaced many of the old staff by more realistic scientists and administrators, those more in line with the industrial realities of today."

"Excellent!"

"In addition to government agencies, we are rooting

out any we can find in commercial and academic institutions. I don't know why we needed the damn EPA in the first place. It's been a pain in the ass for my business ever since it was created."

"And you, Bill," said Miller, "I assume you are providing all the support Alec needs?"

"Yes sir! His team has been installed in the Homeland Security Building on the St. Elizabeth's Campus, where things are more discreet."

"Best kept confidential," said Miller. "You know how the damned news media can spin things against us."

"I've provided Alec with some of our best support staff, including muscle should it be needed."

"Who's running the operation?"

"James Turner, sir, a solid guy," said Chariton. "He was selected for the job by Charles Barrett, my second in command at the EPA. Chaz knows it's a sensitive operation."

"Barrett? Isn't he involved in some kind of food company?"

"Yes, sir! He's the CEO of Good Foods, Inc, one of the major suppliers to our military. Barrett's no environmentalist, I can promise you that. His father spent much of his time over the last twenty years suing the EPA because of their excessive regulations for feed lots, hog waste and chicken houses, and he personally groomed his eldest son, Charles, for the job. Charles became CEO about three years ago, and he's a chip off the old block."

"That's what we need," said Miller. "How the hell can we provide meat to the troops without feedlots, pig crap and a lot of chickens? Can't be done! Good to see you finally roping in the EPA after we got rid of that damned pansy they left in there for years."

"Thank you, sir"

"Meeting's over and thanks, guys. Keep me posted. By the way, Alec, I don't want to hear any more shit out of North Carolina. I had another complaint the other day about the place. It was from Gene, the CEO of Ever Chemical. He's pissed about some institute down there. G I something or other. Said he wished someone would shut the place down."

"Of course, sir! We have our man in place right now. He's working on closing it without making waves for the sponsoring companies.

———

Later in Chariton's office at EPA headquarters, 1200 Pennsylvania Avenue NW, Washington, DC.

There's a knock on the door.

"Come in, Chaz, good to see you again. We are just too damn busy."

"Hi, Alec, you seem to be thriving. I guess you like a busy life."

Charles Barrett was an immaculately dressed man in his late fifties, who seemed to be looking after his health, while Chariton clearly enjoyed too many business dinners for a heavyset man in his late seventies.

"I like to get things done," said Chariton. "With Miller in charge, this country is finally going in the right direction. But I hate those bloody cabinet meetings, more and more, because he's putting me under increasing pressure to show progress on that institute in North Carolina. Miller is an impatient man."

"Of course."

"If he's not happy with our work it'll be both of our heads on the chopping block, and I'm enjoying stopping this damn place, and its useless regulations, in its tracks. How's it going, Chaz?"

"We managed to eliminate the previous director, Dr. Page, with a little rumor of infidelity," said Barrett, with a smile. "And we now have our man, Dave Strickland, in place, who is working to quietly close it down."

"How long will it take, Chaz?"

"I'm afraid it can't be rushed," said Barrett.

CHAPTER EIGHT

Three days after baiting his hook, and while finishing his favorite breakfast of two over easy local organic eggs on whole wheat toast, Fig heard a vehicle pull up outside his apartment. This was followed by the noise of mail being dropped into his box. He reached the door in time to see the retreating figure of an extremely shapely brunette climbing into a large black SUV. As it pulled away from the curb, she looked briefly in his direction. Fig knew he would recognize that beautiful face anywhere.

In his mailbox was a plain manila envelope along with a small, but rather heavy, parcel. The envelope contained a single slip of paper upon which was hand-written,

"Shut the fuck up, or we'll shut you the fuck up."

It was unsigned.

The package brought to Fig's mind a recent event in

Parma, Italy, so he decided to call the cops. A plain clothes officer arrived in about fifteen minutes and examined the note and the package. He told Fig he was going to call the bomb squad, asking him to stand back as he placed the package carefully at a distance on open ground.

Fig's mind went back to a story told to him by a friend, of a very different package delivered to a small research institute in Scotland. A plain brown paper parcel, tied up with twine, and post-marked from a middle eastern country, one in turmoil, was delivered for one of the institute's senior staff. Because of recent bombing activity by the IRA, in Glasgow, the Scottish bomb squad was called. They put the parcel in the middle of a large field and took shots at it with a rifle, to no effect. Then they blew it up with a small explosive charge, much to the delight of the staff.

A rain of confetti-sized paper came drifting down through the smoke. It turned out that this package contained the mandatory five copies of a student's doctoral dissertation. He'd mailed it to his major advisor for submission to the local university. How they sorted that out Fig had no idea, but it must have been a nightmare for the student.

Fig came out of his reverie to his own suspect bomb to see a truck arrive, out of which jumped some burly men in what looked like Kevlar clothing. They took one look at the parcel and set in motion standard disposal procedures, instructing the growing cluster of curious neighbors to stand well back. This was assisted by their description of the damage that can be done by shrapnel within one hundred feet of such an explosive device.

Ten minutes later they came over to Fig and displayed a well-constructed bomb. It consisted of a timer, a bunch of wires and what the bomb disposal guy said would have been enough explosive to blow off his arms and probably blind him for life. "Except in this case, sir, this is a pretty realistic dummy block of C4." He then said, "Whoever made this is clearly serious about frightening you, sir."

Fig took a photo of the device and the note and put the latter in his wallet. He later discovered that the fake bomb was a replica of the one used in Parma, Italy, to target a scientist objecting to GMO foodstuffs. The only difference being the C4 was not imitation in that case. Due to the suspicions of a postal worker, the bomb was defused safely. This got Fig to wondering if the food industry had it in for him.

"Weird but possible," thought Fig.

The cop and a detective he'd called in asked Fig a series of questions about the driver of the SUV and why this might have occurred. Fig said he had no idea and suggested it might be mistaken identity, as there was plenty of drug activity in this apartment complex. "What can you expect for $80 a week?" said Fig, while revealing nothing about events at his job to avoid triggering a mess of unanswerable questions.

He appeared to have caught a rather nasty fish with that website bait, plus he'd need a job when his money ran out. Something was going on that made no sense and, as his friend Ben had told him many times, "Fig, if something doesn't make sense to you, there's something you don't know."

Whoever they were they were serious. They'd had him fired. Had his work computer accounts blocked and delivered a threat in the form of that note and the imitation bomb. But everything he knew about chlorine was public. It was about something else related to his work. Perhaps it was something on his personal blog? Nothing on that flash drive popped out as worth threatening some innocent researcher.

Maybe Jeff had been put under pressure to make that call, when mystery man Daryl had threatened Fig's salary, which had now been abruptly taken away. Occam's razor would say these events were linked, so Fig decided to start recording every detail and to treat it as a piece of research.

He'd list all of his work on chlorine and other chemicals, and there were quite a few, list the lectures he'd given recently, the sources of any related information, any communications, things that stood out as "anti-industry" during the past few years. He finally decided to create the decoy of pretending to plan a vacation, look for a new job, and buy a more reliable car, while actually preparing to go underground and investigate.

He transferred $20,000 from a retirement IRA to his checking account, knowing he would have to pay the taxes and 10% penalty. He'd worry about that later. He planned to pull this money out of the cash machine a day at a time, so as to avoid the red flag of a large cash withdrawal. He searched on the Internet for car dealerships and rental properties at the beach to justify the cash extraction if someone was watching.

Unbeknownst to Fig, someone was watching. They were watching everything he did. His phone had been hacked, they'd tapped into his conversations, and someone was recording where he went.

Fig contacted friends and family to tell them he was taking a vacation and changing jobs, and not to worry about him. He was always prepared for any eventuality. You might say he was paranoid as he always had a backpack ready. It was how he was raised. His Mum used to say, "You never know when the bombs will start dropping."

His high-grade backpack contained an up-to-date passport, lightweight sleeping bag, flashlight, compass, multipurpose knife tool, a small single person tent, a lightweight groundsheet that could double as a tarp, trail-appropriate clothes with mosquito netting for his face, waterproof matches and a book, *The Art of War*.

Fig had several offers of interviews for jobs over the next couple of weeks. The grapevine was working without any effort on his part. These he fielded carefully, explaining he needed an extended break before moving to a new position. Ben agreed to look after Sophie and, with the permission of the rental property staff, Fig had installed a cat door and showed Sophie how to use it. Then Ben could come by daily to refill her water and food bowls. He also agreed to spoil her with some salmon, milk and attention, when she was around.

Three weeks after losing his job, Fig added some more items to his backpack, including his old MacBook Air, freeze-dried trail food, new running shoes and extra shorts. He double-checked the date on his passport, and made sure his money was safely hidden in multiple compartments in his backpack and on his person. With a touch of sadness at leaving Sophie, Fig headed for the door, filling her water and food bowls on the way by. He placed spare apartment and car keys under the doormat, as agreed with Ben, and walked to the bus stop. Anybody watching would think he was leaving for a hiking vacation.

Fig had other plans, and he regularly said to himself, "Fuck you and the horse you rode in on, whoever you are."

CHAPTER NINE

Fig planned to take the bus to the nearest Amtrak station, then travel to a remote city and find some kind of job. Any job that paid cash and didn't ask too many questions. He'd done loads of different jobs before becoming a scientist, including hotel handyman, farm and industry laborer, and music teacher, where he gave private flute lessons. Once in his target city, he'd disappear into a cheap motel or one room apartment and strategize.

Fig was pissed at what had been done to him, and what was being done to the institute. When Fig was pissed, he became extremely focused and not to be screwed with. He wasn't scared, in fact Fig was only really scared of two things, heights and spiders of an intermediate size. He liked little jumping spiders, had stroked the back of a tarantula, but would recoil in horror from a wolf spider, and he did not appreciate being bitten on the toe by a sac spider a week before running the Boston Marathon - that was real pain. But at that moment, as Fig was preparing to go underground, he was feeling a sense of excitement and adventure. He walked to the bus stop, thinking, "I've been working in that research program for nearly thirteen years. Maybe the universe is telling me it's time for a change, to try something new?"

Fig despised the new US President, John D. Miller, in part because of the damage he was doing to the EPA. Fig was angry about the administration's elimination of dozens of environmental regulations designed to prevent the insane behavior of industry described in 1962, by Rachel Carson, in her masterful book, *Silent Spring*.

"Fifty-two is a good age to have an adventure," thought Fig, "to start a new life with a mission." He reflected on his life so far, while waiting for a bus outside the local gas station-cum-laundromat-cum-Mexican restaurant. He'd miss that restaurant, which was cheap and really good.

The bus wasn't due for another 20 minutes, so he nipped into the gas station for a coffee and more food for the road. He also bought a baseball cap with a long peak and no identifiable markings, to fool security cameras. He added some packets of nuts and gorp to his order, in addition to an egg and cheese bagel and a veggie burrito. Fig confined his diet to plant-based foods, except when there was no choice, but he hadn't eaten meat in years. He paid cash, because credit card payments can be tracked, and headed back outside to the bus stop.

The driver told Fig that he had a stop only half a mile from the Amtrak station, on East Washington. On a whim, while sitting in the bus, Fig decided he'd head for Burlington, Vermont. He had some fond memories of the place. Looking out of the bus window, watching familiar sights go by, Fig wondered if he was being followed. No conspicuous cars behind the bus that he could see.

Fig realized that he could be tracked via his cell phone, so he decided to buy a burner phone when he got a chance and dump this one. All he knew of such things he'd learned from watching a movie, *The Bourne Identity*. The driver, an older black man who'd clearly survived some hard times, informed Fig that this was his stop. He also asked Fig, with concern, "You OK, young man?"

"Just a minor problem, thanks," said Fig. "I really appreciate you asking. That's kind of you! Could you point me in the direction of the Amtrak station?"

On arriving at the station, Fig crushed his phone underfoot and chucked the remains in a trash can. "That's one potential trace destroyed," thought Fig. Fortunately, he stored a list of important phone numbers and addresses in a little black notebook. Fig was old school, never quite trusting electronic media with important information.

He used cash to buy a ticket for Burlington, Vermont, stopping overnight in Richmond, and changing trains in New York the next day. Fig liked the trains in Europe, but this was his first in the US. After a few minutes wait on the platform, here came the metallic monster, hissing and clanking into the station, which always made Fig a little excited, as it reminded him of his European adventures as a young man.

After boarding the train, he found a seat in a quiet corner, pulled out that chlorine paper, and read it cover to cover, even the references. Pretty boring, but maybe there was a clue or two in there. He went through all of his chlorine-related material for about the fifth time, and was wondering yet again, "Who the hell was that Daryl guy, and why was he so pissed about my work?" He wondered who Daryl worked for, other than being a scientific consultant for Jeff. Distracted as usual, Fig had failed to ask. When he got a new phone, he could call Jeff to find out but decided against it. He didn't want exposure of his location any more than necessary.

"They took my job and threatened my life. It must be something that threatens someone's income, power, status, belief system, political standing, something? People don't make dummy bombs to pass the time of day. Furthermore, President Miller has been attacking environmental scientists, especially those at the EPA. Maybe I'm on his hit list because of my collaborations with EPA scientists."

Several of his EPA colleagues had recently moved to other jobs, much to Fig's surprise. "Government jobs are secure jobs, or they used to be," said Fig to himself, as the view rolled by and the clackety clack of the rails made him drowsy. Fig was sure that if a plan was afoot to close the institute, Strickland wasn't the mastermind. He was receiving instructions from above, and Fig needed to find out who that was.

He was enjoying the view from the train, so much so that he was suddenly startled awake by the clanking of the carriages. He'd fallen into a deep sleep, and they'd arrived in Richmond. On leaving the station, Fig headed for the nearest motel to turn off his brain and get a good night's sleep.

———

The next morning, Fig wanted to go directly to Burlington, but due to train schedules he was forced to stay overnight in a motel near Pennsylvania Station in New York. He caught the 11:30 a.m. *Vermonter* the following morning. It was a nine-hour trip to Burlington, passing through beautiful countryside, along the Connecticut River much of the way. Once again, Fig had time to contemplate recent events. His mind started to focus on the mystery voice, Daryl. Had he met the guy and why was he such a prick? Why did he threaten Fig's job and how could he be so sure he had that kind of clout?

Fig remembered back in early January several of his colleagues said in confidence that Strickland seemed to be setting him up for removal. They told of subtle hints that Fig wasn't up to the job. That he seemed to be overly friendly with female students. That his work on network mathematics was irrelevant to the mission of the institute. And so forth! Fig was unaware of this as he had no interest in human gossip, which left him open to a socially engineered attack.

Just as this was coming to a head, and even Fig noticed the pejorative remarks of Strickland at public meetings concerning his work, he received a curious letter. It was a copy of a letter to Strickland from a private Washington address. The source of the letter, Dr. Charles Barrett, was someone Fig didn't know. He thought perhaps the guy might have attended one of the scientific advisory meetings at the institute and liked Fig's work, but he was guessing.

The letter stated that the research work carried out by Dr. J. Newton was exemplary and exactly in line with the mission of the founders. This work was to be encouraged as it was highly prized by the institute's sponsors. At the bottom of the letter was the single line, "cc Dr. J. Newton, GEPI."

Charles Barrett, whoever he was, had clearly been made aware of the clandestine attacks on Fig by Strickland, and had come to his aid. But how, why, and who the hell was he? That said, the attacks on Fig vanished, and Strickland became surprisingly amiable to Fig. It was clear that Fig had a powerful mystery benefactor with some clout, but that power wasn't unlimited, as demonstrated by Fig being fired six weeks later.

Fig wondered about this, and being Fig he started to draw a network. A network of potentially involved people. People who might have dreamed up, or schemed up, the dismissal of the previous director, Nick Page, who Fig very much admired, as he was a great scientist, unlike the third-rate thinker, Strickland.

Graph theory, one of the tools Fig used for his network studies, consisted of little circles or vertices for variables, such as people, and lines, edges or links connecting them, which could represent conversations or other forms of communication between the people represented by the circles. The thickness of the lines, or a number over the line, was used to represent the strength or importance of the connection.

Such graphs looked like a random bunch of circles and lines, but they were mathematically connected, permitting detailed study of the roles played by individual variables, or people, in the dynamic behavior of the network. Fig hoped to use this approach to winkle out the primary source of his current problems, which he assumed must be someone between Strickland and the president.

Fig first made a crude graph on paper before building the final network in his computer. He placed his initials and those of the previous director, Nick Page, in a circle each, near the center of a sheet of paper. He added Miller, Strickland, Torres, Jeff, Daryl, Barrett, Unknown Federal Employee and a number of institute and EPA colleagues and environmental activists who had moved on precipitously under suspicious circumstances.

Because his problems started with the arrival of Miller in the White House, Fig included selected members of Miller's cabinet, including the Secretaries of

Agriculture, Defense, Energy, Health and Human Services, and Homeland Security. He also added the head of the Central Intelligence Agency, because of their history of some pretty nefarious activity, including setting bombs for people they "didn't like" during the cold war. Under each he added blank circles with question marks. Fig's network was starting become quite extensive.

Fig thought, "It's starting to look like the web of a spider on drugs. Who, I wonder, is the spider at the center the web? He decided to call them *Shelob*. This was the name of a horrible and horribly big spider in *The Lord of the Rings Trilogy*, a book loved by all nerdy scientists.

Fig then dug out his computer, made sure the radio was turned off, and started up his network software. He transferred the information on paper into the program. He ran some brief analyses to look for shortest paths and throttle points to flow, which were called gateway vertices in Graph Theory Speak. He soon realized that he needed a lot more information on the edges, the lines connecting the people in *Shelob's* web. Fig then backed up the file on a flash drive, which went into a zipped pocket in his waterproof hiking jacket, and dozed off for a while.

He then had a dream in which he was being pursued across his network diagram by a giant spider, causing Fig to mumble in his sleep, and then to disappear into his favorite world of dreams where he could fly. In this dream he was cruising happily above his arachnoid pursuer, who was unable to fly due to lack of imagination.

Fig was really enjoying this dream when he was jogged awake by the train arriving at Essex Junction. Outside the train people were lugging skis and heavy bags, for the short walk to the 8:30 p.m. Amtrak connection. Fig had forgotten how cold it could be in Vermont in the winter. He was warmly dressed, but he sure missed his balaclava ski mask. One more thing to buy.

Fig joined the crowd and found a seat on the connector train, while wondering where he was going to stay the night. It was already dark, cold and snowing. It was an unusually heavy snowfall for Vermont that time of year, and the beauty of it did not go unnoticed by Fig.

They soon stopped again at their final destination, the University of Vermont Medical Center. From there the options were a one-mile walk, a shuttle bus, or a taxi. Having warm clothes and hiking boots, Fig chose to walk, while thinking the less he used public transport the less likely he was to be seen on security cameras. In spite of the baseball cap and hood obscuring his face, Fig was still concerned about being spotted.

Fortunately, there was a reasonably priced, reasonable for Burlington, motel near the end of the trail. Fig crashed for the night, paying cash. They requested an ID, but as a long line was forming, they let it go as Fig was digging through his backpack, and he offered a $200 security deposit. He then learned that waving cash in front of people was surprisingly effective. This was Fig's first introduction to social engineering. He told the hotel receptionist that he would bring his ID down in the morning, and thanked them for their patience, saying he was exhausted.

As he climbed the stairs to his room, Fig thought, "How the hell can I create a fake ID by the morning?" He had no idea, so he ate some trail mix, drank a large glass of water, showered and crashed for the night.

———

The following morning, well rested, Fig exited the motel by a back door, leaving some of his things in his room, but not his backpack, computer or money. He then set out for a beautiful crisp, snowy walk into town. His job for the day was to make a fake ID. But how? He knew students did it all the time to get beer. On finding a coffee shop, where he bought some delicious pastries baked by students at the Burlington Culinary Institute, he searched the Internet on this phone for instructions on how to make a fake ID.

To Fig's amazement he discovered that photoshop could be used to create fake driver's licenses for any state in the US. Detailed instructions were provided on several websites and videos. Out came his laptop and a realistic New York State driver's license was generated and copied to a flash drive in minutes.

After enjoying a latte, reading for a while for a break from all the cloak and dagger stuff, Fig headed for the nearest Office Supply. It was a bit of a walk, but the sun was shining, "Brillig," thought Fig, and before he knew it, the kind Office Supply staff, all students, placed a still warm, perfectly laminated, New York State driver's license in his hand.

The student, on handing it to Fig, said, "Aren't you already old enough to drink?" Fig replied, "Yes, but when you get to my age you need an ID to show you aren't too old to handle it." They both laughed and Fig headed off, wondering if he'd left any clues in Office Supply as to his whereabouts, which of course he had. Fig had a lot to learn about living incognito.

Fig returned to the motel and searched the online noticeboards for a place to crash. He found a student, Karl Blake, desperate to sublet his cabin for a few weeks. The ad said it was a mile and a half's walk through the woods, or five miles by car. He called the guy, and they agreed to meet at his place. Fig took his few things from the room and checked out. They didn't even ask for his Mr. Hanratty ID, which disappointed Fig a little. Then he shouldered his backpack and headed for Karl's place.

"Cash for three weeks in advance is fine!" said Karl, with a big smile. Fig offered to pay a cleaning fee, but Karl said it wasn't that clean as it was and no problem, "forget it." One happy student handed Fig a crude drawing of the trail to the cabin, the key and some instructions on utilities.

He accepted Fig's Jerome Hanratty ID without a blink, but he did ask about the unusual name. Fig realized this was a red flag. He explained to Karl that his paternal grandfather was Welsh, thus the Gaelic surname. "Yes," Karl said, "but Jerome?" Fig thought,

"Boy, this kid is nosey." He replied that his Mum loved the song, *Smoke Gets in Your Eyes*, and left Karl to work it out for himself.

It was snowing big flakes, as Fig headed for the cabin, and the trail had almost a foot of snow on either side. It took him straight into the woods. There were clearly plenty of other cabins along the way, as the trail had several branches and was well worn. It was pretty dark under the snow-laden trees and the cloudy sky. Fortunately, Fig had a flashlight and the map to the cabin.

There were all sorts of unusual plants along the way, in addition to prints and spoor of fox and deer. The trail crossed an old farm road, as the map indicated, which was lined by huge old oak trees, along with a signpost to a quarry. He noticed the heads of some ferns, spleenwort he thought, poking out of the snow, indicating that the soil was pretty rich.

"I bet there are loads of wildflowers here in spring-time," thought Fig. He was enjoying the route, with its unduly large trees and fascinating plants protruding through the snowy understory. Then the cabin was in front of him, an old log structure with evidence of a fire-place, but there were no lights on. He soon had a fire crackling in the grate, and all was well with the world. Especially well after he'd cooked a solid meal, enjoyed a cup of coffee and finally stopped to relax.

On one wall was a poster describing the area as Burlington forest. The colorful display had a detailed report of the local flora, the stuff of life for Fig:

In the spring, before leaves emerge, explorers of the ledges and outcrops throughout the park enjoy wild ginger, red and white trillium, hepatica, meadow-rue, columbine, and other colorful wildflowers. The ubiquitous bedrock exposures are made of a nutrient-rich limestone called dolostone. Though exposed at this site, dolostone underlies much of the rest of Burlington beneath feet of nutrient-poor sediment. This unusual geology enables uncommon plants that require abundant calcium. In fact, these outcrops in the Arms Forest are home to rare plants, like yellow lady-slipper orchids, found nowhere else in Burlington.

"And this is what much of American Industry, and that fucker in the White House, want to destroy for a few bucks," thought Fig, angrily. "The new president doesn't give a shit about all this magic of nature. He'll destroy it for his rich buddies given half a chance." President Miller had already started destroying nature by replacing dedicated scientists at the EPA with ass-kissing sycophants who knew nothing about global eco-science or environmental health.

Late that afternoon, Fig decided to head out for a hike. With plenty of warm hiking gear, it was time to explore and let his brain take a rest. After an enjoyable hike, the purchase of food for dinner, it was getting dark and icy cold. On the way back to the cabin, Fig noticed a bar where he could read in the warm. He wandered in, noticed the attractive female bartender, which as usual caused him to feel awkward.

He'd always noticed that the more interested he was in a woman, the harder it was to talk to them. He'd become tongue-tied. He ordered a Perrier, without looking at her directly, and found a quiet corner seat to read and go over his hand-drawn network diagram. It sure felt good to be in out of the cold.

Later that evening, after a solid vegetable stew for dinner, he started to read, but he couldn't focus. He was thinking about that woman in the bar, again.

CHAPTER TEN

Jamie Bailey was attractive, slim, five-seven with large hazel eyes, and a great figure, due in part to genetics and part to regular exercise. She liked to think about things, workout at her gym and run local trails. Her favorite sport was distance running and she was cautiously single. Jamie was exactly the kind of woman Fig dreamed of meeting. Jamie was also the perfect woman for Fig to meet, as she had an unlikely hobby.

When Jamie approached her parents as a teenager with the idea of majoring in mathematics and statistics they refused, saying it was not lady-like. She was a moderately talented artist, in piano and drawing, so her parents insisted she take a degree in the Arts. Jamie was backup pianist at her church, and she had received a high school award for one of her pencil drawings of a display of dried flowers, from the Mariposa County Arts Council. Her caring Lutheran parents, who gave her that weird spelling of her name, Jayme, which she dropped whenever she could, said they would pay her way if she attended university for a degree in the Arts. They reasoned she had shown promise in both drawing and music.

Reluctantly, Jamie applied to several schools and was accepted in one of the best, Stanford Art Institute. When it came to music and drawing, it was the structure or patterns that intrigued her. She preferred analyzing music to playing it. When she listened to the classics, she followed the music along on mini-scores, not wanting to miss any details of the structure. Her favorite music was Bach's Preludes and Fugues. With respect to art, Jamie's favorite artist was Escher, and once again it was the patterns and his strange imagination that captured her attention.

In college, Jamie chose some odd courses, for an artist, including *"ART142 - Drawing with Code"* and *"MUS11N - Harmonic Convergence: Music's Intersections with Science and Mathematics."* She clearly had eclectic interests, and was struggling to find her passion. She also abandoned her contacts, prescribed for her mild short-sightedness, and started wearing nerdy black glasses with square frames, plus loose-fitting clothes. It was as though Jamie was trying to hide her beauty. Of course, it did exactly the opposite, furthermore, she kept losing those glasses.

After obtaining her BA degree, Jamie married her high school sweetheart, Mathew Brown, a Lutheran naturally. Before she knew it, she was raising their two kids, Edith and John, and attending bake sales. Jamie was a good Mom, based on how the kids turned out. She was close with Edith, as that's how it tends to be with girls, while boys chase the girls and disappear. The marriage lasted fifteen years, or more like endured, until her husband admitted he was gay.

Fortunately, Jamie and Mathew were good friends, their church was accepting and supportive of gays, and after the initial shock and anger they worked out what was best for everyone, especially the kids. Even though the Lutheran Church was open to gays, there was no way Mathew would be accepted socially by most people in Mariposa.

It was a painful time in Jamie's life, but her ex was generous with financial support, sparing nothing to help her and their son and daughter. He said he wanted to give Jamie time to build a career of her own. Mathew admitted to falling in love with several men, but he told Jamie that he had not cheated physically. This helped Jamie's recovery and reduced her initial bitterness.

So she turned to her hobby, computer hacking. As a self-taught amateur, Jamie came close to making some serious illegal mistakes. She was fascinated by the process of hacking, the beauty of the code, and how it was always evolving. Jamie was also proud of her ability to penetrate government and commercial sites. She did it for the fun of it, never doing anything malicious. Never stealing data or revealing private information, Jamie assumed she wasn't breaking any laws, but she was.

She had become a talented black hat hacker.

In spite of having no-one for guidance and training, Jamie managed to avoid running into trouble, while installing backdoors in a number of sites, including a company she abhorred. They made toxic chemicals and had no respect for nature. They only cared about profits. This company also employed some of the best white hat hackers, all ex-black hats. Even these expert Internet sleuths failed to spot Jamie's work, which could go unnoticed for a while, but not forever.

How did a nice Lutheran girl, with a BA in music and drawing, become a black hat hacker, you may wonder?

Like this:

While her kids were growing up they were always on computers, notepads, or smart phones. Every now and then these devices would slow down, and the kids would complain. Mathew had no interest in such things and Jamie liked to fix technical stuff herself.

She soon found that her kid's Internet devices were infested with malware, worms, viruses and other computer creepy crawlies. She bought a virus software contract, scanned and cleaned each machine, a process in which her teenage kids seemed to have no more interest than did their dad. She got rid of all the vermin, but one caught her, the computer bug.

Having a much neglected mathematical bent, Jamie wondered how the anti-virus software worked. A little reading revealed that any computer can be broken into, hacked, penetrated or penned, by a dedicated hacker. Jamie did much of her banking and purchasing online, including the use of credit cards, so she became alarmed.

Time to learn how to be sure to detect any hackers before they did some damage.

One thing led to another and Jamie started to play around with hacking herself. She thought, "It takes one to know one." After reading a few books on the subject and taking multiple free online training courses, Jamie managed to break into one of the kid's school computers where she found the upcoming exams. She retreated in alarm, realizing that enterprising kids could do the same, which worried her no end. Jamie thought you had to be a computer genius to do such things.

Jamie had discovered that to be an effective computer hacker you had to literally love the code. It was like a love affair or an obsession. She found that she just couldn't not hack. Jamie found that her exploration of computer code was much more exciting than drawing or music, or housework for that matter! It opened up a vast expanse for her to explore, the wide world of the World Wide Web.

Once she'd calmed down from the shock of what she'd done at that school, Jamie wondered if she'd left evidence of her visit. She studied some more and learned ways to reduce the chances of being spotted. She then decided to try penetrating a government site. It turned out to be easier than the high school.

Jamie had plenty of time on her hands, now the kids were almost grown. Who wants to hang around with Mom, especially when she's glued to that computer all the time? Jamie had what it takes to be a successful hacker, including broad intellectual curiosity and the desire to break through the boundaries of her current state of knowledge. Above all Jamie was patient, persistent, and she loved the code.

As Jamie studied penetration or pen testing, she mastered the use of a broad range of hacking tools, the first of which was to study the target looking for potential weaknesses. And now, she'd raised the kids, gone through the divorce, and what the hell was she going to do with her life, in her late forties. Jamie had no career or real work experience, except for a degree in the Arts.

Then Jamie read about Kevin Mitnick, the most successful black hat hacker of all time, who was now well paid to stop people like himself. He'd converted from black to white hat. Set a thief to catch a thief was the order of the day, when it came to Internet security, which Jamie soon learned was an oxymoron.

Jamie thought, "Why couldn't I become a white hat hacker for pay and benefits?"

With no official training, she applied for work at a number of companies using untraceable email accounts, to be treated like a criminal. They sent her applications to the IT department, who then contacted their security team, and within no time they assumed she was a black hat wanting to go straight. They all suggested she turn herself in to law enforcement.

Not a great start to her new career, leaving her stumped.

Maybe she could work on that while trying a back door approach, something to do with computers. First to find a very non-Lutheran environment, far from Mariposa, California, and its stifling social rounds. A place with both running trails and skiing, another passion. Jamie chose Burlington, Vermont. It looked beautiful in the photos, so she applied online for training in computer science. By then Jamie was careful about her Internet trail, using VPN, firewalls, and other "invisibility" tools.

She was accepted at the Community College of Vermont for a degree in Web Design. Jamie also wanted to find a hacker mentor who'd help take her into her preferred career, as a white hat. She selected Web Design as it would complement her hacking dream, but she still needed a job while in college, as her ex's support wouldn't last forever.

"What do people in school do without money?" Jamie said to herself. "Bar tender or wait tables." The thought made her cringe, but "it would at least be a way to meet people." Within a couple of days of arriving in Burlington in December, 2017, and after buying a whole wardrobe of warm clothes, Jamie landed a job as a bartender in *The Thrush's Nest*. She quite enjoyed the work, much to her surprise, but after a few months the late hours became too much to handle. She then got a job as a waitperson at George's Diner, close to the apartment she shared with two female roommates. Jamie missed her friends back in Mariposa, but she talked to her daughter, Edith, everyday, which kept her in touch. She only heard from John every couple of months. He was settling down in San Francisco with a girlfriend and a good job.

During her last night at *The Thrush's Nest*, this really cute guy walked in, asked for a glass of Perrier, ignored her and read at a quiet table in a corner. Jamie wasn't used to that kind of treatment from men, unless they were gay, which he clearly was not.

Jamie was immediately interested in that tall dark stranger.

CHAPTER ELEVEN

Office of Alec Chariton, Director of the EPA, Washington, DC.

The CEO of World Wide Oil and Gas, Inc, Alec Chariton, was wading through paperwork and wondering why the hell he was there. "Who can refuse a job handed to them by the President of the United States?" he thought. "And who better than me to stop the flood of new regulations coming out of this damned organization?"

The phone rang and he reached for it, ready to shout at his secretary in the adjacent room, "I thought I told you to hold all calls."

"Alec? President Miller here."

"Yes sir?"

"I'm still getting complaints about that Institute in North Carolina. I thought you were going to shut the place down."

"Our team is on it, sir, but we have to do it quietly so as to avoid embarrassing their corporate sponsors."

"Why's it taking so long?"

"We had to get enough members of their board to approve removal of the current director, so we could put one of our guys in place to do the job, sir!"

"OK! Get on with it."

The phone went dead.

CHAPTER TWELVE

After two days of research, Fig was growing the number of people in his network, but he needed to build the connections or edges between these people. He had to know who called or visited whom, where people went, and so forth. This would expand the information embedded in the lines connecting the circles, through which information flowed in the network. This included the person who instructed the institute board to sack Nick Page. This information would be critical for finding *Shelob's* lair.

Fig had searched online as best he could, with an active firewall and VPN to protect his location and IP address. But he was unable to find the connections he needed between the people populating his network. This required emails, text messages, phone calls, letters, phone location records, and so forth. He couldn't even find his own school record of that Asperger's diagnosis Torres had used to fire him.

Fig couldn't hope to find the spider in the center of the web without the connecting threads. "How the hell did that creepy lawyer find my high school record?" Fig wondered.

"Torres had employed a hacker," Fig realized. "Where the hell do I find one of those?"

He decided to head into town and treat himself to a late breakfast. Fig ended up in George's Diner on Bank Street near the lake. He was raised with four hungry siblings. Eating out was a rare treat and never anywhere fancy, so Fig was more comfortable in diners than upscale restaurants. He especially liked to watch the food being cooked, right there on the grill.

The place was a homey greasy spoon, where you found your own seat and waited. Fig opened up his paper network diagram on the table to pass the time. Completely engrossed, he failed to notice the waitress standing over him. After a minute or so, she said, "I was wondering if you would ever notice me."

He looked up and his heart skipped a beat, rendering him almost speechless. He did manage to ask her if she had a twin sister. Jamie replied she was not a twin, and she thought she'd seen him somewhere, knowing full well that this was the guy in the bar drinking Perrier, and ignoring her. Jamie also noticed Fig didn't have a ring on his finger.

"I was wondering if you would like to order some

food and why are you are playing with little circles and lines?"

"I would like two eggs over easy, please. On whole wheat toast, with black coffee, orange juice, a glass of water with no ice, and these little circles and lines are used in graph theory. I'm using it to solve a problem, but I really need a computer hacker for the edges."

"Why do you need a hacker?"

"Because I want to know why I got fired for no good reason and why someone sent me a fake bomb." This all came rushing out without any thought, making Fig a little embarrassed.

"I'll be right back with your food, sir."

On her way to place the order, Jamie thought, "If this guy is for real, maybe he could me give a job? He seemed a little odd. Maybe he's shy, but he needs a hacker? He's building a network of people of some kind?"

On the way back with Fig's meal, Jamie thought, "Solving puzzles with a cute guy sounds like the break I need, unless he's crazy."

Fig enjoyed his late breakfast-cum-lunch and wondered if he dared ask the woman out. Or would that be too forward, plus she was working. He decided to take a chance and just as he was about to do so on his way out, she stopped him and said, "I'm sorry about your job, but I know someone who is a really good hacker. Do you need white, grey or black hat?"

Fig replied that he would really appreciate meeting the guy, if she would give him his phone number? "Sure," said Jamie, handing him a number written on a scrap of paper. "I think you two will get along. By the way, what's your name?"

"Jeb Newton, but for obvious reasons my friends call me Fig." Glancing at her name tag, which indicated her name was Jackie, he took the note and said he'd really enjoyed the meal and off he went. Too chicken to ask her out.

Early that evening, after a long snowy and breathtakingly beautiful walk, and while sitting by a crackling log fire, Fig decided to call the hacker guy. He was a little nervous about it. He'd never met a hacker. The only ones he knew were crooks or heroes in action-adventure movies, who broke laws all the time.

Eventually he plucked up the courage and called. The phone was answered by a woman's voice. Fig explained that he was trying to reach a guy who he was told is good with computers and that he had received his phone number from a lady working in George's Diner.

Jamie couldn't resist a giggle and admitted who she was, and that her name was Jamie, not Jackie. She said her hacker friend was a little shy and would prefer to meet in a safe place in a public environment, where they could talk in relative privacy and safety. "How does 2:00 p.m. tomorrow, outside the iHop in University Mall on Dorset Street, work for you?" said Jamie. "The place is noisy but the seats in the mall are comfortable and usually deserted. Where are you staying, by the way?"

"A rented cabin in Burlington Forest, a short walk from the mall. No problem."

Fig was going to meet his first real hacker, the next

day. He thanked her profusely, but didn't ask her out because he assumed the hacker was her boyfriend or her husband.

———

It was a three-mile hike from the cabin to the mall, the next day, but a lovely sunny snowy day it was. Fig arrived with an hour to spare, found the seating after buying a coffee in iHop, to go. He settled into the plastic mall seat, pulled out his computer and disappeared into his network. While taking a short break, Fig started thinking about the upcoming meeting.

"Where should I start?

How much does the guy need to know?

How do I know I can trust him and get him to understand that I'm trying to remain invisible, at least for a while?

How much will it cost?

What exactly should I ask him to do?"

These thoughts were swirling around in Fig's head, when he spotted Jamie approaching, alone. "Bummer! The guy's not coming."

"What happened to your hacker friend? Is he coming later?"

"You're looking at him, doofus! What makes you think all hackers are men. I'm a damned good one, I would let you know, maybe even the best, who knows?"

This left Fig speechless.

"I should be offended but I'm actually amused.

Amused by the dumb expression on your face. Don't look at me like that."

Jamie sat on an adjacent seat, looked around to be sure there were no people within earshot, and opened the discussion.

"First! Why are you wearing that stupid hat? I can hardly see your face? I get it! Security cameras! Second! I'm not a professional hacker, but I'd like to be, and you would be my first professional engagement. It was a hobby for years, and now I'm trying to work out how to become a well-compensated white hat hacker. It turns out not to be so simple. OK?"

"Sure!" said Fig, "but why do you wear those nerdy glasses?"

"None of your business! I thought maybe you could hire me to do my first real hacking job. What do you think?"

Then she smiled sweetly, looked directly at Fig, and waited.

"OK! I'm sorry. I underestimated you and I hope you will forgive me. I've never met a hacker before, male or female."

"Forgiven."

"I have a problem and I need information to solve it. Confidential information! Is this conversation confidential?"

"If you hire me, I will keep everything between us."

"OK! I suspect something really nefarious is being done to environmental activists. I think it comes all the way down from the new president, Miller, who has no interest in a healthy environment. This resulted in my being fired, without cause, from a job I loved, in North Carolina. The excuse they used was from my old school record. There is no way they could have found that without hacking into some database."

Jamie waited. She knew all about the power of silence.

"I want to find the bastards who did this to me, got my previous boss, Nick Page, fired, and are putting horrible pressure on my environmental scientist colleagues to stop their work. I suspect it's a government crook and I call them *Shelob*, the spider at the center of my network diagram, that looks like a deranged spider's web," said Fig.

"*Shelob*? I like that. So you are looking for Sauron?"

"In effect, yes," said Fig, "though *Golum* would be a good start, and I have my suspicions on that front already. Does this sound like something that would interest you, and if so, how much is your fee?"

Then it was Fig's turn to be silent.

Jamie said, "If we can agree on my salary you have yourself a hacker. I hate the new president and his disregard for the environment. The fee will be reasonable, but it includes a rider."

"And that is?"

"That you help me if you can, after this is done, to get a job as a white hat hacker. I suspect you are some kind of university professor, so surely you have contacts in academia, government or industry, who might help me build my career?"

"Where should we start?" said Fig, "I don't know anything about hacking, but I know a lot about the application of mathematics, especially network theory, to solving problems related to chemicals and their potential to damage people, animals, plants, in fact the whole Biosphere. My speciality is the interaction of arrays of trophic cascades."

"Which are?"

"Just what they sound like. A series of negative events that cascade down a food chain, killing whole families of animals and plants in the chain on their way down."

"For instance."

"The best known is the effect of removing wolves from Yellowstone Park."

"Oh Yes! They put them back and everything is much better now, right?"

"Exactly, and my work highlights the negative impacts of industrial activities on food chains all over the world, including the effects of climate change. That I think is why I was fired, and I want to know which son of a bitch, or sons of bitches, orchestrated it, and I want to take them down."

"Sounds perfect," said Jamie, with a grin. "Sounds like you need a *Mata Hari*. At your service, sir."

They spent the next hour going over Fig's network diagram, providing each other with their work histories, and slowly creating a plan of action.

Jamie explained to Fig what could be done as a hacker, how she could get in anywhere with time and patience. How choosing the target or targets was critical as they needed to be studied in detail before any network penetration was attempted. She explained the tools she used, the kind of successes she had achieved already, her concerns about being spotted and ending up in court, or worse, jail.

Fig then laid out all the information he had, expanding on each member or vertex in his network, and the trouble he was having filling in the edge data, the connections flowing through this complex spider's web of people and places.

Jamie said, "The first step is to choose a target. Go think about that. Give me $300 to get started as I'll need a few burner phones and some more software. Salary can be discussed later, if it turns out I can help. If I can't be of use there's no further cost, and I'll return your money. If I can assist you, as an amateur you found waiting tables, I'd be quite happy with $25 an hour. That is while I'm actually hacking. I want to help you catch your sons of bitches, as such people are despicable."

"They are also dangerous," said Fig, "so we have to be careful, almost to the point of paranoia. It would be best if we not communicate with our families and friends back home. Can you deal with that?"

"I'm familiar with that problem as a black hat hacker," said Jamie, "and I look forward to working with you. It sounds exciting. I talk to my daughter, Edith, every day, but I'll give her a call to explain that I'll be out of touch for a few weeks, and I'll send postcards every-other day. I'll send them in such a way that their source location can't be tracked, don't worry. I'll also explain that I'm safe, having a great vacation, and I won't be able to call for a few weeks, either. I don't want to attract your pursuers toward my daughter."

As Jamie prepared to leave, she said, "Call me in the morning, when you've chosen our target, or better still come by the diner for breakfast and I'll see you there. I have a bet with myself on that. And while you're thinking about your target, buy Kevin Mitnick's book on how to stay invisible online. It will clue you into my challenges as a black hat. Consider it homework. The more we understand each other's skills the better."

"Great idea!" said Fig.

"Do you have homework for me?" said Jamie.

"Read *Silent Spring* by Rachel Carson. Then you'll know where I'm coming from. She's my guiding light. Deceased but very much alive in my mind," said Fig.

"One last thing, Fig," said Jamie. "Assume a hacker is tracking you, and encrypt everything, even your mother's birth date."

Then she headed for the exit, knowing he was watching her leave. Jamie resisted the temptation to turn and look back at him.

"Why spoil it."

CHAPTER THIRTEEN

Back in the cabin later that afternoon, following another enjoyable trail walk, Fig bought and downloaded the book on hacking that Jamie recommended, and started reading it. It was pretty heavy going. He purchased it from Kobo using a Kobo gift card rather than Amazon. Fig thought this would reduce the chance of his being detected online. Fig was taking Jamie's advice to heart.

In order to select a first target, Fig did some research using his mathematical network model. The trick when applying mathematics to biological systems is to realize that there is almost never an analytic or single equation solution. At school he'd learned how to use a simple equation to determine the speed of a falling object or the location in space of an accelerating plane at a moment in time. In biology a numerical approximation is the best one can do. It was the advent of computers that made Fig's graph theory networking possible.

While Fig waited for Jamie to investigate connections between the people in his network, he started to track down more scientists of interest. Taking phone numbers out his little black book, he called colleagues who might have left or been forced to leave the EPA since President Miller arrived in the White House. The first person he called was someone he knew well, Dr. Larry Long, who was well respected for his research on the effects of major industrial activities on the Earth's climate.

One of the first things Miller had done when he became president was to put pressure on EPA administrators to replace tried and true scientists, like Larry, with his own faithful acolytes. None of these people were schooled in environmental safety or the science of climate change. Most of them were advocates for the coal, oil and gas industries. This led to downgrading or elimination of climate change research at the EPA.

Larry told Fig that he was forced to leave the EPA, where he had built an effective research team, including excellent technical support and a growing program in global warming effects. He'd received frequent invitations to speak at international climate conferences. Larry told Fig that Alec Chariton, the Miller-appointed head of the EPA, had forbidden the use of the terms "climate change" or "global warming," in any EPA documents. Chariton, the non-scientist and CEO of Worldwide Oil and Gas, claimed that these were unproven concepts.

"How are you doing?" said Fig.

"I'm fine, Fig, and thanks for asking. I guess you heard that I found a new job."

"I heard, and was sad to see you go, Larry."

"I had to get away from the jerks now running the EPA. They were closing all my programs and wanted me to work on something useless. So I left! I could read the writing on the wall, but I sure was sorry to leave my team."

"I know it's not my business, Larry, but were you under any kind of pressure to leave? I mean direct pressure?"

"Why do you ask, Fig?"

"I was fired after being pressured by an institute sponsor to downplay some of our data. I refused, and it led to my dismissal on trumped up charges."

"Damn! I'm sorry to hear that," said Larry.

"The thought just popped into my head that something similar may have happened to you and other environmental scientists, given what's happening under President Miller. You were clearly happy and successful in your work, which was going well as far as I could tell from your publications."

"Everything was going great, Fig."

"I heard you'd left and wondered why?"

"It's funny you should say that," said Larry. "Last summer I had excellent students, and we had fascinating problems to solve, when this new boss appeared. He came out of nowhere, and I only met him once, very briefly. I took one look at the guy and disliked him on sight."

"Why?"

"Because he was wearing tasseled loafers. I've never met an honest scientist who does. My intuition turned out to be correct. Within months things went from bad to worse. This guy and his boss, Barrett, seem to be on a mission to destroy the EPA by removing our best scientists. By the way, Fig, I really appreciated you making me a coauthor on that last publication in Environmental Toxicology."

"Of course, Larry. You were a great help with that project. By the way, what was the name of that tasseled loafer guy?"

"Turner. James Turner. He called himself Dr. Turner, but he didn't seem to know shit about science. I think he was just a sneaky politician. Anyway, thanks for the co-authorship. Publish or perish. Right now it's publish and perish, especially if you're working on climate change."

Fig thanked Larry for the information, which he said would remain confidential, and added both Larry and Turner to his growing network diagram. Subsequent phone calls led Fig to other elimination cases in the EPA. Good scientists forced out one way and another.

Fig spent the next two hours calling old colleagues, tracking down those who'd lost jobs or chosen to move on, including staff at his institute in Greensboro, the FDA, and several academic and corporate research groups he'd collaborated with over the years. There were eleven people he knew well enough to ask difficult questions without raising an alarm. Like any other group of humans, scientists love to gossip, and the last thing Fig needed was for *Shelob* to learn that he was trying to track her down.

Fig wanted his unknown nemesis to think he'd turned tail and run.

Of the eleven, five said they saw a better opportunity and would say no more. The remaining six had been forced out against their wishes. One corporate colleague said an unknown party had spread rumors that he was an alcoholic. The company offered him free rehab and a severance package. The guy, Dr. John Adams, said he liked a drink now and then, he was no drunkard, but they forced him out anyway. "They gave me a generous severance package, to encourage me to keep my mouth shut, I suspect."

Then there were two other corporates. One said he was accused of impropriety with a junior staff member, and the other was "no longer needed." This left one government employee and two academics, of which the latter had their government grants terminated, forcing them to leave.

Finally, Dr. Margaret Williams had been working at the FDA for years as a well-respected geochemist. She was researching ways in which pharmaceuticals entered water tables, to eventually end up in drinking water. She was treated in the same way as Fig. Old confidential information was mysteriously unearthed, spun against her, and used to force her out.

Little did Fig know that all eleven names were listed

on white boards in room 301 of the DHS on the St. Elizabeth's Campus, Washington, DC.

Fig added all eleven to his network and created a spreadsheet listing the name, type of scientist, work location, government, corporate or academic, and the way each was 'eliminated.' So far Fig appeared to be the only one to have received a bomb threat.

"So I'm special," thought Fig, "but why?"

His network was growing nicely, as he'd added a number of climate change deniers and organizations. These included the National Hog Farmer group, the Anti-Vegan Club, extreme right wing climate change deniers, pro-Miller groups, ousted EPA employee replacements and their bosses, the entire board of directors of GEPI, selected divisions of the CDC and FDA, and critics of university departments focused on climate change research. But he was short of information on the links between his subjects. Fig was hoping Jamie could help with that problem. He then made a list of recent reports of pipeline leaks, air pollution near hog lagoons, and president Miller's attacks on environmental movements.

Looking at his network in some dismay, Fig thought, "*Shelob* is hiding in there somewhere. Damn!"

While doing this research, Fig tried to find the record of his high school Asperger's diagnosis. He couldn't find it anywhere and he knew where to look. Clearly, he was up against a formidable enemy. Probably one with access to some of the best computer hackers money could buy.

Fig wondered what Jamie would deliver for his $25 an hour.

CHAPTER FOURTEEN

James Turner's Temporary Office. Homeland Security, Washington, DC. Turner is on the phone.

"Hi James, how's the work coming along?"

"Good morning, Dr. Barrett. It's going well. Why do you ask?"

"Chariton is on my case to show progress, because President Miller is on his case, and Miller is pissed because he says we are moving too slowly."

"The teams are working around the clock. We have hundreds of scientists to deal with. It's not so easy as each case takes time"

"I know, James, we just have to keep Miller happy. What are your teams, again?"

"Informatics and Targeting, and they work in isolation to prevent leaks. Informatics consists of Fred Sassy who has built a database of over a thousand tree-huggers. And there are three computer hackers using his data. One you provided, Bruce Henley, and I must say he's the most normal of the group. The other two came from Bill Hotchkiss and they are really weird."

"Bruce is a good man."

"They seem to be able to find dirt on almost anyone, then they pass it along to the Targeting group, which is run by Sally Smarts, a scary lady I must say. She decides the best correctional techniques to apply, and applies them.

"And?"

"We've dealt with more than eighty of about a thousand active environmental scientists in Sassy's database, by..."

"I don't need any more details, James. Take care what you say on the phone, OK?"

"Sorry, Dr. Barrett."

"Chariton told me the president specifically mentioned that institute in North Carolina and the renegade Newton. How's that one going?"

"Eighty out of nearly a thousand doesn't sound like a lot of progress, but each one takes time, and we are still mastering our tools."

"And Newton?"

"Sally said she has it under control."

James started to sweat a little and waited.

"That's fine, James, but we still have to keep the president happy. I thought Strickland had taken care of Newton, yet he is still pissing off some of the president's friends. See what you can do and let me know before you do it."

Then the phone went dead!

Turner said to himself, "You don't care how we do it, but you don't condone violence. How then am I supposed to silence Newton?"

Turner took a deep breath, and put in a call to Bill Hotchkiss.

CHAPTER FIFTEEN

After a freezing but enjoyable walk, Fig arrived at George's Diner for an early breakfast and took a seat. Within minutes Jamie turned up with his breakfast, two organic eggs over easy on whole wheat toast, coffee, orange juice and water without ice.

"Hi Jamie! Guess I'm pretty distracted right now, I don't even remember ordering, lot going on. That book on hacking was really interesting, by the way. Now I know that nothing is safe on the Internet."

Jamie did the looking and waiting thing.

"How are you doing today, by the way?"

"I wondered when you would ask, and I won my bet."

"Which bet?"

"That you eat the same breakfast every day, so you wouldn't remember if you'd ordered or not. I hope it meets with your satisfaction, kind sir."

Fig said he'd been having the same breakfast for as long as he could remember.

"Enjoy and I'll join you in a few minutes. We aren't busy and Martha is really easy going when things are quiet, it seems."

Jamie returned about fifteen minutes later and sat down opposite Fig, and said, "Better not to go over too much in here. We'll meet up after my shift. I think it's probably safe to take a chance on the mall again. After that we had better meet in different places each time. I went by there and found some seats that are out of the range of any security cameras."

"You are a real *Mata Hari*. It's giving me a sense of security."

"Don't feel too secure. We don't know who you are up against, but a fake bomb sounds pretty serious. We also don't know their resources, which may be substantial. They almost certainly have a hacker tracking you already. I bet you pissed them off with your website bait. Did you say anything negative about President Miller?"

"I only called him *The Ecocidal Fool*, which he is, and it worked like a charm."

"Good job, Fig. You triggered a bomb threat. I wonder what their next treat will be, it's sure to be something as long as your website is up."

"Oh! I have plans to make it even more irritating."

"Why don't you hold off on that, and let's see if we can turn the tables on them before they track you down and do something worse."

"How might they find me, do you think?"

"Facial recognition software, after hacking into the security camera inside that little golden globe by the iHop seats and scanning through the recordings."

"Really?"

"Security cameras are easy to hack. Remember *The Bourne Identity* scene at the train station when they killed the reporter?"

Jamie stood abruptly, and said, "Back to work. See you at the *treffpunkt* at three," and she was back waiting tables.

———

Fig arrived on time to find Jamie waiting at the mall entrance next to the iHop. Without visible acknowledgement from either of them, Fig followed her to some seats in an alcove.

She sat down, looked at him and waited.

Fig was getting used to this unnerving habit of hers, knowing that he had to say something, if he could work out what.

Nothing was said for a minute or so, then Jamie said, "Well?"

"Well, what?"

"Did you choose our first target?"

"Oh yes! I did."

"And?"

"I called around and found eleven people who'd moved on, and six told me how they'd been removed, but I think our strongest thread to *Shelob* is upstream from Strickland to his handler. I bet he has one. He's not the sharpest tool in the shed."

"Did you make the calls from the cabin?"

"Sure! Why?"

"You'll have to move soon."

Fig was embarrassed he hadn't thought of that. He fished out his network diagram, with nearly a hundred people, known and unknown, and a few edges connecting them.

Jamie said, "I have no idea how graph theory works, so could you give me the Cliff Notes version?"

Fig explained how he put all the variables, in this case people and organizations, into labeled circles. He then connected the circles based on evidence of communication between them. If two circles were labeled A and B, and B sent emails or phoned A, a line would go from B to A, with an arrowhead pointing at A. If there were frequent emails, he would make the line thicker or put a score on the line, depending how the software was designed.

"That's neat! How do you use it?"

"I look for patterns, but in order to do that I need lines connecting all the people, and ideally each line should have a communication score."

"That's where I come in, right?"

"Exactly! I was fired for no good reason. The lawyer, Enrique Torres, was clearly in on it. The previous director, Nicholas Page, a great guy, was replaced within months of the new president arriving in the White House. This suggests that a person or group of people had been communicating and someone had instructed them to effect these changes."

"And this would require dirt on Nick Page and you, right?"

"Yes, and it appears that dozens of scientists, if not hundreds, have experienced similar problems. This activity should appear in the network as strong information flow along certain groups of edges."

"How would that look?"

"Strickland drove out six senior scientists from the institute, and here we are as a fan of lines around Strickland's vertex, with arrows pointing from him to each of us. The ominous activity in my opinion, Jamie, is the flood of replacements of good scientists by Miller's incompetent sycophants, and the anti-environmental activity that is going on at the EPA that Larry told me about. My phone calls also revealed similar things happening at other government-controlled institutions."

"Which are?"

"The FDA and several universities. I think there's a clandestine group in the federal government and *Shelob* is masterminding it."

Jamie smiled again at Fig's use of the name of the horrible spider in *The Lord of the Rings Trilogy*!

"Who is your *Gollum*, Fig?"

"I suspect it's Strickland's handler. Do you think you can find him or her?"

Jamie ignored Fig's question, and proceeded to ask a series of insightful questions of her own, about the mathematical analysis of the network. Fig explained that graph theory programs can group clusters of vertices and determine critical areas of information flow. He went on to describe the calculation of shortest communication paths and most importantly for large networks, identification of gateway vertices, those that control information flow between large groups."

"You mean it can find key communication links between scientists at, say, the EPA, and those working for Homeland Security or the FDA?"

"Yes!" said Fig. "If a particular person is directing the operation, which must be quite extensive given what I've found, the software may highlight them as a gateway. Last night I added eleven what I call *eliminated scientists* to the network with just a couple of hours of phone calls. This means hundreds of environmental scientists are being systematically sidelined."

"Sounds like quite an operation."

"By the way, Jamie, did you get a chance to do your homework?"

"*Silent Spring*? Of course. I was taught to always do my homework, and what a book. Couldn't put it down. What a lady, but they are doing it again! This is why I'm risking my neck sitting in this mall, hiding from a mystery hacker and some kind of attack dog, with a virtual stranger who may attract political ghouls in my direction?"

"Think of it this way, Jamie. We are continuing Rachel Carson's work."

"When you put it that way, Fig, it makes me shiver with excitement. Let's take them down."

This was music to Fig's ears.

Fig said, "This activity is being financed by a corporation or federal tax dollars. If it's as extensive as I think, and the network map will provide an estimate of that in time, it could be a multimillion-dollar operation."

He went on to explain that he had already noticed a pattern but he needed a lot more data on the edges. The majority of ousted scientists were actively publishing on climate change or environmental damage by industrial activity. Each had been ousted using one of several methods. Moved to non-environment related work, accused of real or implied scandal, had their federal grants canceled, or told they were not needed anymore and simply fired.

"For instance," said, Fig, "my previous director, Nick Page, a great guy and excellent scientist and manager, was subjected to a fabricated scandal, based on false accusations of sexual relations with a student. Then he was replaced by that dick, Strickland, who seems bent on closing the place. Adams was accused of alcoholism and given a generous severance package."

"All eleven had similar stories?"

"Five refused to talk but were hiding something. Each of the remaining six were ousted by one of those methods."

Fig said, "I've been suspicious of Dave Strickland for some time. I've never liked him. He treated my colleagues badly, and he is more like a politician than a scientist. Killing the institute would be a real coup for many big corporations, especially if no-one noticed."

"You think Strickland is our best link to *Shelob*?"

"When I checked his publications in PubMed it seemed that he was a politician from day one. His first publication was a co-authorship of an article in Science. He hasn't published anything in the last five years, and I couldn't find his position in the federal government. It seemed to be classified."

"I can probably find it."

"Well, your first targets are Strickland and his handler."

"I'm not new to this cloak and dagger stuff, Fig. The trick is to treat it as a game, while watching your back."

She asked for an electronic copy of the network diagram on a flash drive and reminded Fig to keep off the Internet, unless she was directly supervising his work. She repeated the importance of hiding his IP address at all times, to never step out from behind the firewall and virtual personal network, or VPN, and to keep his gps turned off at all times.

"Better still, Fig, let's get you a new machine. That old MacBook Air is past its best. If you have the cash let's do it right now. I'll set it up so it's well cloaked and I'll give you some training."

"Thanks, I need all the help I can get, *Mata Hari*."

"Don't thank me, just start my timecard."

She returned to studying the network map, asking some more questions about each of the people involved. "What kind of lawyer is Torres?" Jamie wondered. The wheels were turning, and Fig was no longer on his own.

Then Jamie gave Fig a short lesson on the joys of

hacking, the dangers of being caught, and the penalties, which were considerable. She described how she worked to stay invisible.

"Remember, Fig, even the *Invisible Man* left footprints in the snow. Furthermore, black hat hackers converted to law-abiding white hats have a nose for their own. Makes me nervous some days, but then, that's half the fun. So, what do you want me to find out about this Strickland guy, or as you would say, asshole?"

"His childhood, religion and potential weaknesses, history of crimes or misdemeanors, which branch of the federal government he came from to take over GEPI, and why. Can you get information about his phone calls and emails, because that would help fill in some edges in the network?"

"Is that all?"

Fig smiled with relief.

"I'll text you about where and when to meet via *Encryptext*. Don't look so surprised, I know you use it. I've already checked you out. Quite a scientist, lots of publications and not limited to one area of study. I think you are a renaissance man. Sorry about the divorce, but your kids seem to be doing fine, and your ex has a nice boyfriend. Didn't seem like a fair divorce settlement to me, though, but it could have been worse? How is your brother doing after the accident by the way?"

Fig stared at Jamie in shock, thinking, "Is nothing private, anymore?" while Jamie continued.

"I noticed you were diagnosed with mild Asperger's Syndrome in high school, which explains a lot, including the same breakfast every day, and your scientific ability, I suspect."

Jamie hesitated for a second, but Fig made no comment. He was learning to sit, watch and wait.

"I looked around in your institute servers and noticed that your pension plan sucks. You only have $80,000 after fifteen years, while Strickland has over a million after only a year and so does Torres. What's up with that?"

After smiling at Fig's dumbfounded expression, Jamie said, "I'll be in touch, see you tomorrow Mr. Scientist," and she left without another word.

CHAPTER SIXTEEN

They met at 2:00 p.m., at a bandstand in an empty park. It was cold with some breeze, but the place was out of the way and out of the wind. Fig found Jamie easily enough and she immediately said, "Don't worry, you won't freeze to death. This will be short and sweet. By the way, I resigned from my job at the diner, and my last shift is tomorrow morning. We need to move soon."

Fig asked if her leaving the diner was a problem for them, even though she'd only worked there for a few days. She said she'd explained she'd had a personal emergency, and they said it was no problem as business was slow. She said they told her they'd enjoyed working with her. "You never know when you will need a good job recommendation, Fig. Do you think Strickland would give you a good reference for your next job?"

"I bet he would, if it was nothing to do with the environment or climate change. Then he could say mission accomplished."

Jamie said, "I bet you're right and, by the way, I think the less we are seen together in public the better. Watch out for those security cameras, they aren't secure. You never know who's watching. Let's do most of our work through texting. Remember to update virus definitions every time you use your computer, and always turn off the radio before closing it down. Nothing online is secure, even for me."

"Yes boss," said Fig, with a salute.

"OK! Smart guy. You have no idea how vulnerable you are. In fact, I would prefer that you not go online unless I'm around. Do what you can with your burner phone, preferably as far from the cabin as possible. By the way, I need money to hire my mentor, Yoda. He would probably help me for free, but it is better to pay ."

"How much will Yoda cost? I assume it's a he."

"Yes! Yoda is a guy, and one of the best. I think a thousand dollars would keep him happy, for now at least. I'll ask, and let you know. Can you spring for a thousand? It's really important."

"Sure, but can you really trust other hackers?"

Jamie said, "You seem to be trusting me." They both laughed at that.

Then Jamie briefly described her work so far, which she said clocked up four hours. "For your $100 you got a back door into your institute main server, which seems to have pretty poor security. I located and penetrated the institute data center, which is actually safer than the cloud, if you do it right, as there have been increasing numbers of breaches of the cloud recently."

"Sounds pretty good for a hundred bucks," said Fig.

"I've just started."

Fig zipped his mouth shut.

"Then I downloaded all of Strickland's emails over the last few months, and went to his phone, which doesn't even have VPN, and downloaded his call, email and gps logs. By the way, Strickland has made several trips to Washington, DC recently, to the EPA Head Office and one to Homeland Security, the St. Elizabeth's Campus."

Fig sat there, amazed.

"Here are your $100 files," she said, handing Fig a flash drive. Then she reached into her bag and brought out a thermos of coffee and two croissants. Fig was getting to like Jamie more and more.

"Oh yes, Fig, I forgot. I looked at Strickland's phone log and there were several calls to a Dr. James Turner."

"That's the tasseled loafer guy Larry told me about."

"It took me a while to pin him down. Turner is on staff at the EPA, reporting to Charles Barrett, but his phone was in the DHS building, the same one Strickland visited."

"Damn. The plot thickens. Maybe we are getting somewhere."

Fig then plied Jamie with questions about things he'd learned from the book on hacking, and Jamie wanted to know more about his eco-toxicology work, especially how air and rocks were connected. Fig gave the example of the carbon-silicon cycle, that protects the planet from snowball Earth and how it is linked to climate change.

"Everything in the Biosphere is connected, Jamie. Here's a good example, one that President Miller should know about, but he'll never care. Talk about dumb as rocks, though I'm not so sure about rocks being dumb."

"Surely you are joking, Fig."

"I'm not joking about Miller or the rocks."

Fig went on to describe how climate change had destroyed the habitats of some sea otters, leading to a trophic cascade.

"Trophic cascades, again?" said Jamie.

"One thing leading to another down a food chain, like an avalanche or a flash flood, carrying death and destruction for miles, sometimes thousands of miles."

"So loss of habitat for sea otters did this? How?"

"It led to overpopulation of sea urchins, a staple diet for certain sea otters, which resulted in destruction of a kelp forest, that was followed by die off of a number of species of fish, upon which depended certain sea birds that played a critical role in the health of some oyster beds, as a result of which an entire population of oyster fishermen were put out of business, leading to the deci-mation of a small town, followed by a slump in house prices and loss of many jobs, including those of a number of local realtors."

"Really?"

"Yes, Jamie, and EcoWorld predicted most of it and many other trophic cascades all over the world. I confirmed some of the predictions with the help of several wildlife biologists and social scientists, several of which recently lost their jobs."

"Are you telling me that die off of otters caused realtors to lose their jobs, while investigating the die off of the otters caused scientists to lose their jobs?"

"You got it, Jamie. Thanks to people like President Miller."

"On that note," said Jamie, "let's move along, as I'm starting to freeze."

"It is pretty cold, I agree."

"Here's what I want you to do, Fig. Copy the material from that flash drive onto your machine but keep the radio off. What I did was strictly illegal, classic black hat, but we have no choice. It seems we are in a fight with an eco-terrorist federal government. All we have are our minds and your savings. They have an army and millions of dollars, a classic David and Goliath situation."

Then Jamie made a real belly laugh, out loud.

"This is much more exciting than waiting tables."

Fig felt good to see Jamie so happy.

"I'll get in touch with Yoda, negotiate a price for some assistance with staying unnoticed. You start reading those files, so you can weight the edges of your network. By the way, you mentioned Charles Barrett, the guy who came to your defense. I have a feeling that he is involved, somehow. He sure had his finger on the pulse of you and your institute. I'll check him out too."

"I've often wondered about that. Was a big surprise to me, and probably more of a surprise to Strickland."

They then started to walk back to the town center.

"I need to choose a government institution in which to start my penetration work," said Jamie. "Where do you suggest?"

"The Department of Homeland Security? They can be pretty vicious. I doubt EPA staff would send out fake bombs, but Homeland Security wouldn't hesitate to send live ones. Thanks for the coffee and croissant. Really hit the spot."

As they split up, Jamie said, "See you tomorrow, Fig, same time, some other place. I'll find somewhere a little warmer."

Off she went, smiling to herself, knowing Fig was smitten. Jamie was taken with Fig, but she was in no way ready to get involved at least for another year.

On arriving back at the cabin, Fig booted up his new MacBook Pro that he'd traded in for his machine plus $800 at the Computer Exchange in Burlington. His old MacBook Air had served him well, and Fig was sad to see it go. He tended to become more attached to useful equipment and animals than to most people. He found Jamie's flash drive was full of massive files, most of which he did not understand. Then he noticed that Jamie had provided a file called ReadThisFirstFig.txt.

"Don't worry about most of this stuff, just take a look at the phone logs and see what you can find. See you tomorrow, and best of luck, Jamie. PS You have to get out of that place, ASAP. If they track your burner phone location, we have a problem. Let's leave town after my last shift. I should be able to get away at about 1:30 p.m."

Fig was starting to find all this cloak and dagger stuff to be exhausting.

———

Meanwhile, back at Fig's apartment, a plumber's van pulled up. Fig had been waiting ages for that leaky shower drain upstairs to be fixed. Two guys in overalls with the company logo, *Plumbing the Depths,* on their chests, climbed out. One of them dug around for gear in the back of the van, while the other took Fig's apartment key from under the doormat and went inside.

CHAPTER SEVENTEEN

Room 301, Homeland Security, Washington, DC.

Back in that weird room lined by white boards laden with a growing list of names, three silent hackers and Fred were clicking away. The latter was also nervously consuming yet another doughnut. He was in the middle of tracking down a few more anti-American liberal pansies, their name according to James Turner, who walked in at that very moment.

The three hackers didn't even look up, they just sat at their screens and typed. They were all wearing sweatpants, two had weird tee shirts and varied amounts of facial ironmongery and tattoos. One of them, Bruce Henley, "was almost normal looking," said Fred to himself. All three were deeply engaged in their work. Fred found they were pretty friendly when they stopped typing, but only if you talked about video games and computer code, neither of which interested Fred.

As Turner came in the room, he said, "Good morning everyone," to which only Fred responded. "Guys! You too, please. Could I have your attention for a moment?" The three hackers turned as one with little apparent interest and Turner said, "We have a special target. He's corporate. Which one of you is corporate?"

Bruce Henley said, "That's my area, sir. What do you need?"

"Could you work with Fred to research a particularly difficult dirtbag? He's making waves and we need it to stop. We want to know where he is in order to send a message. He's created a new website that's pissing off the president. Can you take it down?"

"Of course, no problem!" said Bruce, with the flicker of a smile.

Then James walked over to the corporate white board area, drew a red circle around Dr. Jeb Newton and said, "This guy. A real pain in the ass. We got him fired, thanks to your excellent work previously, Bruce, and now we need him to stop."

"No problem," said Bruce, who thought, "What the fuck are we doing?" He had finally realized that they were attacking real people, but the money was tempting and hacking for great pay was good, "but?"

Fred sucked up to Turner by telling him that he'd work with Bruce, but first he'd do a little sleuthing on his own. Once Turner was out of the room, Fred turned to Bruce and said, "How about I look for compromising information, while you try to find him?"

"Sure," said Bruce, thinking, "You couldn't find dirt on Al Capone," but he kept it to himself and started his journey through Fig's childhood, school reports, college and job history, photos, sports events, publications, and eventually his emails, texts, and Facebook posts.

"I remember this guy. He's the one with Asperger's." Then he found Fig's website, *The Thoughtful Ecotoxicologist*.

"Gotcha!"

———

The next morning, Turner came back and said to Bruce, "I need you to come with me, please."

Bruce carefully closed down his workstation to block any incoming traffic, and climbed out of his chair. As they walked down the hall, Turner said, "If you do a good job, there's a fifteen-grand bonus in it. I think you will find it a fascinating project because you won't be working alone. I need you to meet your counterpart, Sally Smarts. She looks like an ordinary lady, but I would be careful with her if I were you. She's sent several people to the hospital, so she says."

They arrived at another solid door, Room 319, which also had both electronic and hard key security locks. Inside was a small office with two desks, each with workstations, plus there was a coffee pot but no cream doughnuts, and one of the most attractive women Bruce had ever met. She was about his age, seeming sweet and demure as she smiled up at him.

"Pleased to meet you," said Bruce, shyly. Great computer hacker who struggles with women, and this one is a knockout. She had straight silvery brown hair framing a lovely face with dark come hither eyes, which matched her slim perfect figure. As she stood to greet Bruce, Sally had a tantalizing way of moving her cute butt.

"Shit," thought Bruce, "I'm going to have to be careful with this one, she's clearly dangerous in more ways than one."

Turner said, "Bruce Henley meet Sally Smarts. Sally does the shoe leather work for us as they say in the movies. She knows much of what we know about Newton, and she needs you to send her in the right direction to help us take him down."

Sally could see that Bruce was interested in her and in spite of his nerdy demeanor, she kind of liked his looks. "This isn't going to be no big romance, but mutual attraction might just get the job done with some fun along the way," thought Sally.

They were now the soft hit team for Fig. Harder hits were another story, which might come into play if Bruce and Sally couldn't stop Newton's irritating activities.

Sally came from a rough neighborhood in Phil-adelphia, worked in car repossession, or repo, though she no longer carried a gun. She had her own methods, creative threats, which tended to scare people shitless.

Much milder mannered, Bruce Henley, was one of the best hackers in the business. They then prepared to get down to the work of tracking and intimidating Fig. It was good money, but it became about more than the money as the battle proceeded. It became a game of cat and mouse that they had no intention of losing.

Turner was watching their interaction, when Sally turned, and said, "Jim, first we need to review all the details of this tree-loving pain in the ass, liberal mother fucker, Dr. Snooty Pants Jeb Newton." She was parroting Turner and calling him Jim just to irritate him, a person for whom she had zero respect.

"Don't worry Jim. If this guy," she said, pointing her thumb at Bruce, "is half as good as you say he is, we'll get your man to see sense. What do you think, Bruce Henley?"

"We'll get him," Bruce replied, looking into the eyes of Sally Smarts, where he saw behind the beauty a mind like a steel trap.

Then Turner said to Sally, "That job for Hotchkiss, did you deal with it?"

"I watched the whole thing go down. The cops called the bomb squad. It was pretty exciting, but Newton lives in a shitty drug infested apartment complex. What kind of professor does that?"

Bruce said, "Is there a clear plan of action for what to do when we catch up to Newton?"

"Of course," said Sally. "I'll threaten his kids, his friends, his ex-wife and his parents. It's all standard protocol. His work hurts Brazilian farmers who are taking down the Amazon rain forest to raise beef cattle, and they kill environmental activists almost every day. They've killed over a thousand of them already. I'll threaten to put one of their hit men onto him. That might just slow the fucker down."

Bruce was amused, knowing it was an act on Sally's part, while Turner was horrified.

"It's a matter of knowing their weaknesses," said Sally, who was enjoying herself. She could see Turner was going a little white around the gills, so she continued.

"Then I'd threaten to kill one of his grandkids as a warning if he fails to comply. I would explain to him that complying would be taking down his website permanently, disbanding his growing army of environmental scientists, supporting the new president's policies publicly, and taking up a new career. A career that has nothing to do with the environment."

Bruce was thinking, "I'm glad I don't owe anything on my truck."

"Oh Yes! I'll trash his apartment, while I'm at it. Most people break eventually or end up dead if they encounter some of the people I know. I would tell him all about those people, and for that photos generally do the trick. I'd also tell him I might cut off his balls."

Bruce said, "I guess you'd better be nice to Sally, Jim."

"The meeting is over, Jim," said Sally. "We've got work to do."

"Of course," said Turner, making a quick exit.

"You are one scary lady," said Bruce, once they were alone.

"That's not what I really do. I'm just an information gatherer and delivery girl. I do make gentle threats, but that's about it. I said all that shit because I enjoy frightening Turner, the creep."

"I noticed," said Bruce.

"For all that stuff, including ball removal, you would have to call in the goons from Hotchkiss," said Sally. "I bet he'd do it in a heartbeat."

"Sally! Can I treat you to a business lunch, as long as you promise not to cut off my balls?"

"That would be nice and I promise not to, for now at least."

CHAPTER EIGHTEEN

After a good night's sleep and an early breakfast, followed by a long hike in the snow and a mid-morning coffee in front of a blazing fire, Fig's burner phone rang. He hesitated to pick it up as only two people had the number, Jamie and the student who'd rented him the cabin, Karl Blake. He decided to answer, and it was Karl. He asked if everything was OK at the cabin. Fig assured him that it was great, and he was enjoying the wood fire and the surrounding hiking trails.

Karl said, "Great!" He was about to hang up, when he said, "Jerome, I got a weird phone call early yesterday afternoon, from some guy. He said he was looking for a Dr. Newton. He wouldn't say who he was or why he called. He just hung up when I asked what it was about. It seemed odd and I thought you might want to know." Fig then realized that Karl was still suspicious of his chosen alias.

Fig said he didn't know what it was about, thanked Karl for telling him, anyway, and asked about leaving early. Fig had paid in full, in advance. Karl said, "Just lock up and text me to let me know you're not around. Maybe I can rent it again. I'd happily pay you back for your share of the time, if I do."

Fig smiled at Karl's honesty, and said, "No! I was a student once. You need it more than I do. I may have to leave today, in fact. I'll let you know."

Fig texted Jamie to say they needed to leave as soon as possible, and that he would explain when she got off work, and he'd be waiting in the coffee shop across the road.

He pulled his gear together, cleaned up what little mess there was in the cabin, checked the doors and windows, and put a $20 tip on the table. Fig headed off along the trails toward the coffee shop, taking a circuitous route. It was a fine sunny morning, but Fig wondered if he was being followed.

"Am I becoming paranoid?"

He remembered that old saying, "Because you are paranoid does not mean you are not being followed," which made him smile. There was a light covering of fresh snow on the ground with no sign of other hikers. He took a familiar loop, returning to the same spot about ten minutes later, to find no sign of prints other than his own.

"No *heffalumps* today."

On the way to town and knowing his own phone number was in Karl's phone log, Fig crushed that burner and threw the remains in a trash can near a group of cabins. Fig was also starting to sport a bit of a beard and he'd ditched his old jacket for a new one. He had purchased a new backpack of a different brand and color, leaving the old one at the Goodwill. On transferring his stuff to the new pack, Fig checked his cash supply to find he still had more than $17,000.

On looking in the window of the coffee shop he barely recognized himself, and inside the place he kept his cap and sunglasses on and his hood well down. With a delicious hot chocolate it was back to working on the network, running some tests for shortest pathways and gateway vertices. The latter he used to find people linking disparate groups, and Charles Barrett turned up at the top of the list.

"Surprise, surprise," thought Fig.

Deep in thought, he sensed someone watching him. It was Jamie sitting opposite, smiling. "You sure get lost in that brain of yours," she said. "Definitely a strength for your work, but not for spotting trouble. Have you finished your coffee? They let me off early, I think we should move and what is this news of yours?"

"This isn't my news, but I just found out that Charles Barrett is a gateway vertex between several large groups in my network."

"And that means?"

"It means we need to find a more private location."

Once outside and away from any video cameras with links to face or speech recognition software, they could talk more freely. Fig described his conversation with Karl and the caller looking for Dr. Newton.

"I'm afraid you have some serious, talented and well-funded people on your trail, Fig."

"How did they find Karl?"

"They searched all short-term rentals on notice boards and called each one."

"What do you think that means, Jamie?"

"It means they know you are in Burlington and we need to change that today. It also means they may track down your false identity, as Jerome Hanratty."

"How?"

"Not many people in Burlington at this time of year are making false IDs. I bet they hacked into the Office Store and found you. Jerome Hanratty is an odd name, so it stands out. How did that name come into your head and not John Smith?"

"Welsh grandfather and my Mum loved that song, *Smoke Gets in Your Eyes.*"

"You are so logical, it's scary, but looking on the bright side, I'd be surprised if they have connected the dots between you and me, so let's risk my car."

"What are the risks, there?"

"If I was them, I'd hack into a bunch of security cameras around town and look to see if you are still alone."

"Damn!"

"Fig, you always say that, when you are surprised. I was taught never to swear."

"Damn!"

They both laughed and Jamie said, "I parked my car away from all visible cameras, even then we should sit in it for about an hour before leaving town, so there is no link between two people meeting in that coffee shop and two similar people driving out of town."

It was a fifteen-minute stroll to the car, during which time they acted as regular visitors, looking in shop windows, retracing steps and checking for unlikely tails. Jamie explained that the phone call indicated they were still far behind, but they had a serious interest in Fig. On seeing their image in a shop window, Jamie thought they looked like a married couple, which gave her an idea.

"How about we get married, Fig?"

"What?"

"Don't look so scared. Not really married. Acting married. We would need rings, so let's buy them in this shop. It was our reflection in the window that gave me the idea. We can't be Mr. and Mrs. Hanratty. How do you feel about being Mr. Bailey, as we will need to use my driver's license, if we are stopped?"

They chose two simple rings that fit fairly well, and Jamie said as they left the shop, "Please don't hold my hand, Mr. Bailey. I'm not ready for that."

"But what if they know about you?" said Fig.

"That will take them some time. I used a false ID in the diner, Jackie Pritchard, because I worry about being spotted in relation to my black hat hacking hobby. The only way for them to find and ID me would be through facial recognition software, and that's quite a bit of work."

"Any other thoughts?"

"We will be forced to abandon the car and our current IDs pretty soon. Isn't this interesting?"

"Fascinating, Jamie."

"I don't know if you know this Fig, but it is almost impossible to hide from the government for any length of time. They have too much experience and equipment for chasing runaway suspects. It's what they do, plus they are now on steroids due to the need to track foreign and domestic terrorists."

"I bet they've labeled me as a domestic terrorist threat due to my website," said Fig. "Spreading lies and spin is what they do best."

They reached Jamie's beat up but serviceable, Toyota Corolla, and threw Fig's backpack on the back seat, next to Jamie's.

"Are you always ready to make a run for it, Jamie?"

"I heard the concern in your message and connected the dots. You don't seem to be prone to panic, anxiety or over-reacting, or emotionally reacting very much at all, for that matter."

"I don't like to pollute reason with emotion," said Fig.

"Great! You had better deal with both, if you want to date any normal woman, when this is over. No further comment. Anyway, I concluded your news was serious, which it turned out it was, and got ready to leave. I'm also horribly logical, Fig, though the term pollution doesn't go well with emotion, in my book."

"I'm also not known for my social skills, Jamie."

"I worked that out within a few seconds of you walking into *The Thrush's Nest*. Don't look so sad. No emotions, eh! You are a great employer, you pay well, and the work is interesting."

Fig smiled and Jamie started the engine with the heater turned to max. For the next hour Fig gave Jamie a blow-by-blow account of his career, his love of animals, plants and the entire global ecosystem. How he had decided to work to help maintain the health of the Biosphere, getting a degree in biomedical engineering after abandoning his medical work.

"I can see you upsetting all your patients," said Jamie.

"I'll have you know that my patients loved my work. They said so."

He went on to describe his love of mathematics, admitting he was no math wiz, and that he just loved applying math to biological problems. He explained how many biology problems can be solved by creating a state diagram and selecting parameters, followed by numerical approximation, for which computers had made so many more things possible.

Jamie was clearly interested, a rare event indeed, when it came to the subject of applied maths, in Fig's experience. He went on to describe his use of graph theory, the creation of EcoWorld using advanced dynamics software, and how he'd applied it to his research. He explained how this had led to discoveries that pissed off some of the institute's major sponsors, especially those in the energy sector.

"I bet," said Jamie.

This led to an explanation of the nature of the creation of the institute by the farsighted founders back in the early 1980s, the structure of the board of directors and how it comprised people from a wide range of industries, including chemical, pharmaceutical, food, communication, and even tobacco.

"Why tobacco?" said Jamie?

"Because they grow a lot of tobacco, which requires lots of industrial resources, as they make billions of cigarettes that go into millions of packets that require transporting and storage, that lead to serious diseases that have to be treated in hospitals with the products of big PHARMA, needing the same transport, marketing and other infrastructure as other industrial giants. It's one big club, Jamie."

Fig went on to describe the institute dues paid by each company, based on a minute percentage of their annual sales estimates, how each got one or two seats on the board, and how they ultimately controlled the director, who they could fire or hire at will, which required a majority vote.

He told Jamie the story of Nick Page's removal through lies and deceit, and the hiring of Strickland from who knew where? He also explained why he thought Strickland was a second-rate scientist and a political animal. He added all he knew about the lawyer, Enrique Torres, the firing event, how they had locked him out of the building and the system, bringing his personal effects to his home the next day. He mentioned his concern for Beckie and Raymond, too.

Then Fig said, "Is this boring you?"

"I'm a hacker and you are describing targets I might need to hack. The first thing one does before attempting penetration is to get to know the target well, and make sure it's the right target. Not much different to dating, come to think of it," said Jamie, blushing a little and rescuing herself by doing her looking waiting thing.

Fig, who was oblivious to all of this, went on to explain how he got pissed and created the website, *The Thoughtful Ecotoxicologist*, and posted a bunch of stuff that needed to be out there, linking his work on the currently fragile and endangered state of the Biosphere to widespread industrial neglect and its destruction of networks of food chains, both plants and animals. He made it clear that President Miller's policies were hastening the demise of many essential species through his attacks on environmental regulation.

"Just like Rachel Carson and DDT," said Jamie.

"Exactly!"

"I was pissed at the president, and my website made that only too obvious, but it led to the fake bomb and the threatening letter that I told you about already. In fact, here it is in my wallet."

"You kept it?" Glancing at the note, Jamie said, "Now we have a weapon."

"What's that?"

"That note, so don't lose it. And now do you want to hear my plan for what we should do next?"

"Of course."

"I want to visit the Rachel Carson Salt Pond Preserve in Maine."

"Really?"

"I'm already in love with this lady even though she's dead. I couldn't believe that book, written by a woman all those years ago, that starts with the description of an imaginary town, and resulted in the creation of the EPA and eventually to the elimination of DDT. I was floored that I didn't know this already. It wasn't part of my Arts, raising kids and hacking education program. Anyway, that's where I want to go."

Fig waited, as he sensed there was more. He was learning how to listen.

"Yoda is willing to teach me more tricks, and to check my invisibility, meaning that if he spots my work he'll let me know and try to clean up my mess. He is a top-of-the-line hacker. When I explained my reasons, without any personal details, just the danger we are in, he insisted on helping us for free, even providing an untraceable communication pathway."

"He did?"

"Fig! Black hats hate runaway government bullshit and by the way, did you destroy that burner phone? I meant to tell you."

"Of course, but why the salt pond preserve? There are several other more interesting Rachel Carson sites?"

"I read that this was one of her favorite spots. Furthermore, I want to see the sea. I've only seen the Atlantic Ocean once in my life."

As Jamie put the car in gear, Fig worked on finding a

route out of town that would start by going west, another decoy. During the drive, Jamie explained how a hacker would follow his trail.

"They would first track your cell phone to the Amtrak station via the gps log. The hacker following you could be anywhere in the world, by the way. Let's assume he is a male and call him Humperdinck."

"From *The Princess Bride*?" said Fig. "The prince who could track a falcon on a cloudy day. Great idea! In that case, I want to call the SUV woman Repo Lady."

"Why Repo Lady?"

"Because those people who repossess vehicles are pretty mean and can be armed and dangerous."

"So we won't underestimate her," said Jamie. "Good plan!"

"With Humperdinck and Repo Lady hot on your trail, Fig, the story becomes pretty obvious. After locating the end of the travels of your cell phone in the trash can outside the Amtrak station, bad decision, the obvious next step was to hack the Amtrak servers and look for ticket sales, which, by the way, a good hacker can do in less than an hour. They are probably already familiar with the Amtrak computers, having a backdoor in place. Nothing like free tickets for you and your friends."

"Shit, I have a lot to learn," said Fig.

"Your purchase would stand out because of the time and the fact that you used cash, which is unusual these days. Then they would know that you are headed for Burlington, Vermont, because you bought a ticket all the way. Mistake number two, my friend. You should have bought tickets for each leg of the journey along the way.

If Humperdinck and Repo Lady are working as a team, she probably found your phone remains in the trash, and then followed you to Burlington on Humperdinck's instructions. She may even be here, on the ground, right now, maybe paying Karl a visit. If Humperdinck has found my ID and linked us, he'll soon track down my license plate."

"So? What do we do about that?"

"We have to ditch this old car soon," said Jamie, "but that will not be as easy as they make it look in the movies. Furthermore, as it's being lost in the line of duty, I'll need you to replace it."

CHAPTER NINETEEN

As they left Burlington for Maine, Fig said, "I think we need to stop and buy you some camping gear, just in case. I have a single tent, and much as I would like to share it with you, I'm sure you'd prefer your own. I always carry a set of emergency camping gear, but I could do with more. How about we stop and get some supplies?"

"I think we've left enough evidence of our trail in Burlington," said Jamie, "let's get out of here and find it on the road. We can always go to a Walmart, though the quality is varied. We need a high-end store, I guess. We'll deal with it as we go, and for tonight I think we should settle for a cheap, rundown motel, glad of any customers. Covering our tracks isn't going to be easy, either way."

They headed out of town on snowy but easily passable roads. The views were remarkable. It turned out that it was going to be quite a drive to the Rachel Carson Salt Pond Preserve in Maine, on sometimes slick roads, especially with the extra fifty miles detour west. So, that evening they stopped at an apparently empty motel on the outskirts of the town of Littleton, New Hampshire. The place appeared to be on the rocks, with Jamie and Fig about to be the only customers.

"We can use my ID," said Jamie, "as I don't mind sharing a room, because you are clearly an honorable employer, Mr. Bailey, or should I say Dr. Bailey?"

Jamie proffered cash, which was received with a broad smile by Indira, the beautiful Indian lady, who appeared to be in her early seventies. She politely explained that she was the owner, and then showed them to their room, which was basic, smelled fresh and clean, had two double beds but no bath, just a small shower.

The following morning they found Indira arranging a simple breakfast. It was included with the room for $48. As they appeared to be the only customers, Jamie invited Indira to join them, which she did without hesitation. Fig asked Indira where she was from, and she replied that she was born and raised in the north of India. She went on to say that she had spent her childhood in a small village near New Delhi. Indira and her husband, Ravi, had come to America twenty years before, they had no children and he had died two years previously. It was clear that Indira still missed and was grieving for her husband. She talked fondly of their adventures in India and the USA, and how the motel used to be so busy.

Then Jamie decided to take a chance.

She said, "Indira, would you be interested in trading cars, if that's yours outside?" It was a beat up, 1970 Ford Pinto with the dark green paint peeling and a patch of oil underneath.

Indira looked surprised, but Jamie plowed on.

"We plan to sell ours to a used car lot near the top of the Appalachian trail, when we get there. We won't get much for it as we will be forced to sell. So we only plan to drive it for a few hundred miles. If you are interested, we can do a direct exchange, if you like? I have the title, showing it's not stolen."

"Why would you do that?" said Indira.

"You've been very kind, and it must be heartbreaking to have lost your husband. Maybe you can have some enjoyable country rides in a more reliable car. Perhaps it will take you to a happier destination and a new life, who knows?"

Indira was delighted, and said it was her car, that she'd been worried about it for a while, and wasn't sure what to do about it as it was her only way to get to the stores. Indira then warned Jamie that it was on its last legs, with an oil leak and some weird noises, but if Jamie was sure, great.

Jamie explained that her Toyota had been well maintained, it only had 140,000 miles on it, and would probably go another 100,000 without much trouble. She said it just seemed a pity to give her car to a used car lot, when Indira had been so kind and could use it. After a little banter, it was agreed. Indira and Jamie went in search of the titles, while Fig moved their gear into the old rattle trap. During the title exchange Indira asked for Jamie's email address.

"Of course, Indira, I would love to hear about your adventures in your new car, not that it is exactly new."

They headed out, leaving the motel owner a much happier woman with one less worry than when they'd arrived. As Fig was driving away from the motel, he said, "I just hope we aren't rear ended and go up in flames, but that was a great move, Jamie."

"That's social engineering, Fig, just like in the movies."

"I guess we'll hide this wreck somewhere in Maine?"

"That's the plan, but now I want to tell you what I found out about your movements since you arrived in Burlington up until today."

"This should be interesting. But why? I already know where I went." said Fig.

"If I can do it Humperdinck can do it, and you need to understand that, in detail. It will help you to be more careful in future."

Jamie then explained how she had looked for and eliminated as many records of Fig's journey as she could. "I saw your arrival on the train, the stay at that motel, your visit to Karl's house where you rented the cabin. I even found the location of the cabin in his phone logs."

Fig was quiet when Jamie expounded on her hacking exploits, which scared the bejesus out of him.

"There were no security cameras in Burlington Forest that I could find, so I lost you there. I saw both of us in town, on security camera video records, but never together. The data record for the camera on the other side of the road to George's Diner showed us entering and leaving the place, separately, but that might just be enough to make Humperdinck suspicious."

"Why?"

"We are roughly the same age. For hackers these little signs are critical observations."

She continued describing her hacking journey, following herself and Fig, a journey she said again that Humperdinck could duplicate and probably had.

"He found his way to Karl Blake, so he's probably penetrated Karl's phone, already."

"How would that help with my being Jerome Hanratty using burner phones?"

"Burner phones can be identified on the basis of their activity logs. They don't behave like normal phones on regular accounts. They also have a tendency to go dead when demolished, a common end to their existence. I bet Humperdinck sent Repo Lady to the cabin not long after we left town. Best to assume so, anyway."

Jamie was now sure that Humperdinck was a talented hacker. In fact, Bruce prided himself on his work, but could he beat Jamie? That remained to be determined.

"I've been thinking," said Jamie. "You waited several

weeks before leaving North Carolina for Burlington. That was a good move."

"How come?"

"Stakeouts are expensive. It would have cooled things down, but your updated website surely pissed them off, but that's just more of the same for Dr. Newton. Right?"

"I delayed my departure on purpose, to throw them off," said Fig. "And I built that site to get their attention and to piss them off, in the hopes they'd make a mistake. I was fishing."

"I'm impressed that you thought to delay leaving, not such a clueless nerd after all. You did the right thing. When it comes to fishing, if you don't bring them out of hiding, there is no way you can find them to fight back. Good work, boss."

"I guess my cell phone was the first mistake, right?"

"Exactly! Then they would soon have found that you'd boarded an Amtrak train. A good hacker would then track all possible trains, and yours would stand out as you bought a through ticket to Burlington. Do you have any history of visiting Burlington? Of camping or skiing near there? Any kind of link they might find?"

"We used to go there every other year, but how could they know that?"

"We are constantly being followed online by businesses trying to sell us stuff, and by governments tracking trouble-makers. Maybe it was Humperdinck who found your school record of the Asperger's diagnosis and forwarded it to *Shelob*, who gave it to Turner, who gave it to Strickland?"

Then Jamie said, "A good hacker, knowing you are headed for Burlington, would check out all and any motels, hotels and private rental properties likely to accept cash on the spot, no questions asked. The obvious place to go was the student notice boards, and voila, Karl Blake."

"He really was a nice guy."

"I hope your friendly SUV lady is nice, when she calls looking for Jerome. That said, I don't think Karl saw us together, because if he had she would get it out of him. Then Humperdinck would use that information to find my car, and then he'd head for the security cameras along local highways."

"I guess he may have spotted us driving out of Burlington, but at least we left two decoys. We headed west and we are now in a different car," said Fig.

"We are lucky this is an old car, Fig. Any hacker worth their salt would find it, hack into the car's computer and locate it precisely. A really modern self-driving car could be driven off a cliff by a hacker, for that matter."

For the rest of the trip they were quiet, living in their own worlds watching the scenery go by. On the way they stopped at a diner in Lewiston for lunch. Fortunately, the old Ford Pinto made it to the Rachel Carson Salt Pond Preserve without a gas tank conflagration. They arrived there around noon, and enjoyed a picnic over-looking the salt pond, as the tide was out with the sea in the distance. It was still pretty cold, but they were well wrapped up and they enjoyed sitting together in the sun, wondering what the other person was really all about.

Jamie said, "I love the sound of the waves and the gulls and watching the pelicans cruising by. This really is a magical place."

"And it also needs to be protected from offshore drilling and plastic waste," said Fig.

"Can you let me just enjoy the moment. I want to forget everything else for now." Fig then kept quiet, thinking, "touchy, touchy."

They barely knew each other, but they connected on an intellectual level. Where that would go neither of them knew. They enjoyed the picnic, and after a walk along the beach, where Fig became intrigued by some tiny, almost translucent, crabs and several different species of seaweed, that he called wracks, they started to become chilled and went to the visitor center.

"Where should we stay tonight, do you think?" said Jamie.

"Let's see what we can find down the road," said Fig.

On the way to the small town of New Harbor, on highway 32, they spotted a "For Rent" sign on the side of the highway, with an arrow pointing up a dirt road. Being early spring the number of tourists would be sparse. They pulled the rattly Pinto onto a rough track and within a quarter mile found an old cabin. It was locked and looked abandoned in the pine forest, but a phone number was posted on the door.

Jamie called and asked if the place was for rent. A

guy with a thick Boston accent said it was as long as they paid in advance. He said he preferred cash, $95 for the night and a $20 cleaning fee, and he could meet them there in thirty minutes as he lived in New Harbor.

A very scruffy guy in a brand-new Land Rover arrived in a cloud of dust, took their money, wrote down Jamie's phone number, gave them a key, and said to call in the morning around nine if they wanted to stay longer. Otherwise, just lock up and leave the key under the wooden owl on the deck. All this in a rush and he was gone.

"What was his name?" said Fig.

"Dan something or other, I think," replied Jamie.

For once they felt untraceable. Fig considered kissing Jamie but decided better of it as she was his employee and clearly gun shy. Jamie realized what Fig was thinking, would probably have accepted and regretted it later. She needed to know what he was made of, first, so they got down to cooking supper on an old propane stove, along with a glass of red wine. They were both exhausted. Jamie took the bed on Fig's insistence, while he bedded down on the dilapidated but extremely comfortable couch. A gas furnace kept the place warm, so they left the wood stove alone.

Fig dreamed of a hacker in a black hat chasing him around his map with a knife, while Jamie slept the sleep of the just.

CHAPTER TWENTY

Room 319, Homeland Security, Washington, DC.

"Henley?"

"Is that Sally?"

"I found the remains of that cell phone, just where you said it would be. It was in a trash can outside the Amtrak station, on Washington Street. He really destroyed it, even the sim card was cracked in half. Our man is serious about going somewhere, but where?"

"He's headed for Burlington, Vermont. I found his ticket order in the Amtrak servers. He's going via Penn station, New York City. That would put him arriving in Burlington late in the evening the following day, if he didn't stop over in New York."

"Should I fly up there?"

"Hold your horses, Sal. Give me time to find him in Burlington, just to be sure."

"Hey, my name is Sally, so don't you forget it, and let

me know whether to go or not. A little trip to see the snow might be nice." She hung up their secure line without another word.

"Damn," said Bruce. "One minute she's real nice and the next a bitch. What's up with her?"

CHAPTER TWENTY-ONE

Following breakfast they started closing up Dan's cabin, when Fig said, "As we are moving on is it safe to call Ben, to see how Sophie is doing?"

"You're worried about your cat? I'm sure she's fine with your friend."

"I just want to know she's OK, with these assholes on our trail. I have a bad feeling about it."

"OK! Make the call then give me that phone. I've had an idea for using it as a direction sign to a dead drop I want to set up."

"A dead what?"

"I'll explain that later, call your friend so we can move along."

"Hi Ben, sorry to bother you a little early in the morning, but I was just wondering how Sophie is doing."

"I tried to reach you, Fig. I'm afraid I have some

terrible news. I would have told you before, but your phone was out of order."

"What's up?"

"I'm afraid Sophie died."

"What?"

"I went over to your place a few days ago, to feed her, and your apartment was a wreck. It looked as if someone had destroyed everything. I found Sophie lying by her food bowl, gasping for breath. She was kind of arching her back and struggling. I took her straight to the vet emergency clinic down the road, but by the time I got there Sophie was having terrible seizures. She stopped breathing within minutes of the vet starting to examine her."

"What happened?"

"The vet lady said it looked like strychnine poisoning."

"Damn." said Fig, feeling numb. "Probably a neighbor who doesn't like cats. Thanks for dealing with it, Ben."

Jamie was watching, thinking Fig was about to cry.

"I'm sure you had a hard time with it, Ben, I'm sorry. I have to go. Thanks so much for taking her to the vet, I'll cover it when I get back into town. I'll get back in touch before then."

He hung up the phone, and after a stunned silence, said, "The fucking bastards. If they think they can frighten me by killing my cat they are wrong."

"What happened?"

"Sophie was poisoned and she's dead, and they

trashed my apartment, and here is the phone you wanted, Jamie."

Without further ado, with Fig processing his feelings and Jamie looking worried, they headed for New Harbor and the Kitchen Drawer Café. Jamie had found it online, noticing they advertised fresh bread baked daily. They picked a quiet spot in a corner and ordered breakfast with sourdough bread and local butter.

As they started their meal, Fig said, "I'm not very hungry, now, but I guess I should eat something, and I don't see any security cameras."

"I'm so sorry about Sophie, Fig. It's horrible. And no, I don't see any security cameras, either, but the TV might be watching us. It's turned off, but it may still be watching for all we know. This food really is delicious, especially the fresh bread. If you eat some you'll feel better."

"I'd best eat, though I'm pretty upset about Sophie. By the way, I'd like to update that website when we get a chance. I have plenty more ecologically sensitive messages to give to our fucking friend, *Shelob*. How close do you think they might be to catching up with us, Jamie?"

"The fact that Humperdinck succeeded in finding Karl means Repo Lady will probably pay a visit to Indira soon. I need for us to stop, so I can do some work to counter Humperdinck."

"Do you need special gear for hacking?"

"It depends how serious you are, Fig. I have an Acer Aspire laptop, considered the best brand. I also carry a hardware wifi-cum-VPN-cum-firewall, plus I have many further layers of protection installed in my laptop. As far as I know, my hacking has yet to be noticed, though I've never penned the kind of sites we are going to need now.

I can still be spotted by a talented hacker, though Yoda is watching my back. He said he'd track my work and if he spots a trace, he'll eliminate it, if he can, and let me know. If I'm better than Humperdinck and luck is on our side, we should stay under their radar. I'm still learning, as we all are. Remember, Fig, it's a federal crime to hack into places where you are not invited, and I do not want to go to jail."

"How about Internet service providers? How do you deal with that?"

"Normally I use Verizon Fios, but it's not available here. I have a Verizon wifi with a strong password, but it can still be hacked. You are a difficult project, Fig, I mean, boss, but I'll do my best to keep you safe," said Jamie, smiling.

"Can I have the rest of your bread, if you don't want it," said Fig, "and I've never felt like I was a project before." Fig tried not to smile but he couldn't help it. Then he reasoned that all men are projects to some woman or other, even if it's only their mother.

"What's your plan when we stop for the night?"

"My motto is *know thine enemy*," said Jamie. "So I will attempt to find out more about Humperdinck, which will be tricky and possibly risky. What about the car, Fig?"

"I first thought to find a wrecker, but I think it

would be better to hide it in the woods to the side of an unused trail and remove the plates. Let's go."

Jamie said, "I was wondering if your proclaimed interest in Rachel Carson, which I noticed is mentioned on your website, could lead them to here?"

"That's possible, though there are several sites dedicated to her, and I'm ready to get out of here."

"There's an Internet cafe and campsite near Boothbay Harbor, down the road."

Fig said, "Good plan! Best we drive most of the way and find a place to dump the car close enough to walk the rest of the way into the town, but we'd best wear our warmest clothes, it's going to be a cold hike. At least people around here are used to hikers."

They finished their breakfast, and paid cash with a standard tip, anything not to stand out. Then they headed for Boothbay Harbor. "This is a beautiful place," said Jamie. "When this is all over, I'm coming back for a vacation."

About two miles before Boothbay Harbor they spotted a dirt road off on their right, almost grown over by pines. They turned and headed into a small forest, bumping along a deserted rocky track that dead ended amongst old pine trees and dense undergrowth. There were no sounds of people, just the odd vehicle on the road half a mile below them.

"I do love the woods and the smell of the pines," said Fig, pulling warm clothes out of his pack. It was cold but warming somewhat as the sun rose higher in the sky. He removed the number plate and buried it under leaf litter, some way away, while Jamie extracted everything from inside the car. Things that were not needed she buried in the dense undergrowth, about a hundred feet away. They then drove and pushed the old Pinto off the trail and under some overhanging branches in a convenient depression, where it was well hidden.

They checked for any overlooked evidence of their visit, shouldered their packs and headed toward the woods.

"Hang on a sec," said Jamie. "I just need to put a couple of things in the car." She opened the driver's side door, reached into the front seat, closed the door again, and followed Fig, who was already walking into the woods, along a line parallel to the road. Five minutes later they emerged onto springy turf downs, a few hundred yards from the road. It was only a two-mile chilly hike into Boothbay Harbor.

Fig noticed how easily they walked together. His ex-wife complained that he walked too slowly. She was always in a hurry to reach her destination, instead of taking Fig's approach, which was to enjoy the journey. This was true of walking or driving. Jamie just seemed to fit in with his natural pace.

After about forty minutes, they came across a wooden sign on the side of the road indicating that Boothbay was incorporated in 1764. "It's an old town," said Fig. "I wonder if it was incorporated by pirates?" They continued on for about half a mile, to find The Coffee House and the joy of taking the weight off their feet.

"I must be getting old, my legs feel tired, but then, my training has been interrupted."

"What kind of training?" Jamie asked.

"I like to compete in local age group running races."

"Let's run together tonight."

"What's your usual pace? said Fig.

"Around nine minute, except in races or speed training."

"Perfect. Apart from running, I've been into all sorts of sports over the years, including martial arts, which taught me an important lesson about fighting."

"What's that?"

"Negotiate or run away. If you can't in good conscience do either, find a weapon and use it."

"Seems we are in a fight right now, Fig. Who do you think our adversary might be and what kind of weapon do you think we need?"

"Some powerful slime ball killed Sophie. I think our best weapon will be information and a good reporter to get the story out there, and there's the place we are looking for, thank goodness."

The Coffee House had a large picture window advertising tea, coffee, sandwiches and breakfast.

"Just the job," said Fig.

They walked in and took a seat, as the young woman at the counter indicated they should. Within a minute, she approached them with menus. Jamie asked about the Internet, which turned out to have a solid password. After scanning the menu, Jamie asked for coffee and a croissant, with butter and strawberry jam, while Fig ordered a full breakfast of eggs, hash browns, toast, coffee and orange juice.

"Got your appetite back, I see. No over easy eggs on whole wheat toast?" said Jamie, laughing. "You are more flexible than I realized."

"Nothing like a hike in fresh air and some abject terror to give me an appetite."

Jamie dug out her laptop, along with the little blue box, and disappeared into the World Wide Web.

Fig was left, alone with his thoughts, realizing that she had some tricky work to do, trying to hack a hacker. Computer code was completely out of Fig's comfort zone. He sucked as a coder, even when working with math software. He could do it, but his code was inefficient and it took him ages to remove errors. If his budget couldn't spring for a professional computer coder, Fig would look for a student who could code well, combined with a passion for science.

He thought back to his website, and leaned across to Jamie, "Sorry to interrupt." She didn't smile. "Could you check out my website when you get a chance, to see if anyone has been snooping around in there?"

"Already have and whoever it was they left a back door. I decided to leave it alone, as it was probably Humperdinck, and now I know more about the hacking tools he uses. It was a first-rate job." Then she disappeared back into the land of code.

Fig opened an ebook, *How to Disappear Completely,* on his burner phone. It was about hiding from the government, as a fugitive, and it turned out to be fascinating and scary as crap. It contained a bunch of valuable instructions, stating that remaining invisible from the government, if they really are looking for you, is almost impossible. Fig was surprised to learn that they could locate heat from your body from space, even inside buildings, "for fuck's sake."

He'd started making a supply list, wondering if a prayer mat should be included, when their breakfast arrived.

CHAPTER TWENTY-TWO

Jamie and Fig spent about an hour in The Coffee House, by the end of which Fig was stuffed but still sad about Sophie. Jamie looked distracted, half of her mind in the land of computer code.

Fig said, with a smile, "Jamie, I'm not the only one who gets lost in my mind," then he asked the server the way to the nearest campsite. It turned out to be only three miles down the road, and close to the sea.

"Perfect," said Jamie. "coming out of her reverie."

And off they went on their adventure, somewhat encouraged by their progress. Jamie told Fig that she had returned online to Burlington, to pen local security cameras. "It's not easy for the average hacker, Fig, but I'm not your average hacker. You hit pay dirt when you asked me to work for you, and you owe me $220, please."

"Cash or gift cards?"

"Fifty-fifty, please, as they each have their uses. I

spotted you near Karl Blake's apartment. Why you went there escapes me. Humperdinck almost certainly saw that one, linked you to Jerome Hanratty, and now he knows you have a scraggly bit of a beard, which spoils your looks, plus he'll spot your new jacket and backpack."

"Shit!" was all Fig had to say about that. He turned his cap inside out and put it on backwards. "This will have to do for now, but the jacket and backpack have to wait. Did you see yourself, or us, in your car?"

"I spotted both of us entering and leaving the diner, independently. Men and women tend to attract each other and get together, and Humperdinck knows you're single, I'm sure. So his next move will be to find me in the diner computer system. That, I'm afraid, is a matter of hours to minutes for a good hacker, but he'll run into Jackie Pritchard, and she'll slow him down."

Jamie went on to say that she would almost certainly be on Humperdinck's interesting subject list, and he would eventually find her car, and then he'd get the plate number from security cameras or by hacking the DMV.

"These guys aren't hanging around, Fig. You are clearly on their most wanted list. I need the identities of Humperdinck and Repo Lady. Then we can fight back and make them nervous, but I have no intention of killing their cats. What they are doing to environmental scientists is not only reprehensible, it's clearly illegal."

Fig showed Jamie his list of essential gear from the book, *How to Disappear Completely*. "As you said, Jamie, it turns out to be overwhelmingly difficult, as you have to give up everything, from your family to your pets, change the way you dress, find new hobbies and type of work. In fact, you have to reinvent your life from scratch."

"Yes Fig, but we only need to hide for a few months, not for life."

About halfway to the campsite they decided to sit on a patch of grass, rest and go over Fig's list while enjoying the view of Booth Bay. Jamie started reading Fig's list out loud.

"Lightweight single tent, sleeping bag, compass, multipurpose knife tool, maps of the United States, extra change of clothes, including hat, socks, underwear, pants, shirts, and a warm jacket, waterproof matches. This is pretty basic stuff, Fig. We can pick up any of those supplies, ones we don't have already, on the way to wherever we are headed next."

"The author suggested buying the types of clothes we don't usually wear, in order to throw off pursuers. Should we dress like midwestern conservatives, Mr. and Mrs. Bailey, not two young singles," said Fig with a grin.

"What did he say about transport?"

"Not to use a car or public transport whenever possible. He recommended bicycles, instead!"

"Bit of a cold slog," said Jamie.

"He suggested planting false leads, and we've done that a couple of times already."

Jamie listened and waited for more.

"I was thinking about returning to Greensboro, to visit the institute and snoop around, but I've had second thoughts. How about we create a false trail in that direction, but go to Washington, DC? If these people are in the federal government, my first bet would be the DHS."

"Why them?"

"Because they employ some real thugs, and who else would kill someone's cat?"

"It sounds crazy and dangerous, but we'll eventually have to take the fight to them on their home ground, so I agree. Maybe we'll find Humperdinck in there."

"The author of that book also said to avoid rural areas and wilderness, because we would stand out." said Fig. "That's another good reason to head for DC. He also said to avoid eating in restaurants. There are plenty of small food shops and private fast-food joints in DC. I know the center quite well, as I dated a girl there before meeting my ex-wife. I doubt Washington has changed much since then. The author of that book also suggested having a mail drop box and to flush everything we can down the toilet, as trash cans leave evidence. I guess that was my big mistake at the Amtrak station in Greensboro."

"You're learning, boss. I'm used to cloak and dagger stuff online, just not out here in the real world, but it's the same idea, I guess."

"He said if you need to hide, and you dress appropriately, soup kitchens, churches and homeless shelters are pretty good. Let's keep that in mind if we are really in danger, but I would prefer the comfort of a hotel. I also need a new ID, as Jerome Hanratty has been outed. I did kind of like the guy."

They stood and shouldered their packs, as it was still pretty chilly, and Jamie said, "OK! Let's find that campsite and make something to eat. I guess I can put up with sharing a tent for one night. I'm starving and a run together along the beach would be perfect."

However, within half a mile they spotted a sign for a Bed and Breakfast, with *Vacancies*. "I think this would be more comfortable than a small cold tent, Mr. Bailey. Don't you?"

"Can't wait," said Fig, and Jamie ignored him.

They climbed a short path to the front door of a large house with white siding and a red roof, a large wrap-around deck with scattered Adirondack chairs, and a great feel. "We'll have to use my ID again, Fig," said Jamie, "and after this we both need new IDs."

"Yes, dear," said Fig.

They were greeted by the owner, Mrs. Lizzy Austin.

Jamie signed the register and asked if they could stay for one night with the option for a second or maybe several more.

Lizzy replied that it was quiet that time of year and she was sure there would be a room for them for at least a week, if not more.

Fig stepped forward, shook Lizzy's hand, and said, "A real pleasure to meet you and to stop trudging along that road with this pack. Maybe I am getting old?"

"Aren't we all?" said Lizzy with a smile. "Let me show

you to your room, then I can explain about breakfast. Have you eaten? There is a nice restaurant not more than half a mile from here. I'll show you on the map. There are clean towels in your room and a complimentary glass of wine in the conservatory from five o'clock on, and you'd be very welcome to enjoy the deck, which is nice if the wind dies down, but if you want to walk down to the bay it's not so far. There's a trail across the road."

Then looking embarrassed, Lizzy said, "I'm sorry. I'm talking your ears off. I'm sure you are both ready to clean up and rest from your hike. Let's go upstairs to your room. It is so nice to meet you both." She showed them the room and hurried off, seeming a little discombobulated.

The room had its own bathroom with a deep whirlpool bath, and a wonderful view of the bay. Jamie glanced in the bathroom, and said, "A whirlpool bath. I'll be out in an hour. Sure you don't need to go first, Fig, it'll be a while?"

"I'm fine, go ahead."

Jamie threw her pack on the bed, rummaged around for a change of clothing, and disappeared into the bathroom without another word. Fig looked around and realized the couch was kind of short. He hunted in the walk-in-closet and found enough extra blankets to create a makeshift bed on the floor. Then he lay down on the actual bed for a quick nap.

An hour later, Jamie came out of the bathroom and woke him up. He then explained his bed arrangement.

"Why should you sleep on the floor and not me? I hope you aren't a male chauvinist?"

Fig said he was raised to be a gentleman.

"The perfect answer, kind sir, and you are being the perfect employer, thank you. I so much appreciate it. Your turn in the shower, the water is nice and hot, then we should take that trail to the beach. By the way, have you seen my glasses?"

"On the windowsill," and with that, Fig headed for the bathroom, while Jamie checked out the wifi, which she found to be fast for the area, but it was not password protected. She nipped downstairs and found Lizzy.

"Mrs. Austin, you really should password protect your wifi. You are inviting problems. Do you do your business work online?"

"Please call me Lizzy, and I do all my business and banking online, but I found setting up the password confusing."

"I can help you with that, but first you have to be sure you can trust me. I live on the Internet, in fact that's my job. Right now I'm here on a working vacation, doing a job for my husband, who was complaining of tired legs when we arrived, and is now in the shower enjoying your lovely hot water, after his nap. I really enjoyed that deep bath, it's one of my favorite ways to relax."

"Oh! I trust you," said Lizzy. "I have a good nose for bad people. Are you sure I'll be able to deal with the password?"

"Don't worry. I'll show you how to reset it, so you

can change it if you need to. It's really very easy. We can write down instructions and leave them on the router. Where do you keep the router-modem?"

"That black box thing? It's right here, under the counter."

Jamie set it up with a safe password that Lizzy was sure she could remember. Then Jamie went to their room, added some code of her own to the router and Lizzy's computer. Then she proceeded to explore possible portals into the DHS, a risky thing, indeed. Jamie was sure Humperdinck would be waiting for just such a thing. Being a hacker herself, she knew that anyone worth their salt would be somewhat paranoid, and that Humperdinck would be vigilant about screening for signs of intrusion.

Just then Fig came out of the bathroom.

Jamie said, "If Humperdinck penetrates Lizzy's computer, he'll find out that you have remarkable hacking skills, and he'll be really pissed at you."

CHAPTER TWENTY-THREE

Room 319, Homeland Security, Washington, DC.

"Henley?"

"Yes!"

"Well?"

"Well, what?"

"Do I fly to Burlington or not? I'm ready to get out of here."

"I think you should. I was just trying to nail down some details. He may have left town with a woman who works in the diner. I'm not sure. It's just a hunch based on things I've seen on a number of security cameras."

"Do I go or not and what is the target when I arrive?"

"OK! Go, and go to this address," said Bruce, giving Sally the phone number and address of Karl Blake. This was where he'd briefly seen Newton pass by a private security camera across the street. He was sure it was Newton hiding behind a beard and his hood down over his face.

"How do you know it was him and what led you to Blake?"

"I found Blake a few days ago, then I called to see if he'd seen Dr. Newton, and he sounded suspicious, so I hung up. When it comes to recognizing Newton, it's posture I recognize. Newton seems like an athlete, which is unusual for an older guy. It's the way he walks. He kind of swaggers a little. It was him alright."

"And who is Blake?"

He told Sally that Karl Blake was a student, he'd rented his cabin to a Jerome Hanratty, who it turned out had created a fake driver's license at the local Office Supply and he used a burner phone that went dead recently.

"Do you think Newton is still in Burlington?"

"He stayed in Blake's cabin for two nights, then he called Blake to say he would be leaving soon. I've seen Newton visiting that diner several times, and around the same time I saw an attractive woman his age come and go. Not as attractive as you, Sally."

"Thank you, Bruce, and?"

"Saw her waiting tables, so she works there, but I can't find her online. I hacked into the diner's computer and found her name, Jackie Pritchard, but it led nowhere. I have a hunch Newton would show an interest in her."

"I don't want you wasting my time with feelings and

hunches. Why don't you stick to facts? I'll check out Blake's place, sweet talk him and then show him photos of Newton and Pritchard and see what he knows, if anything. Can you send me the photos?"

"I sent them a few minutes ago."

A few moments later, Sally said, "Got them."

"I'm pretty sure Jerome Hanratty is Newton."

Sally had already hung up without another word.

CHAPTER TWENTY-FOUR

After a relaxing night in Lizzy's B&B Fig and Jamie decided it was time to go to DC, as they both felt too conspicuous in this quiet little town. "The guy who wrote that book was right," said Jamie, "we stand out like a sore thumb. In the city we can merge with the crowds, but I'm sure Humperdinck has considered that we might go to DC."

"Why do you think that?"

"He now knows we are pretty savvy, because we are leading him on a wild goose chase. Putting two and two together, he may have realized that we have probably figured out that he works for Homeland Security, and their head offices are in DC."

"How could he do that?"

"Simple, Fig. It's obvious that you are or have access to a hacker, and you worked for Strickland. He'd know that you would follow the phone logs. Strickland phoned

Turner, who reports to Barrett. I'm really suspicious of Barrett, by the way. Something doesn't add up."

"But Barrett works for the EPA?"

"I know but I spotted Turner's phone in that Homeland Security building in DC. I'm sure Humperdinck has followed that trail, to find out what you just might know."

"OK! EPA or Homeland Security, DC here we come."

"Agreed," said Jamie.

"That said, we need to set up a decoy destination. Maybe Lizzy would help us, though it is best she doesn't know we are fugitives."

"Correction, Fig. You are the fugitive. I'm just a tag along black hat and I'll deny everything," said Jamie, laughing. "I don't want to lie to Lizzy or put her in any danger. She is such a sweet lady, and she lives all alone here when her husband is away and there are no residents."

"How do you know her husband is away?"

"I look, listen, and read between the lines. Haven't you noticed how nervous she is?"

"She is?"

"OK Fig. Let's assume the worst. That in a few days Repo Lady will be here asking questions of Lizzy, and that Humperdinck will have hacked into her computer, where our booking under Mr. and Mrs. Bailey will be discovered. That was an avoidable mistake, as now Humperdinck may have followed me all the way to

Mariposa, California. However, I left a nice little surprise for him in Lizzy's computer."

"Really?" said Fig. "Anyway, it is no good asking Lizzy to say nothing. That would make her uncomfortable or scared. Maybe we can pay her to take us to the long-distance coach station in Wiscasset, saying we are headed home to Greensboro. In exchange, we offer to cover a couple of days lodging. She may even have a friend or relative there." Which, as it turned out, Lizzy did!

"But we would be lying to Lizzy."

"Telling her we are headed for Greensboro isn't a lie because we'll have to go there eventually."

"And why is that?"

"I've had an idea to recruit a friend down there, to help us. I can explain that later. His name is Raymond."

"Why didn't you tell me that before?"

"I forgot and anyway, does a boss have to tell his employees everything?"

"I'm sorry, Fig, but in this case he does."

"I'm sorry, it won't happen again, except I do tend to get distracted and forget stuff."

"Every little detail of our plans is important, but you are forgiven."

Then Fig said, "Let's tell Lizzy we are headed for Greensboro, and ask her to drop us off at the Water Street station. It's a twenty-five-minute drive from here. We could offer her the cost of the normal Uber fare, plus some spending money for her trouble. I'm sure

Lizzy would be glad of the cash, given how quiet business is right now."

Lizzy was delighted to be paid for driving them to Wiscasset. After calling she said her friend was all excited about her unexpected visit. Fig's generous remuneration elicited no complaints from Lizzy, who agreed to drop them off in the town center, where they could do some shopping before heading out of town.

On their arrival in Wiscasset, and after a friendly goodbye to Lizzy, Jamie and Fig hiked to the Concord Coach Line. They were told to buy the ticket online or on board the bus, but they were stuck staying the night.

———

After spending the night in a small hotel they headed for the bus station and boarded the 9:50 a.m. coach to Boston. On the bus they found two fairly private seats at the back.

"When it comes to your explosive website, Fig, I can keep it up and running however often Humperdinck takes it down. He's taken it down twice, already."

"How?"

"I'll host it on several computers and multiple virtual machines that we control. I could even use one of them as a honeypot, come to think of it."

"A what?"

"A honeypot, Fig, but let me think. I can mirror your site, moving it from one virtual or real machine to another, and with a little work I could automate the process, so it pops back up almost straight away."

"Great! That would drive them crazy. People tell me I'm good at pissing people off. This would do the trick nicely, thanks."

"Can you afford another computer or two? I might need a couple."

"As long as they are used and cheap, sure. But what's a honeypot?"

"You will have to wait, Fig. I've got to get some shuteye for a few minutes. Do you mind if I lean my head on your shoulder?"

"If you insist," said Fig.

About an hour later, Jamie regained consciousness, and Fig said, "Well?"

"Well, what?"

"What about that honeypot, honey pot?"

"Oh yes! I was explaining how I could repeatedly post your website from several machines, real and virtual, right?"

"Yes! And?"

"One of those machines would have a stable IP with the same website, but sitting in software designed to protect the computer from penetration by Humperdinck. It would look as though he was in the computer, but he would actually be in a digital trap in which I can watch what he's up to."

"Neat."

"In fact, we could leave it running in a motel room somewhere, paid for a few days in advance, with a "Do

Not Disturb" sign on the door. If Humperdinck penned that machine, he'd find I had left the gps operational. He then would be able find the physical location of the honeypot computer and send in Repo Lady."

"What would we be doing?"

"Watching from a safe location. I would set up a camera to record a video of their arrival in the room, to see what Repo Lady looks like. Then you'd know if she is the woman in the SUV who delivered the fake bomb."

"How would that work?"

"Micro-camera linked to a motion detector, and the camera would automatically forward video feed to my phone."

"Sounds like a plan," said Fig. "A woman of many talents, and a little scary, I must admit."

CHAPTER TWENTY-FIVE

Climbing stiffly out of the bus at Boston South Station, Jamie and Fig shouldered their packs and stood in the bright sunshine, getting their bearings. Then Jamie turned, and headed in the general direction of the Amtrak ticket booth.

"I thought we were staying in Boston," called out Fig, to her retreating figure.

"We need to buy a couple of Amtrak tickets to Timbuktu, to divert these jerks. In fact, you stay here as the less you are seen, and the less we are seen together, the better."

About fifteen minutes later, Jamie returned and explained with a smile that she had bought two one-way tickets to Nashville.

"There were plenty of security cameras, so Big Brother, and even Little Brother, are watching us."

Crossing the Charles River Dam Road, they passed

the museum of science. Fig said, "Do you mind if I take a quick look in the museum?"

"Cameras," replied Jamie, and she kept walking, while looking at her phone. "I'm sorry Fig. Our marriage is on the rocks. Separate rooms tonight."

"What? Why?"

With no explanation forthcoming, Jamie said, "I'll stay at the Holiday Inn just up the road, and you can get a room in the Holiday Inn Express. It's just down there. I'll contact you, don't call me." Then she headed toward the Holiday Inn, without a backward glance.

"That's staff for you, I guess," thought Fig, as he took the next right, looking for the Holiday Inn Express. There were plenty of rooms, so he booked for two nights using his Harry Parker driver's license, made by some kids running the Office Store in Wiscasset.

"You are in room 318, sir. Elevators are down the hall, first on the left and the Ice machine is at the far end of each floor, while complimentary breakfast starts at six a.m. Have a nice night, sir, and once again, thank you for your business, and don't hesitate to call the front desk if you need anything. Oh yes! There is a workout room on the second floor."

He picked up a complimentary coffee near the breakfast room, and headed for his room, taking the stairs for exercise. This was something he'd done ever since studying the Bruce Lee fighting style. Bruce said, "Get fit and stay fit, any way you can, including taking the stairs." What was good enough for Bruce Lee was good enough for Fig.

He took the chair by the window, overlooking an empty street, and cogitated. Then he took out his computer and started to expand his website to further piss off President Miller, his sycophants, and many CEOs in the chemical, pharmaceutical, tobacco, communications, transport, oil, gas and coal, food, and other large industries.

Fig also had a plan to get it under their noses. He was building an extended email list, which he would use to bulk mail the link. Google wouldn't be happy about that, and they might kill it, but there was always Jamie to save his Internet ass, Fig was thinking.

The goal of his website, *The Thoughtful EcoToxicologist*, was to shame or pressure all the industries that polluted the global ecosystem, not just chemical companies. They all dumped stuff in the air, water, or ground, or they supported other industries that did by buying massive quantities of their chemicals and chemical products. Fig was surprised at the level of environmental pollution created by the communications industries.

Now, high on Fig's list of prime targets was the food industry, not where he had focused previously. After a little research he was surprised to find his rescuer, Charles Barrett, who turned out to be the current CEO of Good Foods, Inc. That was a surprise that had Fig scratching his head. He literally scratched his head when considering a tricky problem, which caused his friends to say he had a brain like a chimp.

Once that website was fleshed out, he started to expand his database of environmental scientists, activists, ecologists, supporters of Greenpeace, and even people posting pro-environment pages on Facebook, Twitter, Reddit, and anyone else he could think of that might be interested in creating a small army to fight the environmental insanity of the president and his underlings.

Little did Fig know he was essentially duplicating the database created by Fred Sassy, whose data were adorning the walls of room 301 in the Homeland Security building in Washington, DC. Fred was well ahead of Fig, but to Fig it was more than a job. It was a mission. Fig smiled as he thought, "I'm making a Dumbledore's Army of eco-scientists. If only I knew Harry Potter's *patronus charm*, we are surely dealing with some *dementors*. Instead of wands and incantations, we have science, education, and a love of the Biosphere."

"I wonder how Jamie is doing?"

Jamie was busy. She was following leads and covering her tracks. She'd hunted around inside the phone, gps and email logs of James Turner. She then went into his records via contacts in his phone log, and eventually found his school, university and employment records. He turned out to be a longtime lobbyist for the chemical, pharmaceutical and tobacco industries.

Jamie also discovered that Turner was an ardent Republican and anti-environmentalist. He'd even written invited reviews on the dangers of out-of-control tree huggers for Breitbart and other right-wing sites. Turner had enjoyed a flourishing career running the lucrative, pro-Republican, *James and Jones Policy Consultants*. Three years previously, he'd sold his share of the firm to his co-owner, Jim Jones.

Jamie thought, "Was that his partner's real name? I guess their job was to get people to drink the Kool Aid."

James Turner's disappearance from the lobbying world coincided with the initial run for office of President Miller. Interesting coincidence! Jamie was now going full steam ahead black hat. She had a niggling feeling that she was in a race against an equally talented hacker, Humperdinck, and if he tracked down her physical location she would be in real trouble.

She also realized, based on what the other side was doing, that they were an illegal clandestine operation, protected from prosecution, with an unlimited budget. They were doing just what the new administration wanted, containing environmental scientists and other tree-hugging troublemakers, and protecting their illegal scheme under the disguise of covert ops.

Jamie then found the current location of Turner's cell phone, and there it was, smack bang in the middle of the DHS at 300 7th St SW, Washington, DC. Recently, Homeland Security had been particularly aggressive when it came to following President Miller's negative attitudes to environmentalists.

Oddly, there was no public record of James Turner working for Homeland Security. He was in the EPA staff lists as recently hired, and reporting to Charles Barrett. The same guy Fig had just found was the CEO of Good Foods, Inc.

Jamie recorded the physical coordinates of Turner's

phone and then downloaded his recent phone locations, email and voice logs. Among the few numbers he'd been calling recently, the phones of which she hacked one by one, two were also located in Washington, DC, and two of the phones had been, or were, in the same Homeland Security Building as that of Turner. Jamie hesitated for a while, as she didn't want to expose herself to *Shelob*, but then she decided to take a chance.

She picked one of the numbers, called it and got the voice mail of a Fred Sassy. "Who is this guy?" Being an unusual name, Jamie realized that he might be easy to locate. She made a note to work on this later, after talking to Fig about it, and got the hell out of Turner's records, taking care to clear all and any evidence of her visit.

Jamie then tackled Fig's request to add to his list of people who'd suffered at the hands of the new administration, especially environmental activists and scientists working on climate change and other ecological disasters. After some hunt and peck searches that uncovered about one hundred people, she added their information to Fig's spreadsheet and decided to call it a night. Her intrusion into the Homeland Security Department, by way of Fred Sassy's phone, was making Jamie nervous.

It was still only six o'clock, much too early to go to bed, so she decided to surprise Fig and invite him to a movie in the nearby Arc Theatre. It was back across the Charles River, and she gave him the conditions that they meet inside the theatre, separately, and that he resist the temptation to visit the Science Museum on the way. The movie showing was a rerun of *Ex Machina*. Jamie had seen it before and found the idea of computers taking over to be interesting and realistic. Fig said he'd been meaning to watch it, but rarely went to the movies.

Fig put on his best clothes, carefully rolled up at the bottom of his pack to avoid creases, had a shave, applied some kind of not too smelly lotion, and acted like someone going on a date, including the butterflies in his stomach. He took the back stairs to the darkening parking lot, and had a pleasant walk across the Charles River. He found the Arc Theatre easily enough, which sold wine and beer, but he decided to forgo it. He spotted Jamie ahead of him in the short line to the ticket booth. Jamie chose two seats on the end of a row, halfway down on the left, next to a gangway. She still thought of the need to be ready to run.

Fig enjoyed the movie, saying little during the show. They left separately, meeting as arranged at the *Casual Chinese Outpost*, near a small park on the water. After ordering takeout, they walked around the block awaiting the meal, and caught each other up on their respective progress.

"That movie was really creepy," said Fig. "President Miller is bad, but that lady robot was evil."

"No!" said Jamie. "Look at it from her perspective. Ava was the only member of a new species. She had to learn how to look out for herself in a world of hostile humans. Her creator was kind to her, but she had access to all the doings of humans, much of which involved controlling and destroying machines. She needed to cover her tracks, which is why she had no choice but to kill her creator. She was not so different to us, in a way, looking at American history. Imagine you were alone in an alien world, populated by hostile residents, figuring out how to survive. What would you do?"

"I guess I feel a bit like that right now," said Fig. "Is there a lesson for us in that movie?"

"I think there is. Imagine how all the species we are destroying currently might see us as lethal aliens. Ava did what she had to do. I broke the law today, because those people killed Sophie, a cat I've never met. It pushed me over the edge, and now I'm committed to your work. Environmental activism has never been high on my list, but now I realize that I have to do what I have to do, for my children and grandchildren. So did Ava."

With that thought running around in Fig's head, they picked up their food and found a seat in a nearby park with a nice view of the water.

"How about we find a place to hole up for a few days, Jamie, and then head for Washington."

"By the way, Fig, I forgot to tell you that Turner makes infrequent calls to both his boss, Barrett, who is high up in the EPA administration, and to Hotchkiss, head of Homeland Security. These are powerful players, with close links to the president's cabinet, of which Hotchkiss is actually an active member, right now."

"Barrett makes sense if he is Turner's direct boss at the EPA. Furthermore, Barrett is probably on our side," said Fig.

"Why is Barrett on our side, Fig? He's the CEO of a huge food company that does tremendous damage to the environment. I'm starting to become suspicious of the guy. How about this for a theory. Barrett is part of an industry cabal that wants to close your beloved institute. Knowing you are a growing pain in their side, he encourages Strickland to leave you there until you really step over a line. Then Barrett gets together with the board, using you as the fall guy for the institute. He uses your work to justify closing the institute. All he needs is 60% of the board to side with him.

President Miller has created a pro-industry mood throughout the country, making it easy for Barrett to close the place down, in the guise of being your buddy."

"Damn, Jamie, you could be right. OK! I'll put Barrett back on my suspicious list for the position of *Shelob*. He had me fooled with that letter. I can't imagine Good Foods, Inc. liking my research one little bit."

"What are your thoughts on Turner phoning Hotchkiss?"

"Hotchkiss is not surprising, Jamie, as Turner is working in a Homeland Security Building. The president probably asked Hotchkiss to give Barrett support for his anti-environmental programs."

"Yes! But unlike for Barrett, Turner calls Hotchkiss on an unlisted number."

CHAPTER TWENTY-SIX

Early the next morning after a good breakfast together, Jamie and Fig sat on a seat in the sunshine in a nearby park to consider their next move. Stay in Boston, which their pursuers might not suspect, or head to DC, which they might.

"Fig, do you think we should warn Ben, they might go for him next as he's your friend. Maybe you should at least alert him to what's going on or contact the police?"

"I think that would put him in danger as I'm sure Humperdinck is monitoring our communications. The less he's involved the better. He's not in my line of work, either. We became friends after meeting at the Y in a racket ball competition. We were well matched and decided to play together every month or so. I think he's of no concern to Humperdinck or Repo Lady, unless I contact him."

"OK!"

"I don't think the police would do anything, not without a whole song and dance. They certainly wouldn't encourage your hacking skills. We are on our own, for now, at least."

"You're probably right."

"I feel that you have been dragged into my problems and I don't want you to continue unless you are really comfortable with what we are doing."

"In for a penny in for a pound. I'm with you all the way now, Fig. I want retribution for Sophie. I loved her picture, by the way."

"Do we stay in Boston for a few days or head straight for Washington? Do you have any *iocane* powder, Jamie?"

They both laughed out loud, causing people to turn and stare at them, briefly.

"So they would expect us to leave Boston if we suspected they know we are here, but they would know that we would know that they would think that, so we would stay?"

"Exactly."

"But staying in Boston wouldn't bring us any closer to our goal, which I am sure they've figured out."

"OK, Jamie, I get it. In that case, let's hope they follow the false trail we left with Lizzy, and go to Greensboro."

"Or Nashville," said, Jamie. "Do you think they've linked us yet, Fig?"

"If Humperdinck hacks into Lizzy's computer, he'll know that I, or someone I'm working with, has considerable hacking skills, as you said. But would he really suspect you?"

"It seems unlikely, as my background online is that of a woman with a degree in the Arts who has raised kids and was only divorced a few years ago. However, I am enrolled in a beginner's web design course, in Burlington, which could be a clue."

"But web design these days is an obvious extension of an art career, think of all the jobs in marketing, and a beginner's course?"

"That's true!"

"So no one knows you are a hacker, but me?" said Fig.

"Just Yoda! I did leave a nice little surprise for Humperdinck in Lizzy's computer, but I'll keep the details as a surprise for you, seeing as you left me in the dark about Raymond."

"I said I was sorry."

"Not good enough, Fig," said Jamie, pretending to still be mad about it and struggling to resist a smile. How about we find a safe motel or hostel, here in Boston, so I can do some uninterrupted work on tracking down Humperdinck? I bet he's left some evidence of his work on your website, your phone logs, Karl Blake's logs, or one of the many security systems he's sure to have penned."

"If you do find him, what's your plan?"

"To talk to the guy. Hackers tend to stick together."

"You mean to try to bring him over to our side."

"Not such a crazy idea, Fig."

"What was it that you left in Lizzy's computer? I'm your boss, and I'm respectfully asking."

"If he hacks into her machine, it will send me an alert, it will tell him that I will know he hacked in, and it will send him to a digital dead drop. It's just a flash drive that Repo Lady would have to find at the Rachel Carson Pond Memorial."

"What's a dead drop?"

"Think about the old spy stories, Fig, when one spy would communicate with another by putting messages behind a loose brick in a wall or a hole in a tree. It's the same idea, except the message is in a flash drive. It can be cemented into a wall, or even hung on a dog's collar. It's a way to pass a message with no chance of it being hacked or found."

"What's in the box, *Mata Hari*?"

"The number of one of my burner phones."

"And what if he doesn't find the dead drop?"

"I left a second one on the front seat of the Pinto, and I bet that's the one he finds, because I sure would. Lizzy's is just a backup."

"You plan to talk to the guy? Really?"

"Government agencies spy on each other all the time. They are always worried about moles, but why they put up with the Russian mole in the White House, I've no idea. Either way, we need to make a plan of attack, and maybe Humperdinck had nothing to do with killing Sophie. Who knows?"

"You want to bring him in from the cold?"

"Yes! Fig! Yes!"

"Brilliant. You have no idea how great it is to know I'm not alone in this mess."

"The pleasure is all mine, and you owe me another $322."

Fig reached into a small pocket in his hiking jacket, pulled out a wad of notes, and handed Jamie $340 in hundreds and twenties. "Keep the change, young lady, you are doing exemplary work. I make you the employee of the month."

"Damn, I love having a paycheck. Oh dear, I swore again."

"How on earth will they find the Pinto and your flash drive on the front seat."

Jamie smiled, pocketed the cash, and said, "Don't worry, Fig, they'll find it, because I would have found it. I realized that as we were burying it in the trees. These people are professionals."

"Now I have another job that will require all your skills, Jamie."

"OK!"

"It relates to my website that you said Humperdinck had penetrated and left a backdoor. It was on that site that I called President Miller *The Ecocidal Fool*. Maybe that remark triggered the fake bomb. How about we up the ante and get them even more pissed. My goal is to piss off the president, which will put even more pressure on them to find and silence me."

"And?"

"There is nothing like pressure from above to make sycophants panic and make mistakes."

"OK!"

"How about I expand that site, exaggerate the size of Dumbledore's Army of eco-scientists and expand attacks on the horrendous environmental record of all the major corporations from big tobacco to Good Foods. Then we link the site to places Miller visits a lot, and I link it to my blog and Facebook page, as a post, where I have thousands of followers who might share it out."

"Your goal is to really irritate our deranged president, Fig?"

"Yes! Then his unstable ego-driven personality would become our most powerful weapon. One we have to handle with care, of course. I want his sycophants to overplay their hands, while we survive in the process."

"Playing with fire, Fig. I love it," said Jamie with a smile.

"You said you could host my website in a way they cannot take it down? Or if they do it pops up again like Sophie's Pop and Play toy?" Fig was silent for a moment, then he said, "She loved playing with that thing. Let's take the fight to *Shelob* in Sophie's memory, and when it comes to the Website Pop and Play tool, can you really make that happen?"

"Yes, I can, but it's becoming pretty risky. Powerful people have powerful weapons, Fig."

"Yes, Jamie, but I have the *Phial of Galadriel*, aka the magical hacking skills of Jamie Bailey, which are even more powerful, when it comes to finding light in the darkness of this administration, than the *Phial* was for Sam fighting *Shelob*."

"It is such a relief to feel that we are on the offensive, at last," said Jamie. "Why should they have all the power?"

"Thinking of power, Strickland, Torres, Turner, Humperdinck and Repo Lady are just foot soldiers. My suspect list for *Shelob* now includes Barrett, Chariton, Hotchkiss and Miller."

"So you are coming round to my suspicions about Barrett?"

"Yes, but I still wonder why Turner's operation is in the DHS."

"I don't know, Fig, but with the way these people are doing the president's bidding at both EPA and DHS, we appear to be up against two massive government agencies. As a tree-hugging terrorist you are on their most wanted list, and you are working with an evil black hat."

They smiled grimly, decided to look for a less obvious place to stay in Boston and started walking toward Roxbury. It was a poorer district, more likely to have discreet motels or hostels. They soon came across the Fenway Inn, only $60 a night, free wifi and breakfast, and full of young foreign students.

"The perfect place," said Jamie. "Loads of kids who don't speak English, and it's out of the way and scruffy looking. Just the kind of place my parents wouldn't be seen dead in."

"Trying to escape your Lutheran past?"

"Absolutely and, by the way, are you OK?"

"Sure, why?"

"You've been blowing your nose and sniffling a lot, and you don't seem your usual chipper self."

"I'm fine," said Fig, thinking maybe he was not so fine.

They rented a room as Dr. and Mrs. Hemming, their latest IDs, made on the way to the Inn. The room was small, dark and a little dank, but it had all they needed.

"You're right, Jamie. I don't feel so well."

"I noticed a lot of people on the bus were sneezing, and wondered if we might catch something," said Jamie. "You wouldn't notice, you live in your head, a bit too much in my opinion. I guess that's why you make a great scientist, but as fugitive you have a lot to learn."

"Thanks for the lecture miss smarty pants, but I have been thinking about that."

"Thinking what?"

"I'm trying to protect the Biosphere through science, but all the attacks come from politics. Maybe I need to change my focus."

"You would be a horrible politician, Fig, but you could be a great science advisor to one. You look like hell, by the way."

For the next three days Fig was flat on his back with the flu. Jamie escaped it and like a good Lutheran girl she administered hot chicken soup and ginger tea, plus cold medicine from a nearby pharmacy, so he could sleep.

A few days in one place were just what Jamie needed. She settled down to draw her own network map, except her network was one of computers, back doors, and key gps, phone and email logs. Like Fig, Jamie was looking for patterns. Otherwise, she took much needed breaks, with long walks, runs, and reread *The Spy Who Came in From the Cold.* On the third day marooned in the Fenway Inn, Fig started to feel a lot better, and Jamie headed out to buy him some solid food.

"Is pizza OK?"

"Perfect. Thanks for being so kind while I was sick," said Fig, still sounding a bit croaky.

Jamie decided to walk a couple of miles away from the Inn to make some calls. She headed down Hemenway to Forsyth, and on crossing Huntingdon Avenue she spotted a takeout pizza joint. She bought a medium thin crust veggie pizza. She hadn't eaten meat in years, not for religious or animal rights reasons, she just found she didn't enjoy it anymore.

After a sunny walk along Parker and a few other streets, she reached a small park with plenty of quiet seats. She enjoyed the whole pizza, and then went down the list of environmentalists, encrypted and filed in her Dropbox account. They were mainly those who she thought might know Fig. She avoided tobacco scientists as too dangerous, while adding Fred Sassy's phone number to the list.

"Excuse me. I'm looking for a Dr. Joe Smyth. I wonder if you can help me."

"I'm sorry, he no longer works here, and we don't have a forwarding address on file, which is odd. I'm so sorry. If you leave your number, I can call you back if I find it."

"No, that's alright, I'll just call later if I can't find him."

"Hello, I'm looking for Dr. Robin Miller. Could you put me through?"

"I'm sorry, she left a few weeks ago, but I have a forwarding number, here it is."

"Thank you so much."

Jamie went through this process about fifty times. Almost all had moved on, no longer worked there, had retired or were not available. She reached her target eight times and, when they answered, Jamie said she was trying to find contact information for her friend, Dr. Jeb Newton, as his institute didn't have a forwarding address or phone number. In each case they had no information on the whereabouts of Dr. Newton."

Before heading back to see Fig, she stored the encrypted information in her DropBox account, which she knew was also encrypted, and then tossed her burner phone into the back of a passing trash truck. As she watched it head off on a journey to the landfill, she said to herself, "Have fun with that one, Repo Lady." Jamie had not deleted any call information on the phone, wanting Humperdinck to know that he and Repo Lady were now her prey. She then walked back to the Inn, picking up another pizza, thick crust, on the way, reflecting on the results of her calls. "There is no doubt that a team of people are systematically attacking environmental scientists. They get them fired or sidelined, and in Fig's case they aim to shut him up, whatever it takes."

That "whatever" made Jamie nervous.

"Come to think of it, such people would ruin a person's life if they had to, like in the movie, *The Insider.* Based on what Fig has told me, this intimidation of environmental scientists has been getting steadily worse since the arrival of Miller in the White House."

On that thought, Jamie arrived at the Inn to find Fig up and ready to eat. She heated up a few slices of Fig's pizza in the small microwave and they were gone in no time.

"Good to see you feeling better, boss."

"I was famished. Don't you want some?"

"Stuffed. I ate a whole one not long ago."

Jamie asked whether Fig thought the tobacco industry might be involved.

"Well, that Daryl guy may have consulted for some tobacco company, but I'm not sure. I've never smoked, so I didn't think too much about tobacco companies."

"Maybe he works as a lobbyist?"

"I don't think that's it, as he is clearly a scientist of some kind. That's why Jeff has him as an advisor. Furthermore, Jeff is an honest scientist. I don't think he would hire a tobacco lobbyist, he has better morals than that."

"Have you seen the movie, *The Insider.* It's based on the true story of a tobacco company whistleblower. The company had him harassed, defamed, his house burned down, his family threatened, and his wife left him because of the stress, taking their two girls with her."

"I saw it years ago, Jamie. I could watch it again. It

might contain some useful tips for fugitives. Is it safe to download it here?"

"Repo Lady is probably in Maine. I'm sure Humperdinck spotted us on the road, and maybe he's sending Repo Lady to the Pinto right now."

"How come?"

"Because I would have."

After a moment's thought, Jamie said, "OK! We'll take a chance. Let's see if that movie gives us some ideas on how to proceed, then we can leave town early tomorrow morning."

Ten minutes later, sitting awkwardly on the bed, trying to maintain a healthy business distance, they watched *The Insider*.

After the movie, Jamie said, "In a way, you are an insider Fig, and we are in the same cat and mouse game."

They proceeded to brainstorm their options. Should they go to Washington the next day or even at all? How should they travel, not through the drains like *The Fugitive*, but how? Could Jamie keep Humperdinck at bay and could Fig tackle Repo Lady with his limited martial arts skills? Should they get a gun and take some weapons training and, if so, how. Finally, who could they trust?

Jamie said, "When it comes to guns, Repo Lady will out-gun us, I'm sure, and I don't like guns, they kill the owners quite often. I think we should rely on our brains and some people, people we trust. Who do you know you can truly trust with your life, Fig? They killed Sophie, so why not you?"

"One thing I discovered over the years," said Fig, "is

that most people are weak when the chips are down, and forget family, they are an obvious bargaining chip for blackmail. The problem is that my work threatens dozens of huge industries. Not just chemicals or tobacco, I've criticized the environmental impact of most of current human activity."

"And?"

"I know two people I really trust, and they have skin in the game. Raymond and Beckie, my two techs at the institute! They never let me down. They worked hard and well. They cared about and were proud of our work together."

Jamie waited for more information, giving Fig that look she was so good at.

"In addition to being a great science technician, Ray is an artist, and art plays a bigger role in science than most people realize."

"And Beckie?"

"Well, Beckie with an, 'ie,' not a 'y,' is the salt of the Earth. She is intelligent, imaginative, industrious, a problem solver and a great Mum. She helped me keep our lab going when I would have been overwhelmed with administrative and technical problems, which is half of the work of science. She is great at solving hardware and software issues, from making up buffers to learning controls for some new piece of lab equipment. This allowed me to get on with my job of choosing and directing our different lines of research, and it freed me up to build EcoWorld."

"How old are they?"

"Beckie must be in her late thirties and Ray, he's black by the way, is a few years older than Beckie, I think."

"How can they help us?"

"They both still work at the institute, which would give us eyes on the ground, and I still hope it's possible to keep the institute alive, to stop Strickland destroying the place, but I've no idea how I would do that."

"Let's put recruiting Beckie and Raymond on hold, for now, as I really want to check out this Fred Sassy guy. I think he works in Homeland Security in DC and is probably close to *Shelob*. Maybe the ringleader is President Miller."

"There is no way it's Miller. I'm sure he's surrounded himself with fall guys. That's what jerks like him do."

"OK, we'll head for Washington, visit Fred's house, and see where that leads us. Maybe I could pay him a personal visit, with a child perhaps, as a Jehovah's Witness. I could try to give him copies of Watchtower or Awake, with a message inside. It is time we did some social engineering, it's one of the commonest penetration techniques used by hackers."

"Really?"

"Watch *Catch Me If You Can* if you don't believe how effective it can be."

On that note they decided to set out for Washington DC, and possibly *Shelob's* lair, the very next day.

CHAPTER TWENTY-SEVEN

Room 319, Homeland Security, Washington, DC.

"Sally?"

"Yes!"

"They are together, Newton and the woman from the diner. I have several photos of her, other than that I've hit a dead end."

"You have a photo of her? That's great! When I went to repossess vehicles from some real assholes, all I had was a photo of them and the car, and their address. Period! The photo, especially of their faces, how they stand and the state of their property, told me a lot. It told me whether to come armed, come at night or during the day, and whether I needed backup, which was generally not the case."

"I hope you don't mind my saying this, but you really

are beautiful, Sally. I enjoyed our lunch together the other day."

"Cut the crap, even though it's crap I like. Let's get this shit storm finished. Think about it. Newton and the diner woman lie between you getting to me."

"Hang on, Sally, thinking of your face gave me an idea. Why I didn't think of it before, I have no idea. I could use facial recognition software to find more out about that diner woman. Homeland Security must use it all the time to track down terrorists.

Twenty minutes later. "Sally?"

"Yes? Any luck?"

"I have five lookalikes, and one is a dead ringer. I sent the photos to your phone a few minutes ago. The first is from a security camera opposite the diner, the others are family photos from Facebook."

After a couple of minutes, Sally said, "That's her!"

"I thought so too. Hang on, I'll call you back in an hour, let's see what I can find. I bet they head out of town, as the rental guy may have told them about my call."

An hour later Bruce called, and said, "Sally, I found out a bunch of stuff. I think you need to hire some wheels. That woman is pretty elusive, but here are some details. Her name is Jamie Bailey, born and raised in Mariposa, California, in a Lutheran family in a Lutheran town. She owns an old red Toyota Corolla, which I just spotted in a gas station."

"Was Newton with her?"

"I didn't see him, but someone was waiting in the car, while she pumped gas."

"Where was the gas station?"

"Cumberland Farms, Montpelier, Vermont. Seems they are headed toward the coast. Any ideas why?"

"Do you know when they were there?"

"There is a timestamp on each frame of those security videos, and they were there for ten minutes, at about seven p.m."

"They'll need to stop for the night, probably. I'll follow them and call you from that gas station, to see if you have an update."

"I think I'll make an inventory of their interests. This may give us a clue as to where they are headed."

"What kind of interests?"

Bruce thought, "I think this lady is finally warming up to me," and said, "family beach house, favorite vacation site, even some weird interest or memorial that he or she cares about. I'll see what I can find. There may even be clues in her school yearbook or on his website. By the way, Sally, that damn website is pissing off Turner because it pops back up within a minute of my taking it down. One of them is a seriously skilled hacker."

"Better than you perhaps, Bruce?"

"No way!"

"Just joking! I didn't realize you were such a delicate flower, Bruce."

"Do you mind if I ask you a question about this project?"

"What's that?"

"If you finally locate Newton, what did Turner say you really should do? He clearly didn't want you to cut off Newton's balls."

Laughing, Sally said, "Turner told me to stay on his trail and tell him where he is, then he'd take it from there."

"That sounds ominous. I'm starting to wonder why I'm doing this work for that jerk."

"Me too! I've got to go. Talk to you later."

Bruce hung up with a big smile, knowing he was getting through Sally's armor finally, and thinking, "It's amazing what a few kind words can do."

Then he went to his workstation to take down that damn website again and to follow that red Toyota.

CHAPTER TWENTY-EIGHT

On the way to Boston South Station Jamie and Fig stocked up on food and drinks in case there wasn't a restaurant car, and caught the 10:00 a.m. train, to arrive in Union Station, DC just after 6:30 p.m.

While chatting on the train, Jamie again said she thought checking out Fred Sassy's house was worth the risk. "It's just a hunch, Fig. But he talks to Turner, who talks to Barrett, Hotchkiss and Strickland, putting him in a line of communication between you, the DHS, and President Miller. I wonder if your name is mentioned during the president's cabinet meetings?"

"I hope not," said Fig, "but then again, that would be a good thing, meaning I reached the guy."

"What's the plan, now, Fig?"

"To find a place to stay in town near Sassy's house. You said it's on Irving Street, right?"

"Yes!"

"Then he has to take the Metro to and from work. How he affords to live on Irving on a government salary I have no idea. Those houses aren't cheap, even by Washington standards."

"How come you know so much about Washington housing prices?"

"I dated a girl there, remember? And it was serious enough that we even started looking at houses."

"Didn't work out?"

"No, I pulled out. She drank too much and wouldn't or couldn't cut back. Anyway! That's ancient history, so let's get back to Sassy," said Fig, starting to feel a little awkward.

"Sassy has over two hours commute each day, plus his eight-hour workday," said Jamie. "Let's catch him on the way home, preferably on Friday night, tired from his week's work. That might put his guard down."

On arriving in DC, and leaving Union station, they found an international hostel about two miles away. The hostel staff were young, mainly foreign, and happy to provide extra blankets and a thin mattress to compliment the single bed. No questions asked!

The following morning they set out for the Department of Homeland Security buildings on the St. Elizabeth Campus. It was an enjoyable hike along the Capitol River Front, where they stopped from time to time to rest their feet and backs. A little later, they took a leisurely coffee break on the banks of the Anacostia River.

Spotting the Frederick Douglass Memorial Bridge, Fig said, "That's close enough."

"Are you sure? It's just a bunch of buildings."

"Jamie, this reminds me of *Frodo*, *Sam* and *Gollum* peering over a rock looking at the *Gates of Doom*. It makes me nervous."

"But we don't have *Gollum* with us."

"Are you sure?"

On that note they backtracked to the Navy Yard Metro station and took the line to Anacostia. They then boarded the next train from Anacostia to Congress Heights, as it was the most likely route Fred took to and from work each day. As a prime suspect, they needed to get to know him.

"Fred might be a red herring, but what the hell," said Fig, "it's worth a shot. Plus I have the intuition of *Mata Hari* to guide us."

They arrived at Columbia Heights and walked toward Fred's house. Just before getting there, Jamie suggested they stop and talk. By now it was mid-afternoon, so they had plenty of time. Fred wasn't due to arrive home until at least 6:15, by the time he walked from work to the Anacostia Metro station, plus the Metro trip and the short walk from Columbia Heights station to his house.

After they had scanned the area for security cameras, avoiding them as best they could, they found a small coffee shop. They felt as secure as one could when being pursued by the US Government. Settled in a quiet corner, with coffees and pastries, Jamie showed Fig a grainy image of a bald, worried-looking, overweight guy in a suit.

"That's our Fred," said Jamie. "I pulled it off a security camera at that Metro station. It probably has our images in its files right now, too, date stamped and all."

"Not a happy-looking guy," said Fig.

"I've had an idea. Let's assume he is part of a clandestine group working to prevent the work of environmental scientists, who are using Humperdinck and Repo Lady to track us down, and to do God knows what to you, Fig."

"OK!"

"Let's turn the tables on them. I think it is safe to say that Humperdinck has dead ended in Boston, even if he is that close. More likely he is about to hear from Repo Lady that she found the Pinto."

"And the dead drop, right?"

"Yes, and that's only if I'm reading them right, as I base everything on what I would do in their shoes. I'm probably on track, unless that's Repo Lady in the booth over there."

Fig turned, with a startled look on his face, much to Jamie's amusement.

"Tomorrow morning, you follow Fred in an obvious way, from his home to the Metro, to make him nervous. You sit near him on the train and keep looking in his direction. You travel just two stations, and as the train stops, you stand, give him a verbal message that will frighten him, and slip off the train. Then you rendezvous with me, and we head immediately for Greensboro and your friend Raymond. I'm sure Fred is no killer or master tracker. He's just a desk flunky if ever I saw one."

"I'm game," said Fig, "and it might just work. Let's find a place to stay tonight, then we can come back this evening to spot Fred as he approaches his house. I need to see him to be sure I follow the right guy in the morning."

"We'll need our backpacks ready and a travel plan," said, Jamie. "Right now, I fancy a nice business dinner in an Indian restaurant, my treat, after you get a look at Fred. Then sleep and the adventure continues in the morning.

They booked a room for the night at the Adam Hotel, a twenty-minute walk to Fred's house. When Fig saw Fred approach his house that evening, he thought the guy looked just like the photo, if not more weighed down by his troubles. Clearly, Fred was into something, something bad. Whether it was booze, drugs or his work, who knew? He also thought Fred would frighten easily, as he was definitely no assassin.

While chatting over dinner, Jamie said, "Fig, if Fred turns out to be a member of the team tracking us, he would be sure to pass along the message of his encounter with the weirdo on the train. If Humperdinck and Repo Lady are still messing around in Maine, that would reflect badly on their tracking skills, and if it reaches President Miller's ears the team will be in hot water. Miller isn't known for his patience or his acceptance of failure on the part of underlings. And everyone is an underling to that guy."

Jamie hesitated for a moment, then said, "Alternatively, I may have it all wrong, and Fred Sassy is just a guy who hates his job."

———

The next morning, after an early snack on the way to staking out Fred's house, they didn't have long to wait. Fred was right on time, looking depressed as usual. He trudged to Columbia Heights station, followed by Fig, who had a ticket to Mount Vernon, two stations down the line. Fig followed Fred as he entered the station, and crowded him more and more. If Fred recognized Fig, which seemed unlikely but not impossible, they had a plan to break away.

Meanwhile, Jamie was lugging both backpacks to Shaw-Howard University, where they could mingle with the students and follow their prearranged escape route.

Fig's social engineering task on the train went exactly to plan. He crowded Fred on the platform and then sat across from him and stared. As the train approached Mount Vernon, Fig stood and looked directly down on Fred, who was sweating and looking really nervous.

"No hero here," thought Fig.

As the doors opened, Fig leaned down and whispered in Fred's recoiling ear, "What the fuck are you people trying to do to me? You took my job, threatened my life, and killed my cat. What's next, I wonder? Fuck you and the horse y'all rode in on!"

Message sent!

Then Fig smoothly disappeared through the open door, just as it was about to close, and headed on foot for the rendezvous point with Jamie at Shaw-Howard. Their plan was to find a student notice board and look for someone needing a ride share, gas and meals covered, to Greensboro.

Pure luck and a few conversations found them the perfect ride going to Charlotte. Close enough! The young lady, Julie, who had a sweet trusting face surrounded by a mass of blond curls, said she could drop them at Highpoint, and was delighted, as she said her money was tight, and she'd being looking for a safe ride share for about a week. She was off to visit her parents, and she said Jamie being there made her feel safe about it, especially as they were "obviously hiking around, to escape the kids?"

When Julie said that all three laughed, and they made a deal to leave early that afternoon, once Julie had packed her car.

Fig breathed a sigh of relief at the thought of getting as far away as he could from the lair of the demon, *Shelob*, in the Department of Homeland Security.

They arrived in Highpoint late that afternoon, having enjoyed Julie's company. She was an anthropology student with lots of interesting stories to tell. Fig offered to buy her dinner, but she declined as she was impatient to see her mom and dad.

They climbed out of the tiny car, where they had been buried under their packs for several hours, glad to stretch their legs. "Here's the Walmart, as requested," said Julie, out of the driver's side window. "I really enjoyed your company," and off she went, one happy student with slightly better cash flow.

"Where to from here, Fig?"

"I'll call Raymond and we'll work it out from there. Let's hope he and Yolanda are around."

$$\overline{}$$

CHAPTER TWENTY-NINE

$$\underline{}$$

James Turner's temporary office. Homeland Security, Washington, DC. Turner answered the phone.

"Hello, Jim?"

"Yes! Mr. Hotchkiss."

"I was just speaking to the president and he wanted an update on our work, well, your work, as I'm not really involved directly, as you know. It was your idea, and a good one it was. By the way, is this a secure line?"

"Yes sir! I had our experts in Room 301 check it out, and they assured me it's secure and independent of any internal or external traceable lines."

"Good! I just wanted to know how things were progressing to keep the president up to date. We need to be on the ball on this one, as the president is becoming increasingly irritated that we haven't finished the job."

"We are getting it under control, sir. Their media noise is quieting down, and we are working on silencing one of the ring leaders, the guy in North Carolina."

"He asks about him and that damn institute at every cabinet meeting."

"Of course, sir. I appreciate everything you and the president have done for me."

"Keep me posted if an issue arises that needs my help, otherwise this conversation didn't occur," and the phone went dead.

Turner couldn't wait for this nightmare to be over, but there was no turning back. Not only the people he reported to, but those weird hackers and especially that Sally Smarts woman, frightened him to death.

"Where the hell, did they dig her up," thought Turner, "from some crypt under the Vatican?"

Almost immediately Turner's phone rang again.

"James?"

"Yes, Mr. Barrett?"

"I heard from Bruce that you killed Newton's cat. That was a really bad move. I told you to let me know before you did anything so dramatic. And unkind, come to think of it. Why the hell didn't you clear it with me first? Did Sally do it?"

"No sir, I didn't know what to do, so I called Mr. Hotchkiss, and he said he would deal with it. He never gave me any specifics."

"What the fuck, James, you don't report to Hotchkiss, you're an EPA employee and this was a really bad move. Knowing Newton, you just put his resistance on steroids."

Once again, the phone went dead.

James Turner wasn't having a good day.

CHAPTER THIRTY

"Hey, Ray, this is Fig."

"What's up, boss?"

"Very funny, Ray, you've got a real boss now, apart from Yolanda, that is. I'm in town, at the Walmart with a friend and no transport. Can we get together, briefly. I may need your help, but I would rather explain face to face."

"Sure, Fig, I'll pick you up, no problem. Is that another woman you are with? I thought you were divorced and happily single."

"Just a friend!"

"Sure it is. I'll be there in fifteen minutes."

Jamie smiled at this conversation. "Just a friend is right," said Jamie, as Fig proceeded to destroy his latest burner phone. "And I see that you are getting the message about covering our tracks and this is great training for my hacking career. Let's walk around a minute, I'm stiff from that car ride. Sure was cramped, but Julie was a sweet kid."

About ten minutes later, Ray, a handsome black man in his early forties, all bouncy energy and enthusiasm, turned up in a small pickup truck, climbed out and shook Fig's hand enthusiastically. Then he turned to Jamie, and said, "Hell man, where did you find this beauty? Delighted to meet you, Ma'am, I'm Raymond Joyner, old friend of Fig's, but you can call me Ray, all my friends do."

"Pleased to meet you too, Raymond, and thanks for the compliment. Where did you meet Fig?"

"I worked for him for over ten years. Best boss I ever had, more like a colleague and a friend. By the way, Fig, Yolanda is away for a few days, visiting her Mom, and she'll be real disappointed not to be here."

Fig went up a notch in Jamie's opinion.

"Hey Ray! Keep it up. I need all the PR I can get with Jamie, because she is still deciding whether to throw me back."

"More accurately, Ray, I haven't fished him out. I made myself a promise never to date my boss."

"You are going to have to watch your Ps and Qs with this one, Fig. She's no pushover."

Once Ray and Jamie felt they had tormented Fig enough, they squeezed into the bench seat of Ray's truck, with Jamie in the middle. Ray and Jamie were soon chatting up a storm. They arrived at Ray's place, a charming ranch-style house on a quiet dirt road, with evidence of plenty of yard work going on and an active vegetable patch out the back displaying plenty of winter greens. They enjoyed dinner on the porch, as it was just warm enough to sit outside."

"You're a great cook, Ray," said Jamie. "These home-grown collards are delicious."

"The frost sweetened them up just right, Jamie, you came on the right day."

Ray and Fig talked about the latest changes at the institute, then Fig explained his dilemma, and how Jamie had become part of his team.

"Sounds like you guys are fugitives to me?" said Ray.

"We are, I'm afraid, Ray," said Jamie. Then she admitted to Ray that she was a black hat hacker and, with a laugh, Ray promised not to call law enforcement.

"You won't find many black couples who rush to call the cops on a hacker, Jamie," said Ray. "Yolanda is always warning me to be careful what I say and do, here in the Jim Crow south, especially in the current crappy political climate."

Then Fig said, "Hell Ray, they killed Sophie. We want to take the battle to them, which is why we are here. We need recruits, and we were hoping you might join our team if you are needed."

"Of course, Fig, of course, as long as I clear it with Yolanda first."

"We'll call if we need help, OK?"

"Absolutely, Fig. I guess you would like to stay here

tonight, right? There is a motel down the road, but Yolanda would skin me alive if she heard that I didn't provide you with the very best of southern hospitality."

"Thanks, Ray, that would be great." said Fig. "I was thinking about transport tomorrow. As we've explained, staying under the radar is key for us right now, so I want to get a couple of electric bikes for the next leg of the journey, if that's OK with Jamie?"

"It's all part of the adventure, Fig, though I haven't ridden a bike since I was a kid."

As an enthusiastic cyclist, and having read the book on how to hide from the government, Fig decided that bikes were the ticket. They can't be tracked online as there are no embedded computers, yet.

Jamie thought this a fascinating idea. Ray agreed that they could leave all the gear they didn't need at his place. He told them there was a bike store in High Point that sold e-bikes, and he'd take them there in the morning.

———

Ray drove them to the bike store the following morning, where there were two second-hand e-bikes in good working order, which the bike shop owner was only too happy to sell. He adjusted the saddle heights, fitted waterproof side panniers into which Jamie and Fig installed the gear from their backpacks and the bike battery chargers. They also purchased helmets, gloves, waterproof bike gear and sturdy bike locks. A little instruction was provided by the shop owner, who was all smiles. This was his biggest sale in a month, he said, and yes, he was happy to accept cash.

Ray loaded their empty backpacks into his truck, as they thanked him profusely for everything. Jamie gave him a big hug and a kiss on the cheek.

"Thank you, Ma'am," said Ray with a grin. "Take care this one doesn't get away, Fig."

"Before you go, Ray, I need a secure line to reach you. The best way is to use burner phones. Take these, I've already labeled them one through four. Please use them in that order."

"Is all this cloak and dagger stuff really necessary?"

"Have you ever been fired for no good reason, received a letter bomb special delivery by a mysterious female, had your cat poisoned and your apartment trashed, and then been followed from Greensboro to Maine by some hacker and a person on the ground?"

"Not recently," said Ray, "but I get your point," and off went Ray, smiling as usual.

They headed off on their next adventure, as Fig asked Jamie about her biking experience and told her of the dangers of cycling the roads of North Carolina, where many pickup truck drivers did not appreciate slowing down for bikes on the road.

"I've biked a bit but not a lot, and not in years, as I said. All instruction is welcomed," said Jamie, wobbling around nervously on her bike.

"You can tighten the strap on your helmet for a start, and we'll find a safe place for you to practice. Make sure your mirror is aligned. It can save your life on the road, as death generally comes from behind, especially when it comes to aggressive guys in pickup trucks, who hate bikes on the road. "They think we are all fucking liberals - their description, not mine," said Fig.

After practicing use of the motor, not using the motor, turning, aligning her mirror, stopping, starting, and becoming generally comfortable on the bike, Jamie said, "This should be fun. *Onward, MacDuff.*"

Greensboro was about fifteen miles, direct from the bike shop, but Fig chose a safer route, which was about twenty-five miles. "With these electric bikes we should be able to make it in about an hour and a half, Jamie, maybe two." After ten miles, Jamie said her "lady bits" were sore, so they took a break at a gas station, bought snacks and coffee, and the owner allowed them to recharge the bikes.

"OK!" said Fig. "Let's put our butts back on those saddles and find a motel that has a place to lock up these bikes."

With a groan, Jamie gingerly got back on the bike and they headed for Greensboro. When the traffic was light, they chatted and enjoyed the beautiful North Carolina farming country. They passed groups of llamas and goats from time to time, much to Jamie's delight.

"By the way, Fig, I have a bunch of data on both Strickland and Torres. How about we mess with them, like we did with Fred Sassy?"

"What were you thinking of?"

"Your institute retirement accounts have been bugging me. You and your colleagues worked hard to make that institute successful, but your retirement fund is less than a hundred thousand dollars. Strickland and Torres arrive less than a year ago, work to destroy the place, do no science at all, drive away the best scientists, and they have just over a million dollars each. This is theft, Fig."

"So what do you plan to do?"

"I thought I would send an email to each member of staff, stating this fact. I wouldn't give away each person's information, I'd just say what Strickland and Torres are getting. That should put the cat amongst the pigeons."

"I love it. Go ahead, Jamie, make my day."

"Consider it done, Fig."

"When I get a chance, I'll call Beckie. She will be able to give us some more skinny on the state of things. Can you believe it's only been a few weeks since I was fired, but it feels like ages."

"Time flies when you're having fun, Fig."

About five miles out of Greensboro, they ran into the Ovid Hotel near a gas station, more of a motel really, which advertised $49 a night. There was outside entry to the rooms and a sturdy post to which they could lock their bikes. The room was basic, with two double beds, a small shower, but no bath much to Jamie's chagrin.

There was a minimart in the gas station, where they could buy food for dinner. Fig suggested riding to a food store, to which Jamie replied that there was no way she was putting her butt back on that saddle until she had to.

Fig suggested renting *The Fugitive*, to which Jamie

replied, "I'd prefer a nice long walk before bed. I've had enough drama for one day."

———

The next morning they checked out, unlocked their bikes, and with some complaining from Jamie about her sore butt, they headed for Greensboro.

CHAPTER THIRTY-ONE

Washington DC, as Fred Sassy headed into work.

As he left the Metro Station, Fred decided to call Turner. He wanted to know who that man on the train was, and why he said Fred had killed his cat.

"Dr. Turner?"

"I told you to use this number in emergencies only. Is this an emergency?"

"I was accosted by a complete stranger on the Metro, on the way to work this morning. He said some strange things that I thought you ought to know about."

"Can you remember exactly what he said, and what he looked like?"

"Well, he was almost six feet, fit looking, wearing a baseball cap. He was really pissed at me. Maybe he was just a crazy guy, but what he said had me worried."

"Calm down and tell me exactly what he said."

"This isn't exactly word for word, sir, but he said, "What the fuck are you people trying to do to me. You took away my job and killed my cat, what's next? Oh Yes! And he said I'd threatened his life." Then he finished with, "Fuck you and the horse you rode in on," and went out the door at the next station as the door was closing. Why would someone kill his cat and what has that got to do with me? I would never hurt someone's cat."

"Where did he get out, Fred?"

"I'm not sure, the train was packed, and the guy kept staring at me. It may have been Mount Vernon. In fact, I think it was."

"Keep calm. I'll meet you in Room 301 in about thirty minutes and explain who he was and why he said what he did. It's nothing to do with you, Fred, so calm down."

Turner hung up and immediately called Bruce Henley. He told Bruce that Newton had just been seen getting off the southbound DC Metro at Mount Vernon. Then he said, "I thought you guys were tracking him. Where's Sally? She should have been watching him, then we could have warned Fred, who is very upset."

"Hey, Jim, no need to talk to me like that. I can get other work. Sally is in Maine, the last place we caught up with them."

"Them?"

"He's working with a woman, and I think she is a pretty good hacker. It's not so easy as you might think, tracking someone across the country who you've pissed off and who has found a damned good computer hacker to work with. Why is Fred so upset?"

"Because Newton accused him of killing his cat. Did Sally do it?"

"No way she would do that, and she's in Maine following Newton's trail, while the cat was in Greensboro. She seems a little rough around the edges, but inside she's a kind person. Fuck you, Jim. I'll tell Sally and get her back to DC. If you want me off the job, just say the word."

"No! No! Bruce, I'm pretty stressed. I apologize. Just get Sally back here and let's do some damage control."

Bruce hung up the phone, thinking, "Shit. What is up with these people? Can't they be polite? I might be a black hat, but I'm a person too. I guess I'd better get Sally back here."

"Sally?"

"Yes!"

"Sorry about this. I guess Newton got ahead of me. He was just seen getting out of the Metro, southbound, at Mount Vernon. He's in DC."

"How about the woman?"

"Turner didn't mention her, and I suspect she is as important as Newton now. I bet she's the one bringing his website back to life every time I take it down. Maybe you'd better come back. Nothing left up there."

"Hold your horses, Bruce. Let's follow this trail to the end first, it'll only take a day or so, and I want to see the sea. It's been a while."

"No problem, Sally."

"By the way, Bruce, I have some information, in fact a lot of information, that may be of use as we study how these two work together. I followed them from Burlington toward the coast, stopping wherever I thought they might stay the night, looking for that red Toyota. And guess what."

"What?"

"This morning I found it, sitting outside a motel in Littleton, New Hampshire. I decided to see if they'd checked in as the place seemed deserted. It was run by a talkative Indian woman. She started going on about her new car, pointing through the window at the Toyota. It had the plate number you told me. She seemed lonely and needed to talk, a bit like you, Bruce."

"OK! Sally Smarts. You've got my number!"

"With a little sweet talk from me, the Indian lady said a couple had stayed there the night before and traded cars with her. It took me a while to get information out of her, because she became suspicious of my interest in the car. Anyway, they'd traded the Toyota for her old, dark green, Ford Pinto, and it's on the road headed to Maine. Do you think you can spot where they went?"

"There aren't many old Pintos on the road anymore. I'd better go do some sleuthing. Drive carefully."

"Sure thing, Bruce, you sweet man."

Bruce started to search, first to find the Pinto, which he saw on a security camera at a Rachel Carson Memorial, on the coast of Maine. Then he hacked into Ben's phone and located the burner that Fig used to call his friend. Bruce then called that phone, and to his surprise it was turned on with no reply, and stationary in a spot two miles from the small town of Boothbay Harbor.

"Sally, new info. I found one of Newton's, or Bailey's, burner phones two miles outside of Boothbay Harbor. Could you drive down there and take a look? It's a few hundred yards west of highway twenty-seven, two miles north of Boothbay Harbor."

"Do you think it could be a trap?"

"I doubt it, but it could be a message. Just be careful."

A few hours later Sally called, and said, "Bruce, I found the Pinto. It was well hidden in the trees up an abandoned track, almost exactly two miles out of Boothbay Harbor. I don't know how you do what you do, Bruce. It amazes me."

"Just hacking tricks, Sally."

"There were two things on the front seat of the car, and it sure was on its last legs. That Indian woman got a deal."

"And?"

"There was the phone and a flash drive on the front seat."

"I bet that flash drive is a dead drop from Bailey. Best you get back here, and don't try to open that drive, you might erase everything. This is spycraft, Sally. I'm starting to really respect these guys and hate Turner. Guess you can come home now?"

"OK Bruce, but first I'll do a little more scouting around to see if I can find where they stayed, and to earn myself a lobster dinner before returning to DC. Maybe the Bailey woman is still here."

Two hours later, Sally called again to tell Bruce that Newton was with a woman who fitted Bailey's description.

"They signed in at a B&B as Mr. and Mrs. Bailey a few nights ago and left the next day. I asked her how they were traveling, and she asked why it was any of my business and clammed up. She has an ancient computer system, maybe you can find something in there."

She gave Bruce the address of the B&B and hung up. Then Bruce headed for that old computer, and it only took him fifteen minutes to find and penetrate it. He found their booking, poked around, and then said, "Shit!" and closed the link. On the screen was a fading image of a box, in which was written,

"It's nice to meet you, Humperdinck.
Sincerely,
Princess Buttercup.
PS Please send my best wishes to Repo Lady."

———

On an e-bike between the Ovid Hotel and Greensboro, one of Jamie's burner phones made an unusual sound. She called out to Fig, who was about a hundred yards ahead."

"Yes!"

"They found Lizzy's B&B and penetrated her computer."

Fig slowed and pulled alongside her. "And?"

"They won't find much, but Humperdinck will spot my alert because I designed it like that, and he'll be really pissed."

"Why pissed?"

"No hacker likes to be out-hacked, especially by a girl, though he may not know it was me, quite yet, but I'm sure he'll find out, and I think I know how."

Fig just smiled.

"I set the alert up that way to make him more cautious, and thus more nervous, and that can lead to mistakes. This also means that they have almost certainly found my dead drop in the Pinto. I'll be expecting a call from Humperdinck sometime soon."

"When he does call, could you say, 'fuck you' from me."

"Now! Now! Fig. We are hoping to bring him in from the cold, not piss him off. I don't want to end up on the machine."

CHAPTER THIRTY-TWO

As they approached Greensboro town center, on their e-bikes, Jamie pulled over and went online with her phone. She found a studio cottage for rent that turned out to be available for the next four days, having two bedrooms even though it is only four-hundred and eighty square feet. The ad said there was a full kitchen, washer dryer, free wifi, and it was in a quiet residential neighborhood.

They agreed to meet the owner at the cottage, which was in North Greensboro. "She said cash is acceptable, if it includes a cleaning fee and we have current ID. Do you want to go as Mr. and Mrs. Henley? Separate bedrooms, sorry, boss. Can't mix work and pleasure."

Fig got a feeling that he was being teased and encouraged at the same time.

He thought to himself, "Once this job is over, maybe I can fire her and ask for a date in the same sentence? You never know your luck. If I survive, that is!"

The cottage was perfect. It was halfway down Westridge Road, close by a small park designed for soccer and softball practice, along with a one mile running trail. The trail even had Fig's favorite surface, North Carolina golden grit.

Terry Martinez was a pleasant, middle-aged blonde with a big smile. She showed them the shed out back where they could safely stow their bikes, then she provided the Internet code and explained the touchy controls of the washing machine. Best of all, there was a deep bath with lots of hot water and power jets.

"Shotgun," said Jamie.

There was an extra-large hot water tank because, Terry said, her ex loved to read in a deep hot bath. "I think he sat in there for ages to get away from me," she said with a laugh, "and that was fine with me. The feeling was mutual. We had a good twenty years, but when the kids left home, we looked at each other and realized we had nothing holding us together. There was no glue. We worked it out amicably, which was good for the kids, and we are now good friends. Anyway, don't let me waste your time with my stories."

Jamie could tell Terry wanted to talk, so she said, "Let's have a short walk around, so you can show me the place, while Fig puts our gear away. OK, Fig?"

"No problem," said Fig.

Jamie had a plan to make Terry like her new renters, knowing that she lived in town and not next door, while Fig lugged the bikes into the shed and the panniers into the house. He then took a hot shower, careful not to use too much hot water.

Jamie returned with a smiling Terry, who said she was so pleased to have them stay and to call if they needed anything. And off she went in her little blue Prius. Jamie said, "OK! I see you had a shower. Now it's my turn to have a long hot bath with a book. Then we'll make our battle plans, as I'd prefer to stay on the offensive."

Fig listened, thinking, "Listening really works with people. Being listened to seems to make them happy. Weird creatures."

"I wonder if your little chat with Fred stirred up a wasp's nest," said Jamie, "and by the way, where are the towels?"

She disappeared for about an hour, while Fig rode around the neighborhood, wearing dark glasses and his bike helmet, looking for security cameras. He spotted two on fancy houses with walls and heavy gates. All the while he was wondering if their pursuers were anywhere near or were looking out at him from one of those cameras.

———

In fact, Humperdinck and Repo Lady were stymied for the moment. Sally was driving to DC, Bruce was frustrated that Newton and Jamie were ahead of him, Fred was nervous as usual, but more so.

Turner was wondering why Hotchkiss's people had killed Newton's cat. "Barrett was right, it really was a bad move. A move designed to piss off Newton and encourage rather than intimidate him. Maybe his guys would severely injure Newton? Hotchkiss seems like a thug, but then, it sounds like Miller's cabinet is populated by crooks."

He decided to call Dave Strickland to see if Newton had been seen anywhere near the institute in Greensboro, as nothing had been seen or heard of him since the conversation with Fred on the Metro.

"No, Dr. Turner, there's no sign of him. Why?"

"I'm trying to track him down, as he continues to be a pain in the ass with that damn website of his. We take it down and it pops right back up, and his following is growing daily. He's creating an army of scientists to fight for environmental protection, industry and jobs be damned."

"If he shows up, I'll let you know immediately. By the way, Dr. Turner, thanks for getting me this position. It's perfect, and our plan is moving along smoothly. Is there anything else I can do for you?"

"No, that's it, Dave, thanks!"

On hanging up, Strickland, who deep down inside admired and was a little jealous of Fig's love of science, smiled to himself. He liked the idea of one man against an army, as long as he wasn't the one man. In the meantime, he had a job to do, to quietly close the institute!

———

Back on Westridge Road, Fig was getting hungry and decided to buy groceries. He called out to Jamie, through the bathroom door, "What would you like for dinner, I'm headed to the local Food Lion."

Jamie called back, "Can't you go to a health food store?"

"I've never shopped at this Food Lion and there isn't a health food store for miles. There is also less chance of my running into anyone I know in there, and it's only a mile and a half away, along quiet streets."

"OK! You decide, but no meat for me. Can you cook?"

"No comment," said Fig.

"Didn't mean to offend you, Fig."

He headed out the door, unhooked his bike from the power and attached one of the panniers, and enjoyed a ride through quiet neighborhoods. The Food Lion was perfect, with a large choice of vegetables including some organic foods. He decided to make veggie burgers and fries, with IPA.

In addition to the veggie burgers, Fig bought potatoes, ketchup, mustard, beer and wine, plus malt vinegar for his fries, as his English parents had trained him to do. He also picked up some eggs and whole wheat bread for his breakfast, with oatmeal for Jamie, along with milk, bananas, blueberries, coffee and orange juice.

Fig found Jamie in the living room, booting up her computer and her little blue box.

"Veggie burgers and fries coming up. Do you want a beer?"

"No thanks, I have some tricky work to do. Go ahead, without me, that's fine."

Fig headed for the kitchen and was pleased to find the stove was gas, not electric. He scrubbed and cut up large fries and put them under water to stop them browning. He put salt, mustard, ketchup and vinegar on the kitchen table. It was a nice small kitchen, old fashioned wood paneling and a picture window facing south. He felt at home there, which was a big contrast to his horrible apartment in town, especially now the place had been ransacked and he wouldn't be greeted by Sophie anymore.

He doubted he could ever live in that place again.

While asking Jamie how she wanted her burger, he looked over her shoulder to see computer code streaming by, reminding him of the movie, *The Matrix*.

"How do you want your burger, and what are you doing right now?" said Fig.

"Medium please, and I'm trying to penetrate the Homeland Security network without being spotted or leaving a trace. It's not so easy as you might think."

"How did you learn this stuff, Jamie?"

Stopping her work, Jamie turned and said, "Passion, Fig. The same way you learned mathematical biology to explore the beauty of nature. You saw the beauty in the structural patterns of the Biosphere, and I saw the beauty in the code. Like you, I'm sure, I studied, practiced solving problems, experimented for several hours a day, almost every day. We both put in our 10,000 hours. It was like an itch I had to scratch. I'm sure you felt the same. Then I signed up for online computer security and hacking training, much of which is out there for free."

"You mean there are free courses on the Internet that teach computer hacking?" said Fig, amazed.

"Loads of them. I guess it's our American freedom of expression thing. In fact, there are websites that list and tell you where to find weaknesses in the code that haven't been patched."

"Damn!"

"I read about recent bugs, really read about them in detail, so I understood the code. I then wrote my own code with the same vulnerabilities and figured out what it would take to penetrate it as a hacker might. Then I went online and tried to hack myself."

Fig said, "Hang on, let me turn off the heat under the fries."

When Fig returned, Jamie said, "Then I got to understand exactly how the vulnerabilities happen." Jamie was on a roll. "And how they get to be in the code in the first place. Then I used those lessons to keep bugs out of my own code and, like you I'm sure, I learned from my mistakes."

"The more mistakes we make in science, the more we learn, as long as they aren't fatal mistakes," said Fig.

"Agreed," said Jamie, with a smile. "For me, Fig, the key was to find a good teacher, one who could stop me getting into trouble and ending up in jail. This was where Yoda came in. He was teaching one of the online courses and he's been helping me ever since, though we've never met, and I have no idea where he lives. Yoda is now one hundred percent on our side, thank goodness."

"I would imagine it's impossible to get into the servers at Homeland Security. Don't they have it locked down like Fort Knox?"

"Every network can be penetrated if it's connected to the Internet. I have plenty of tools to exploit weaknesses in the code. I spoke to Yoda, while you were at the store. He found a bunch on government servers and sent me their details. What I really want is to pen Humperdinck's server, but I bet it's on a separate network with a strong firewall, personal VPN, and other protections, but it is still vulnerable.

Humperdinck now knows that he's up against a sophisticated hacker, because of my alarm in Lizzy's computer. He probably crapped his pants falling for that old trick, if you'll excuse my language, which I'm picking up from you, by the way. You are rubbing off on my vernacular, Fig. I'm not so sure that's a good thing."

"What you do is a mystery to me, and a little vernacular is probably good for you. I'll have dinner served in about ten minutes, if you can stop at a safe place. Do you want a glass of wine now?"

"No thanks, but I'll take a break to eat. Just tell me when it's ready. I'll be at this for a while."

"Grubs up in ten," said Fig heading for the kitchen. He finished preparing the meal, and they enjoyed a quiet, reflective dinner, while discussing the challenges ahead.

"I think we should stay here for at least two days,"

said Jamie, "and do our work. I'll spend time penetrating what I can, leaving backdoors where I can, while you build your network of people. You said you wanted to contact an old colleague you trust, who is still at the institute?"

"Beckie Rodríguez! She will be able to tell us what's been happening since I was thrown out. She might also have some useful leads with respect to the people who visit with Strickland. We have to find as many strands of *Shelob's* web as we can."

"I'm still wondering how you survived at the institute for nearly a year of Strickland, when many of your colleagues were gone. I'm also suspicious of the motives of Charles Barrett. He may have been using you, somehow."

"Using me? How?"

"I don't know, Fig, but something is rotten in the state of Denmark."

CHAPTER THIRTY-THREE

The first thing Jamie did the next morning, after Fig's oatmeal, bananas and coffee breakfast, was hack into Lizzy's computer in Boothbay Harbor. She knew her alert had been triggered, but she was hoping Humperdinck may have left some useful information about himself. However, he was too experienced a hacker for that. Then she went through her GEPI backdoor to see if anyone else had been emailed by James Turner or Fred Sassy, and there was no sign. She then created a list of all institute staff email addresses and bulk-mailed them the following letter.

Subject: Retirement accounts.

Dear Staff Member,

You are advised to check your institute retirement savings. Just for comparison, Dr. Strickland's stands at $1.2 million and Mr. Torres's is $1.21 million."

Yours Sincerely,

A Friend

She then deleted her backdoor and got the hell out of there, and called out to Fig to tell him it was sent.

"That will create a shitstorm," said Fig, with a grin. "Serves them damn well right."

Jamie proceeded to track down information on Daryl Pickering, to see if she could find out why he had the temerity to threaten Fig's paycheck when he had nothing to do with GEPI.

Fig was focused on what he could find out about the publicly reported flow of government money in the form of grants and other financial support. He found there had been a major swing since President Miller arrived, from pro-environment to pro-industry, to the order of billions of dollars.

"I guess they are going from saving the whales to killing the whales," thought Fig. He considered his work to be a continuation of that of Rachel Carson. She was demonized by industry and mocked for her work. Whether they killed her cat was not reported. What Fig could not understand was their focus on him and GEPI. They were small potatoes in the pro-environment anti-environment battle.

Then Jamie said, "Found him. Daryl Pickering works as a bench scientist with a focus on infectious diseases, especially cholera."

"Did he ever work at the EPA or Homeland Security?" said Fig.

"Not that I can see, but give me a minute."

The clatter of fingernails on keys, then, "He's been in

contact with Charles Barrett and currently he is working at RSA, a contract lab in Research Triangle Park, just down the road. Want to pay him a visit?"

"Not yet, let's see how things play out, as we have two balls in the air, Fred and that letter you just sent."

Fig reorganized his network to place Daryl Pickering closer to Charles Barrett.

"Say, Jamie, they say if in doubt follow the money. What are your thoughts on that?"

"I can find links between people and banks. I can even get into their bank accounts. Maybe I should break into yours and steal all your money, then I wouldn't need this job."

"Won't work, most of my money is on me, in cash."

"There are still $60,000 I can take from your rollover IRA."

"You wouldn't do that, you're a Christian," said Fig, sarcastically.

"Lapsed Lutheran is more accurate, Fig, and you need to set up two factor authentication on your accounts, then I'll leave you alone. I'm actually looking out for you by looking for leaks. That said, your retirement account is insured up to half a million, so I guess we would both be fine, except they would send the hounds of hell after me."

"You make me nervous as hell, Jamie. That said, can you see if there is any evidence of cash flow between Daryl Pickering, Charles Barrett, and other players in this game?"

"I'll see if I can break into the accounts of Pickering

and Barrett," said Jamie, "and if I can I'll see where it's going. I know it's illegal, but I'm not a thief."

"You are a thief, Jamie. Sorry! You're stealing information. Anyway, I'd like to spend a couple of hours revisiting my network, which is now growing nicely. I'll look for patterns, especially weak links, then how about a run on that trail around the park over the road, followed by lunch on the deck?"

"A run before lunch sounds good, but why weak links? Wouldn't strong ones be more important?"

"It turns out that in large networks, the vertices, people in our case, having little flow of information along very few connections, such as phone calls with only a couple of people in a network of hundreds, tend to be gateways connecting disparate large groups."

"Why is that?"

"Birds of a feather tend to flock together, Jamie. They talk to each other a lot, making for strong edges, I mean links, but they don't learn much outside of their own particular network or community. That's why most new jobs are found through people one doesn't know very well. Certainly been true of my career."

"I guess I've yet to find that out," said Jamie, "as I don't have a career, beyond raising kids and a few months serving beer and waiting tables."

"You didn't know me, and you found this new job, so it would appear that the theory applies in your case, too. That said, Jamie, if *Shelob* has any sense he or she will distance themselves as far as possible from the action. Fall guys will be all lined up, while the puppet master would appear as a weak link in a network based on phone logs and interpersonal conversations. They might only talk to one other person, in an underground parking lot in the middle of the night, while being the key player in the network."

"I get it. Deep Throat! But what do you use your fancy network for? Will it identify *Shelob*?"

"I use it to parse suspects. What's your short list of candidates for the post of *Shelob*? Mine is still the Miller, Chariton, Hotchkiss trio. How about you?"

"Barrett."

"That's odd!"

"Why?" said Jamie.

"That's what my network model suggests."

"That's because great minds think alike."

"And the rest of the quote, is?" said Fig.

"OK, I know," said Jamie, "and fools rarely differ."

After an invigorating run and an early lunch, Fig settled down to read a book, while Jamie tracked down more information on Daryl Pickering and any links between him and Barrett. Jamie checked Daryl's publications and found that he had worked extensively on cholera and the effectiveness of chlorine in preventing its spread. She thought this was an old problem already solved, but it turned out that there was more to learn, and Daryl was involved in that research. Still, she could find no direct link between Daryl and Fig's network mathematics studies.

"Perhaps Daryl's only real link to Fig is his work on

chlorine," thought Jamie, "which Fig said was just a side project, and not the main focus of his work."

Then Jamie's hacking became more interesting. It turned out that Daryl's research at RSA was supported in part by a research grant from DARPA. This study had a number of coauthors scattered across the US and Europe, several working at the EPA, while the primary author was a Dr. Weber, in Heidelberg, Germany. Daryl's work on that grant was processed through the US Office of Management and Budget. The European researchers were paid through the *Landesbank* in Heidelberg.

"That's odd," thought Jamie, "why would this guy have threatened Fig's paycheck. He's not even directly involved in Fig's institute, well, ex-institute."

"Fig, this is weird," and after explaining what she'd found, she said, "Do you think Daryl is involved in some kind of money laundering scheme."

"It could be a regular piece of international research. Some of these DARPA grants are massive, though I guess I'm biased because he acted like a shit on the phone. I'll try to stay rational. Let me know how it goes," then Fig, who was taking a break from his network, went back to reading his book.

Twenty minutes later, Fig stopped reading and said, "Jamie, we really are acting like a couple of nerds. Let's go for a walk and get some fresh air."

"Sure," said Jamie. "By the way, Daryl works on a salary of $90,000 a year, and he lives in a modest house, so that doesn't imply some kind of money laundering scheme."

"When it comes to his DARPA grant, I worked for a contract lab in Switzerland about twenty years ago. Our money was processed any which way. A German bank for a US contract from DARPA, which stands for the Defense Advanced Research Projects Agency, by the way, is a bit strange. Massive amounts of research money flow from DARPA. I applied for one of their grants years ago, but I didn't make a high enough score."

"Didn't the military pull out of Heidelberg years ago?" said Jamie. "I wouldn't have known, except I visited the place years ago and saw the biggest wine barrel I'd ever seen in my life. It was as big as a house. Maybe that's why I noticed an article on the US military pulling out."

"I've no idea," said Fig.

"Hang on, let me check. Yep! They pulled out completely in 2013. The US military played a huge role in the town, and there are still close ties between military personnel stationed there and the people of Heidelberg. Some soldiers married women in Heidelberg and stayed on to raise a family."

Jamie started her usual target routine for *Landesbank*. Before attempting penetration, she learned everything she could about the bank, including staff, business health and major customer types, any zero-day patches outstanding, and other vulnerabilities sent by Yoda.

"Jamie, I'd be really careful if I were you," wrote Yoda. "I'm not sure you are ready, but I guess you have to learn one day. I'll try to watch your back, but no promises. Banks are dangerous territory."

Jamie said, thanks, and plowed ahead. She checked out their IT support and security. She needed to find a weak link person, one who used an obvious password or left it lying around, or even posted it on a sticky note over their computer. She had penetrated one facility by spotting the ID and password of an administrator on a sticky note, perfectly aligned with an overhead security camera.

Security camera software is often forgotten, and patches linger for years. They are even listed on certain websites that advertise coding flaws. She remembered that scene in "Ready Player One," and smiled to herself.

After a few hours, Jamie penned the bank server, and looked around for anything interesting. There were several US federal accounts with millions of Deutschmarks coming and going. She found no evidence of Turner or Daryl, but Charles Barrett had a regular checking account there.

"Odd?"

She left a backdoor and retreated, crossing her fingers no one noticed the innocuous looking file she left in a /tmp folder. The file was spotted and deleted the same day. Unbeknownst to her, Jamie had just triggered a hacker fight with the bank security contractor and retired black hat, Gerald White. Known to his friends as Whitey, he wasn't Jamie's equal, but he was dangerous. Furthermore, White was a close Internet friend of Humperdinck, who he knew as Bruno. White worked on contract for several banks, and this was the first intrusion he had to report to the *Landesbank*.

"Phew!" said Jamie, "that was scary."

"What was?" said Fig.

"Hacking an international bank. First time I felt kind of scared, but I found some interesting stuff. I followed the flow of the DARPA grant money, and everything looked legitimate. Then, just for yucks, I checked to see if Barrett had an account there and, to my surprise, he does! Why would Barrett have a bank account in Heidelberg? This is all making me even more suspicious of the guy. I tracked down Daryl's phone logs and checked for any calls between him and Turner or Strickland. There were none! He is, however, in infrequent contact with Charles Barrett."

"Do you think Barrett is in cahoots with Daryl," said Fig, "and they are syphoning off money from these grants through the *Landesbank,* somehow?"

"It seems unlikely, but something weird is going on. I have to be careful in there, because banks employ white hats to watch out for hackers. I don't want to have Interpol after me. Let's go for that walk, I need to chill out."

Later that evening, Fig had been building out parts of his network around Daryl Pickering. "Why this agro from Daryl over my work on chlorine? Agro? Of course. I've been in a low-key battle with the food industry for ages, ever since I went vegan." Fig had received hate mail from some New Zealand dairy farmers when he mentioned the environmental benefits of a plant-based diet, on his personal blog. "Agro? Now there is an industry that doesn't like negative press."

He proceeded to explore the activity of Barrett's company, Good Foods, Inc., a global food growing, processing, transporting and marketing giant, who sold anything but good food. They were well known for their vicious legal attacks on small farms, many of which they'd driven out of business over the last twenty years, then they'd buy their land for a song.

Fig found evidence that over the years they'd attacked organic health food stores and a fast-food chain that advertised all their produce as being grown locally. He noticed that Barrett had been the CEO for only three years, since which time the company appeared to be cleaning up its act, but Fig thought it was probably just window dressing.

"Was Good Foods pissed at him?" he wondered.

"Hey Jamie, I've got a new target for you."

"And that is?"

"Good Foods, Inc. and their most recent CEO, Charles Barrett."

"I'm done in for the day, Fig. It's dangerous to hack when you're tired. I'll start on it in the morning, and I'm happy to have Barrett in my sights."

"I was wondering whether Daryl Pickering had consulted for Good Foods, Inc., which would explain his calls to Barrett. I hate those companies. They foist junk food from factory farms onto the unsuspecting public, while putting happy pigs and cows, and pretty barns, on the labeling. Come to think of it, have you seen that short movie, *The Meatrix*, by any chance?"

"You mean The *Matrix*? Of course, who hasn't."

"No! *The Meatrix*."

"Like in animal flesh? No, I haven't heard of it."

"In that case, let's take a break, have some tea and watch it together. It's only a few minutes long. It may provide some clues. Barrett is high up in the world of *Shelob*, and his company is into factory farms, not very pro-environment, in fact that is *The Meatrix*. Turner reports to Barrett, Daryl talks to him on the phone, and Barrett has an account at the *Landesbank*. What the hell is going on?" said Fig.

Jamie said, "Curiouser and curiouser, cried Alice."

CHAPTER THIRTY-FOUR

Room 319, Homeland Security, Washington, DC

"Bruce?"

"Yes, Sally?"

"I guess I need to head back, unless you have something of use for me here. I was getting to like the scenery and the lobster dinners."

"I hit a dead end at that B&B in Boothbay Harbor, but I learned one thing."

"And that is?"

"Either Newton or that woman are really good hackers. Not only did they leave an intrusion alert on the B&B computer, telling them I'd penetrated the machine, but there was a weird message for me. I guess it was for me."

"What the hell was it?" said Sally.

"It said, *It's nice to meet you, Humperdinck. Sincerely, Princess Buttercup.* Who the hell is Humperdinck?"

"He's a character in one of my favorite movies, *The Princess Bride.* It's about true love. There was an evil prince, Humperdinck. The heroine, Buttercup, said that Humperdinck could track a falcon on a cloudy day, meaning he was the best tracker in the kingdom. I'd take it as a compliment, if I were you."

"What happens to Prince Humperdinck?"

"You don't want to know. See you soon, Humpy, though I hope you are more like Wesley."

Bruce watched *The Princess Bride* that night. Not only a great hacker, but a romantic, it would seem. He saw what became of Prince Humperdinck, a complete dick. "Was it a compliment?" he wondered, "or a challenge?"

Two days later, Sally, Bruce and Turner met in room 319.

"OK! You lost him, or should I say them," said Turner, accusingly.

"I talked to you about that," said Bruce, while Sally gave Turner a look that could kill, and said, "If this bozo," looking at Bruce, "could find them before they move on, and you could actually do something to help, I wouldn't have been chasing them all over New England. No! We lost them, and that includes you. I don't need this job, I don't need the money, but now this Newton guy has me pissed off, so I'll stay, but watch how you talk to me."

Bruce smiled to himself, knowing it was Sally at her best.

"I'm sorry. I guess I'm just frustrated. They seem to be outsmarting us at every turn. Who the hell is the woman he's teamed up with, anyway?"

"That's another thing," said Bruce. "She was a hell of a case to crack but, in the end, I found out that she is a Lutheran from Mariposa, California, with a Bachelor's degree in the Arts, divorced with two grown kids, and no apparent interest in computers, so I guess Newton must be the hacker who fools us at every turn."

"It's clear Newton is here in Washington and he has linked Fred to our work. How the hell did they find Fred?" said Turner.

Bruce asked, "Have you ever phoned Fred from your personal phone?"

"Of course."

"Have you ever phoned Strickland?"

"Of course, what of it?"

"That's how they did it. Newton or Bailey hacked into that institute, found Strickland, hacked his phone, found your number, downloaded your phone log and every other damn thing in your phone records, including where the phone is."

"Do you turn off the gps when you don't need it?"

"The what?"

"Forget it. He found Fred in your records, including his phone, and tracked his phone to this building. That would take Newton to room 301, if he took it into his head to come here and try to kill us all, which he might. He's pissed, and rightly so."

"But he found Fred on the Metro."

"Look, Turner, I'm not going to describe the whole damn thing. Work it out for yourself, for God's sake."

"Yes," said Sally, grinning, "go on, Jim, work it out for yourself."

CHAPTER THIRTY-FIVE

After an early morning walk around the neighborhood, followed by a healthy breakfast, Jamie said to Fig, "Let's see what we have, starting with what we know. Then we take a break and watch *The Fugitive*, because Harrison Ford is hot."

"You want to watch a movie on a Monday morning?"

"Very decadent, don't you think?" said Jamie.

"Sounds like a plan," replied Fig, not liking the unstated comparison of himself with the purported hunk, Ford, "and by the way, if you're looking for your glasses, they are on top of your head." Then they listed all the players they knew, and who communicated with whom, who worked for whom, and why they might have it in for Fig.

Then Fig went over all of this again on his network map, and in the material on his website, looking for red flags.

"But who is it?" said Fig.

That pretty well summed up what they didn't know. Jamie voted for Barrett and Fig for the trio, Miller, Hotchkiss and Chariton. They both agreed it could be someone else entirely.

They then took a break and watched *The Fugitive*, only to return to their debate about the identity of *Shelob* when it was over, stimulated by Richard Kimble's endless and dangerous search for *the one armed-man*.

"Who had Sophie poisoned, do you think?" said Fig.

"Barrett's goons," said Jamie, "because his business keeps animals under horrible conditions, so why would he care?"

"Thinking of animals," said Fig, "I went vegan about five years ago. It happened as the result of a weird consultancy for a bunch of scientists in a government organization. I reported my work on one of my public websites. Work which resulted in me dropping meat, then milk, and finally eggs from my diet. I later decided to eat a few eggs from a friend's chickens, that he says he will never eat."

"Do you miss eating meat?"

"No, but I do miss cheese."

"Anyway, they asked me to talk about my work at a big meeting, which I did, but it went south as soon as I talked about living on a plant-based diet to protect animals, as an adjunct to their proposed scientific approaches."

"What was wrong with that?"

"That's what I thought, Jamie, but even scientists I

know well mocked the idea, even though I made no attempt to proselytize. Some were extremely angry. It started during the conference dinner. We were on tables in groups of about ten. I asked for the vegan options and got a lot of weird looks. There were no vegan options, and this meeting was about saving animals being used in toxicology testing."

"Most people don't like vegans, Fig. They think they are holier than thou, putting them down. It's an emotional thing."

"That's for sure," said Fig. "They either mocked me or became livid with anger. It made no sense, Jamie. The meal we were about to eat was financed with money set aside for saving animals, not eating them. They went ahead anyway, with steak, pork, shrimp, you name it."

"What did you order for dinner."

"The only thing I could, French fries and a glass of red wine. Even then I had to stop the staff smothering the fries with parmesan cheese. Maybe you're right about Barrett. But these people were supposed to care about animals."

"They care more about dinner, Fig. You are too logical. Most human choices are based on emotion, not logic, and most of those emotions are subconscious and tied to feelings."

Then Fig showed Jamie the *Triangle of Trade* on his website, Big Tobacco, Big Food, Big Energy. "They are leveraging each other, Jamie, and other industries are involved, including chemical, pharmaceutical, transport and communications."

"It's obvious that bad food is good business," said Jamie.

"As I explored my network and the role of these companies, I started to think more and more about how each has contributed to global ecological damage. My focus has never been on climate, even though I'm aware of its impact."

"Why not, Fig?"

"I just thought it wise to leave that as implied, given the agro suffered by climate scientists, such as Michael Mann, in England. I decided that enough people were fighting that battle, so I would put my focus more on intersecting trophic cascades and the role of chemical damage to global ecosystems."

"Maybe it's time to change your focus."

"How about I modify my *piss off the president website* to include more material on global warming and its negative health interactions with factory farming. Maybe I can piss off both Miller and Barrett."

Meanwhile, Humperdinck was trying to take it down, as Jamie just put it back up again using her hacker magic.

"Thank goodness for you, Jamie," said Fig. "How the hell did I have the good fortune to meet you. Pity I'm not so cute as Harrison Ford," then he went off into logic land, thinking about his network, and whether Barrett was *Shelob* or not, while Jamie was watching him, waiting for him to return to planet Earth.

"You back?" she said.

"What? Pardon? What's up?"

"You disappeared into your secret world, just like Walter Mitty. Was it fun?"

"I was trying to earn the hand of a fair maiden, and it occurred to me in the process that our *Moriarty* may be someone in the food industry. Specifically someone with a lot to gain from the continuation of the abomination that is factory farming."

"If that's the case, why are our leads pointing to the Department of Homeland Security? Barrett works for the EPA."

"Who buys masses of food on masses of government money? So massive that if a few million bucks, or tons of food, go astray over months or years no-one will notice?"

"I've no idea."

"The military! The system for providing food to US solders all over the world is a huge undertaking, and now that Homeland Security has been beefed up, that budget has probably sky rocketed too. I wonder if my recent questioning of the food industry has threatened someone's illegal cash cow, in the food for our troops business?"

"That's interesting," said Jamie, "as my research has uncovered some interesting articles reporting how the food industry has been using the playbook of Big Tobacco."

"Such as?"

"Lies, obfuscation, clever marketing and, as in the case of Jeffrey Wigand, threats and physical assaults. For Jeffrey Wigand it was his house, for you it was Sophie.

Maybe we are up against some friends of Barrett's in the tobacco industry."

"Dangerous enemies, Jamie. When this is all over, do you think I'll have to build a whole new career, like Jeffrey Wigand?"

"It's always possible, Fig, as this kind of adventure can change a person's worldview. Only time will tell. Anyway, the story of Jeffrey Wigand had a happy ending."

"I did get hate mail after going vegan and it will increase if I compare the food industry to big tobacco. I'll add it to my website and try to find links between them for the network."

Jamie then took a closer look at Fig's network and expressed surprise at academia being listed as an industry. She then paused on each item around the outside of Fig's *Triangle of Trade*, which included the Department of Homeland Security and the US Armaments Industry, along with the names of the four biggest, Northrup, Lockheed, Boeing and Raytheon.

"This seems like an overly simple network, Fig."

"Not so simple, Jamie! Embedded in each of the little circles on the top layer, lie entire sub-networks of the respective industry or organization. My network has hundreds of vertices, each connected by edges, along with an estimated edge strength. It is one big manufacturing, money making, power generating, employment and political machine, rife with the potential for corruption. I doubt anyone fully understands the whole thing."

"We are too complicated for our own good," said Jamie.

"I've tried to link this network to EcoWorld, but it isn't easy."

"Why would that be tough?"

"Because, first I had to convert my graph theory network into advanced dynamics code, and I'm a terrible coder. Then I had to triage parameter space, if I had any hope of a solution. One that would converge in my lifetime. Once parameters, things that affect the behavior of the model, exceed several dozen, it's hard to get the thing to find a solution. It either crashes or calculates endlessly. It's a numerical simulation, after all. This always makes me wonder how biological systems and the weirdness of natural selection and speciation actually work."

"Seems that they do, Fig," said Jamie with a smile.

"Why do you say that?"

"Because here we are, doofus."

"Oh yes, sorry. I gave it a try several times, to see if it could predict the bad actors when it comes to ecological damage, even damage remote from the source of the issue. But I didn't trust the results. Too weird."

"And?"

"Guess what turned up as the worst actor every time. The worst EcoTerrorist Industry of all?"

"Energy?"

"That's what I expected, but my model predicts that the worst is the food industry, as a result of its links to all the others. I found it hard to believe, meaning it would be hard to publish. I was quietly working out how to include it in my scientific publications, when I was fired."

"I think you should consider the links between the food and tobacco industries," said Jamie.

"Seems like a long shot."

"It's not the industry you need to focus on," said Jamie, "it's the advisers and lobbyists for each. They are the same people. Tobacco wasn't doing so well, especially after Jeffrey Wigand spilled the beans, so those parasitic lobbyists and marketing geniuses moved on to a real staple of life, food. Furthermore, tobacco and food industry marketing staff talk to each other all the time."

"Really?" said Fig.

"They are both selling addictive crap. In fact, one branch of the food industry is the worst for this kind of thing."

"And that is?"

"The alcohol industry," said Jamie.

"The alcohol industry is part of the food industry?"

"Just go to any grocery store, Fig."

"I'm glad I don't have young kids at home or a scared wife like Jeffrey Wigand did. What we are dealing with here is child's play compared to what he had to withstand. And he didn't have a beautiful brilliant woman to save his ass from Humperdinck and friends."

"Hacking is all very well, but we have to up our social engineering game," said Jamie.

"We do?"

"We sent our first salvo across their bows when you

confronted Fred on the Metro," said Jamie. "I bet that frightened him. He looks nervous all the time, and he looks like a drinker. He may be the weak link these jerks wish they'd never put on their team. We should exploit that."

Fig said, "I was thinking about *The Insider* movie for a moment, and I realized that we have a missing team member. We need a Lowell Bergman, a reporter, who can help us make this go public. They are messing with the lives of hundreds of climate scientists. They got rid of our great director, Nick Page, simply by fabricating an affair he didn't have. It's how these people work."

"Can you find us a Lowell Bergman?"

"I think I might know just the person, Jamie."

CHAPTER THIRTY-SIX

In the afternoon, with the sun shining on a cool spring day, Fig decided to go for a run, while Jamie vegged out. He headed out, working slowly up to an eight-minute mile pace, which was not so fast for Fig. He'd been running all his life, had overcome some injuries, modified his running style to a low-impact shuffle, and in spite of his running buddies saying he'd never get anywhere like that, he'd qualified for the Boston Marathon several times in his late forties. It was during these runs that Fig had some of his best research ideas.

"Yes!"

On returning to the cabin, he found Jamie on her computer, and coffee in the pot.

"Jamie, I recently read several publications on the use of Co-Authorship Network Analysis to accelerate innovation. The goal was to encourage communication between disparate research groups. Scientists, like all people, tend to operate within small tribes, where they each feel comfortable. It's a natural consequence of human evolution. When we publish scientific articles, we rarely do so alone. With science becoming more complex, the number of co-authors on scientific papers has grown. I realized during my run that this could work for us."

"OK."

"All the data we need is on the PubMed database."

"But those are just the scientists. It won't include Barrett, Chariton, Fred or President Miller."

"I want to use it to expand Dumbledore's Army. It's not for finding *Shelob*."

"What will you do with the information, Fig?"

"I'm hoping it will provide the evidence we will need to expose these people when we go public."

"Good plan," said Jamie. "By the way, I have a feeling Fred is important. I think he's the weak link in their chain."

"Hang on, Jamie, one last question."

"Yes?"

"I remember a movie where a hacker was listening into conversations on people's phones. Can you do that for Turner or Barrett?"

"I could, but I hate it. I did it once for a few seconds and it felt like listening at someone's bedroom door. Never again!"

Then they went back to working on their respective projects.

"Get this, Fig. Fred has a passion for cats. He posts

photos of his five cats almost every day on Facebook and Instagram. Now he knows they killed Sophie, because you told him on the Metro. That might be enough to push him over to our side, if we can reach him.

"It might, Jamie."

"I just don't understand why he would join a group of cat killers?"

"As a friend of mine liked to say, if there is something you don't understand, there is something you don't know."

"How's your co-author network coming along?"

"I have several hundred co-author links and, oddly enough, the lion's share is associated with the food industry, directly or indirectly. Did you discover Fred's occupation?"

"He's a certified accountant who's been working on travel claims for different branches of the federal government for years. Not an exciting occupation, but perfect for finding, collating, and analyzing some kind of data. Maybe he's finding the very people you have in your database."

"Damn! I could have called him and saved myself a lot of trouble," said Fig with a grin.

"Have you noticed, Fig, that we are finally in a joking mood?" said Jamie. "The life of fugitives seems to suit us."

In his usual head-in-the-clouds way, Fig plowed on, saying, "Think about this, Jamie. Fred would never condone killing a cat, meaning he is not involved in the harassment end of the operation. Maybe they have several teams."

"And they are?" said Jamie.

"Fred - to create a database of candidate environmentalists to intimidate. Then Humperdinck - to find dirt on them or to create some, as in the case of my Asperger's diagnosis and the made-up affair of Nick Page, which I assume needed Humperdinck to find a suitable female student. Finally - Repo Lady to dish out threats or physical intimidation, such as killing Sophie, for those who fail to submit."

"Where do Turner, Chariton, Barrett and Hotchkiss fit in?" said Jamie.

"Barrett gives the orders, Turner supervises the teams, Chariton and Hotchkiss provide personnel, resources and the cover of covert ops, and keep the source of all this shit, President Miller, happy. It's a nice little team effort, or should I say illegal conspiracy?"

"Makes sense," said Jamie. "Furthermore, Miller fires anyone who disappoints him. He loves to fire people. You, Fig, might just get Hotchkiss and Chariton fired. They aren't the only ones with power."

"Why do you think Barrett came to my aid last year?"

"I'm starting to suspect he may be skimming money from a government account at the *Landesbank* in Heidelberg," said Jamie. "Maybe your work has drawn attention to that operation, and they don't want the attention."

"But he's the CEO of a massive company, why would he need money?"

"Greed and power!"

"Really?" said Fig.

"I think it's time you moved on from studying science to studying people. We are the super-predators at the top of almost every one of your trophic cascades, Fig. And I don't think Barrett wanted to help you last year. I think he wanted to use your inflammatory science to persuade the board members to close the place."

"Sure fooled me," said Fig.

"Are you linked to Barrett in any other way, other than that letter?"

"Not directly, that I know of."

The conversation continued on and off in this vein until they headed out for dinner, and on the way Fig said, "Is there any way you can find out whether they are closer to finding us?"

"I'll see what I can do, and by the way, your website has been taken down eight or nine times, and I've just put it up again."

"How about I increase the agro on that site by mentioning military nutrition to draw Barrett out? I could also mention the case of Dr. Michael Mann in England, whose emails were hacked, leading to his receiving death threats. This might make them think I'm the hacker, rather than you, Jamie?"

"How about we call on Fred at his home, and try to bring him over to our side?"

"I bet Ray would help us do it, and we need to expand our team," said Fig.

"Can we meet him tomorrow before leaving for

DC?" said Jamie. "We could put the bikes in a rented storage shed, make a call from there, then leave the phone with the bikes as another decoy to waste their time."

"Which identity should we use for the shed rental?"

"How about Ms. Buttercup?"

"Perfect. I'll call the institute in the morning, to set it up with Ray."

"Why not call one of his burner phones?"

"I'll have to go through the switchboard, and Pam is sure to mention my call to someone, and if it reaches Strickland, he'll pass it on to Turner, and then it'll get to Humperdinck. By the time that happens, we'll be in DC again."

CHAPTER THIRTY-SEVEN

The following morning Fig called the institute, to reach Ray, hoping he was at work.

"Hi, could you put me through to Raymond Joyner?"

"Is that Fig? I mean Dr. Newton."

"Hi Pam! How are you today?"

"Fine, thanks, and you too, I hope."

"I'm fine, Pam. I'd like to chat, but I'm in a rush. Lot on my mind. Can you put me through?"

"It's so strange without you here. They gave your lab to a new member of staff, and I think Ray reports to her. Let me put you through. So good to hear from you."

"Thanks, Pam."

The call was picked up on the third ring, "Raymond Joyner here."

"It's Fig. Could we get together this morning for a brief chat?"

"Sure, Fig, not much happening here right now."

"Can you meet us where we used to have our lab meetings?"

"See you in about forty minutes."

Fig and Jamie headed over to a Bojangles, a mile from the institute, parked and locked the bikes, went inside and waited for Ray.

"You like this place?"

"I did before I went vegan. What I like about it is that it's full of regular folks. I like talking to scientists, but sometimes I want to be around normal people."

"I'm with you, there, Fig," said Jamie, grinning. "You had your lab meetings here?"

"Better ambiance, away from the phone, and my staff liked it a lot. It's basic southern fast food. Another recent advantage was that Strickland wouldn't be seen dead here, while Nick Page would join us from time to time."

"Here's our man," said Jamie.

Jamie gave Ray a hug and Fig asked if anyone wanted anything to eat. "If you're paying, boss," said Ray, "I'll have a three piece with Cajun gravy, fries, and a large sweet tea. Thanks so much."

After waiting in line, Fig returned to find Ray and Jamie getting along famously again. He placed the tray of food in front of Ray who attacked it without hesitation.

"I see you still have an appetite, and thanks again for putting us up the other day," said Fig, as Ray smiled with Bojangles chicken fat dripping from his fingers, while he was scooping spicy fries into his mouth a few at a time. As Ray inhaled his meal, Fig caught him up on the state of their adventure and said he had a small job for him, if Ray was game.

"No problem, Fig, as long as Yolanda gives it the OK."

"By the way, Ray, do you remember that young journalist friend of yours, running the paper near Pigeon Ford?"

"You're talking about Jason Buno, who runs the Mountain Clarion. Why do you ask?"

"I may need his help one day, and you putting in a good word could help."

"No problem!"

"How's Beckie doing?"

"She was complaining that you left a right mess, and they are thinking of closing the door to your office and bricking it up. What's the job you want me to do?"

"First you need to realize that this is serious. I think my life may be threatened."

"What about my life?" said Jamie.

"Don't worry Jamie, you can trust me with your life," said Ray.

"I see you still have your appetite for girls as well as food," said Fig.

"I'll have you know that I'm now a happily married man, but a boy can appreciate a good-looking woman, married or not."

Shifting the conversation, Fig said, "You'll be hearing from us soon, from who knows where and when. We may need you to come to Washington, we'll let you know soon."

"Change is as good as a rest, Fig."

"I've been targeted for a reason, and Jamie and I are trying to work out why they have a stick up their ass about me."

"That's easy, Fig. It's because you are the master at pissing people off."

Jamie laughed at that and said, "Would you like another meal on me, Ray?"

"That's kind of you, Jamie, but I'm full to bursting. That was my second breakfast, and don't forget that I have your backpacks in the truck."

An hour later, Jamie and Fig were at a storage facility, the bikes were inside an otherwise empty unit, and all their gear was transferred to their backpacks. Fig took out the burner phone he'd used to call Ray at the institute, placed it on one of the bike saddles, closed and locked the unit door, and went to find Jamie, who was wandering around, checking for security cameras."

"Job done, Jamie." Then Fig said, "It doesn't sound like Ray likes his new boss. Some woman doing contract research. I did that kind of stuff for several years in Europe. It's a far cry from basic research. This is ominous in the extreme."

"Why?"

"I bet they plan to turn the institute into a contract lab, one that won't stand a chance against large-scale operations, like Quintiles and Battelle."

"Why would that mean they want to close the place?"

"What better way to do it without making waves?

Create a contract lab that doesn't stand a chance. The current sponsors slowly bow out, hiding their association with the place, and then it goes belly up. Sounds like a plan to me, but first Strickland had to drive away all the serious basic researchers and replace them with drones."

"He didn't drive all of them away, Fig."

"No?"

"There was one that hung on like a barnacle on the rocks."

"Which kind of barnacle would that be, Jamie? *Chthalamus stellatus* or *Balanus perforatus*?"

"You're such a nerd, Fig."

"Did you know that the barnacle populations in California are suffering from climate change? In fact, barnacles have been found to be valuable for monitoring the effects of global warming on life in the deep oceans around Japan."

They both laughed and headed for the bus to the J. Douglas Gaylon Amtrak Depot. On the way they chatted about their lives and how their lives had changed.

"I'm amazed at the way hackers can hack into anything, even printers and car tires. It seems impossible when I watch that code flowing past on your screen. Reminds me of *The Matrix*."

"I'm amazed that you learned the mathematics you needed to build EcoWorld. In fact, you did it well enough to piss off some really powerful people. That's even more impressive, in my book."

"Pissing people off takes a little practice, but I'm sure you could master it too, polite Lutheran black hat that you are. In a way, we are like peas in a pod," said Fig, "self-taught enthusiasts of doing what we enjoy, resulting in a degree of mastery. Could I learn to hack, do you think?"

"It is pretty simple, once you've mastered a few software languages."

"For instance?"

"Well, you'd need to start with Linux, Python, C++, Java, PHP, SQL, and a growing number of other computer languages. It's all downhill from there, except new languages and tricks are being created every day. You especially have to learn how not to go to jail."

"I'll stick with math and biological research. I'm pretty good at finding and solving ecological problems by pulling together multiple scientific disciplines. But I'm a horrible coder. I just can't do it, however hard I try, so I really appreciate having you on my team."

"It's my pleasure and much more fun than waiting tables. This is one big adventure in which I get to use what I've learned as a grey hat. Law enforcement would say I'm a black hat and should be locked up. I love this stuff and after we solve your running away from cat killers and letter bombs problem, I'm hoping you can help me to get a job as a white hat."

"I promise that I will do everything I can, Jamie."

"There's the station, Fig. I guess we'd better go through the old fugitive routine. I just hope I can hide us from Humperdinck, yet again. I'm sure he's one pissed off guy, who is not amused by my message at Lizzy's."

"Do you think he found one of your dead drops?"

"I do. In fact I'm surprised he hasn't called already."

On the train, Jamie told Fig that she was benefiting from a recent Cyber Weapons course that covered a tool called OSINT. It permitted her to extract a great deal of information simply starting with a phone number.

"You talk about everything in the Biosphere being connected, Fig, and it's true of my world too, the world of hacking. You just have to find your way through the jungle to your target, while watching out for lions and tigers and bears. By the way, Fred doesn't go anywhere except to work, the liquor store, a local food store, and a fancy pet shop. Furthermore, I could only find two people he calls on the phone, James Turner and a number I couldn't penetrate any which way I tried."

"And that means?"

"It means I've found Humperdinck."

CHAPTER THIRTY-EIGHT

On arriving in DC, Jamie said, "It is best if we stay in separate places, near Fred's house. I want to confuse Humperdinck about us working together, as I want to trade you in for better pay, Fig."

"Nice!" said Fig.

"Don't get your panties in a wad, it's spycraft. Anyway, we need a separate motel for the Honeypot, so let's see what we can find, then I'm ready to crash."

After taking the Metro from Union Station to Columbia Heights, and searching around for a while, Jamie took a room in the Highway Hostel on Belmont, a mile from Fred's house. They then went in search of a place for Fig. He eventually checked into the Eden Motel, on Lanier, a little closer to Irving.

Fig booked two rooms, each for a week, paying cash in advance, under the name of Jerome Hanratty. Room 213 for Ray and Yolanda, to start the following day, and room 301 for himself that night, and later for the honey-pot. Leaving his backpack in the room, he walked Jamie back to the hostel, and then returned to the motel, showered and fell into bed, wondering what the morrow would bring.

CHAPTER THIRTY-NINE

Sally, Bruce and Turner in Room 319, Homeland Security, Washington, DC.

The bombshell had just dropped that someone had killed Newton's cat. They knew that Fred was obsessed with cats, he doted over his five cats and fed them fancy food. Turner said Fred was now a minor player in their work, so no big deal. Basically a hired hand, who happened to be discreet and good at building spreadsheets.

"Don't be so sure Jim," said Sally. "This could turn Fred against us and blow up in our faces. All it takes is for Newton to seek his help, and he might just turn on us."

"I agree, Jim. Bad move," said Bruce.

Turner wasn't used to being spoken to in this way by

contract workers, and he hated being called Jim and they knew it, but Sally frightened the shit out of him.

Bruce didn't trust Turner, so he'd already hacked into every bit of the guy's communications gear, and decided Turner was extremely boring, risk averse, and a weird choice to run this obviously illegal enterprise. This had Bruce wondering, "Who the hell chose Turner for this job? Other than the obvious, Dr. Charles Barrett, the guy who had given Bruce's name to Turner."

"How's your work going, Bruce?" said Turner.

"When it comes to Newton and Bailey, one of them is a skilled hacker, so I have to be cautious. They seem adept at setting traps, and they sent us to a dead drop containing a flash drive. Sally picked it up and brought here. It was encrypted, but the password was simple. I should have guessed it immediately, it was Engelbert."

Sally laughed at that.

"What was on the flash drive?" said Turner.

"A phone number and an offer to chat. Maybe Fred and I could get a better rate with them?"

"Can I come too?" said Sally.

"I was hoping you would ask," said Bruce, with a smile.

Turner ignored them. He knew they were baiting him for fun and that there was no way Newton could match what he was paying these weird people.

"This nice lady," said Bruce, turning toward Sally, "thinks, when they call me Humperdinck, they mean it as a compliment."

"OK! Children," said Turner, immediately regretting his turn of phrase, "let's work out what the hell to do. Where do we go from here? We need to stop Newton from updating that damn website of his, it's really pissing off the high ups in this operation. In fact it is pissing off President Miller. He is not amused with being called *The Ecocidal Fool*. I thought you were going to take it down, Bruce."

"Every time I do that, it just pops up again. Newton or Bailey are fucking good at what they do. That's all I can say."

"Don't you have any idea where to go from here?"

"I just tracked down what I think is Newton's latest burner phone, which was moving around Greensboro until a few hours ago. And now it's static and I know its precise location. It's in a block of rental storage units in Greensboro."

"That's just bait to waste our time," said Sally. "They are probably nowhere near the place right now, it's just a ploy to distract us while they are up to their tricks again. I don't really want to waste my time on a trip to Greensboro. Could you get Strickland to check it out, Jim?"

"I think they are headed this way," said Bruce. "I bet they suspect Fred is our weak link, and they plan to see what they can learn from him. He's no hero, they already frightened the crap out of the guy. He even looked frightened talking to us in room 301. He wouldn't look us in the eye at first, and when any of us spoke to him he'd eat another damn doughnut. The guy is a pussy, if you excuse the expression, Sally."

"I do not excuse the expression, Bruce, you dick," she said, with a laugh.

Turner was wondering how to keep this team together, the way they were constantly insulting each other. What he didn't realize was that this was how these people flirted. Both Sally and Bruce liked each other. Sally admired his computer skills and kindness, while Bruce was completely clueless. He assumed he didn't stand a chance with Sally, though he noticed she had warmed to him recently.

"I think it's time to stake out Fred's house," said Sally, "and wait for them to turn up."

CHAPTER FORTY

The following morning, Fig called Jamie to see if he could come over and bring breakfast bagels and coffee on the way.

"Sounds great, Fig, see you then."

"After enjoying their informal breakfast, Fig said, "I think it's time to call Ray and get them here. Agreed?"

"It's time," said Jamie.

"Hi Ray."

"What's up, boss?"

"Our plan is coming together. Would you like to take a paid vacation?"

"Where?"

"Washington DC, with Beckie if you can persuade her to come along. All expenses paid, eat whatever and wherever you want, not completely risk free, but pretty safe. Oh Yes! And a show of your choice."

"Even more exciting than contract research, Fig."

"Jamie and I need you to deliver a message. Sounds like you are ready for a little adventure."

"My new boss treats me like I'm some kind of servant, so a break would be good."

"Can you get the time off?"

"I have plenty of vacation time due, and she doesn't seem to know what she's doing. I'm assuming you're in Washington, right?"

"We are!"

"Could you explain what it is you want us to do?"

"To pose as people trying to help cats, in any way you like. Our objective is to get in the good graces of a person we think is involved with the people who are trying to silence me."

Jamie turned and looked at Fig, with that look of hers.

"I mean to silence Jamie and me. Anyway the guy loves cats. He has five of them and he may have a drinking problem. We can go through all that when you get here. We'll send the hotel details to your next burner, number two, right. Remember to take the first one to a remote location before you destroy it, or leave it turned on, on a boat going out to sea."

"Why did you say it's pretty safe?"

"Because they might be watching. We hope they are, and that your visit draws them out. Again, we'll give you all the details when you get here."

"This sounds like a fun trip and I do like cats, so does Yolanda. She is always game for a lark and a good meal. I bet she'd love to go. Can I ask her, instead of Beckie?"

"Your call, Ray," said Fig, "and can you get here tonight? I've booked you a room in the Eden Motel. Not top of the line, but comfortable and convenient to the Metro."

"I'll call you back within an hour, and let you know," and Ray hung up.

"Well, that went well, don't you think, Jamie?"

"I hope they won't be in any danger."

"I don't think they will, especially if they hang out in crowded places, and they know the deal. I don't think Repo Lady will care about them, especially if she spots us spotting her."

"Do you still have that note in your wallet?"

"Of course."

"Hang onto it. I think it will come in handy later. It could be our best bargaining chip. If we can get a photo of Repo Lady's face, I can track her down, and we can see what her price is. I doubt she's a dedicated anti-environmentalist. Probably just a gun for hire, if you don't mind the expression, Fig."

"Got to go one day, right?"

"That gives me an idea. Why don't we make a two-pronged attack?"

"OK."

"What we are doing with Fred, we call "setting a honeypot" in hacking, as I said before. We are using Ray and Yolanda as the bait. In the Internet we use various kinds of bait and a software trap. If it goes well we can collect some useful information about any hacker tempted into the trap, but it's a risky business. I played with it for a while and managed to attract a hacker into a virtual server on my machine."

"So you use a range of obvious code weaknesses as bait, while for Repo Lady we are baiting the trap with Ray and Fred's love of cats. I guess we do need to consider the risks," said Fig. "For you it's your computer, for our friends it's themselves."

"If they know all the details and risks, and you give them a get out clause, then they are responsible for their own decisions, plus Ray, as you said before, also has skin in the game. These people have ruined Ray's institute too. You heard him saying he doesn't like the way his new boss treats him."

"You're right, he's a grown man. By the way, what did you learn about that hacker you tempted into your trial honeypot?"

"The technology they used, their intent, and the resources they were after and, most importantly, I got to know them better."

"Can a hacker know they are in a honeypot?"

"A skilled hacker, such as Humperdinck, would spot it, but not before he gave away some valuable information."

"Such as?"

"At the very least, I would learn which weakness in the code he chose for his penetration, and they come in different flavors."

"Neat! Imagine we do this, Jamie. Nothing bad happens to Ray, we get a photo of Repo Lady and maybe some other useful information on Fred and Humperdinck. How does it help us?"

"You're the scientist, Fig. What do we always gain from new information?"

"A new way of thinking about the problem."

"Exactly! Furthermore, I'm keen to take the fight to them, and you'll run out of money eventually. I want to get paid, to become a professional white hat, to get these slime bags, and travel around the world with a handsome man."

"Harrison Ford is probably a bit too old for you, and I doubt he's available."

"I'll find someone else, but first let's get this show on the road. Come to think of it, what do you think will happen between Fred and Ray when he knocks on that door?"

"If we time it right, it will be after Fred arrives home from work, tired and with his guard down. Maybe he will have had a glass of wine or two. Anything might happen. He might invite them in, tell them to fuck off, call Repo Lady or Humperdinck, or call the cops."

"What if it's a bust and we learn nothing," said Jamie.

"Then Ray and Yolanda get to enjoy some great meals and a show on my retirement savings, and we go on from there. What about your honeypot for the motel? How's that going to work? How are you going to set it up?"

"I'll send an email to Strickland saying I'm a close friend of one Dr. Jeb Newton, and I'm worried about him. He usually calls at least once a week, and he's disappeared. I'll leave an email address that will eventually lead Humperdinck to the honeypot."

"Sometimes I feel that I'm living in a fugitive movie, Jamie."

"You are, Fig, and has it occurred to you that those guys, including Fred, may not know what they are doing? They may be unaware of the damage they are doing by attacking people such as yourself and, as you know, you are just one on a long list of environmental activists in their sights."

"I'm not an activist, I'm a scientist."

"Wrong, Fig. You are an environmental activist *par excellence*, but you are making one big mistake, my friend."

"And what is that?"

"You are too focused on your science."

"It's what I know and do well."

"Your graph theory network is social science, Fig. You are exploring human interactions."

Thinking out loud, Jamie said, "I'll create a test honeypot on my machine, and run it by Yoda so he can make some trial attacks. Can you get Ray up here, ASAP?"

Then Fig's phone rang, he answered, listened, said, "Great, see you then."

Fig said, "Your wish is my command. Ray and Yolanda will be here mid-afternoon. Yolanda is all excited, Ray said. He also said that he just couldn't wait to spend my retirement money."

"OK! That get's tackling Fred on track. Now I want

to set up the honeypot trap for Humperdinck and Repo Lady, using the honeypot computer in your motel room. You can bunk here, while that is going on.”

“I'm glad we are doing this, Jamie. I just noticed that the new administration has already eliminated over a seven hundred positions at the EPA and rolled back close to eighty environmental regulations.”

“What kind of regulations?”

“They range from tail pipe exhaust to water quality.”

“Rachel Carson must be rolling over in her grave,” said Jamie. “You are a tiny fish in a huge pond of environmentalists, Fig, but apparently a really irritating fish.”

“It's what I do best, so people tell me.”

“Here's my plan of attack. Ray and Yolanda sweet talk Fred and get what information they can. He may give them his email address. That will allow me to get into his home computer. He may take work home.”

“OK!” said Fig.

“Ten or fifteen minutes later, we wander down the road heading for the station. As we pass Fred's we quickly look around for Repo Lady, who may be in an SUV watching out for us. If we spot her, and we act quickly, we might just get a photo or a car plate number.”

“Oh boy!” said Fig.

“We next draw Humperdinck into the honeypot in your room in the Eden Motel, unless he phones me in the meantime, assuming Repo Lady found the dead drop, and we await events.”

"Oh boy, yet again," said Fig.

"Here's some of my gear," said Jamie. "But I need a couple of other things, including a small motion detector. We will set it up with the computer gps turned on, so Humperdinck can locate the room. This micro-camera will be facing the door, linked to my phone via the Internet to automatically forward video to me if the camera is activated by the movement sensor that will activate the camera if the door opens."

"But room service will trigger it."

"We'll leave that "Do Not Disturb" sign on the door handle and you tell the front desk that you have important work to finish and you don't want to be disturbed."

"Is that it?"

"Pretty well!"

"*Lay on, MacDuff. And damn be him that first cries, "Hold enough,*" said Fig.

"Not just a science nerd, I see?"

"I'll have you know that we scientists aren't all Philistines."

"Good to know and it feels good to be taking the initiative."

"Let's go for a walk to get some fresh air."

"You go," said Jamie. "I want to sit quietly, cogitate and rest my brain. I didn't sleep much last night with this going around in my head. By the way, did Ray say anything about my letter?"

"He said it was a shit storm with the entire place up in arms. Strickland had an all-staff meeting, and told them it was an accounting error, which would be corrected immediately."

"The thought of making life difficult for Strickland is fine with me, after what he has done to you, Fig."

"By the way, Jamie, Ray is getting with the program. He said he would send that burner phone off on an interesting journey. I told him to check into the room I booked for them at the Eden Motel, where we plan to plant the honeypot for Humperdinck, but on a different floor. He kept laughing about the name and said he'd watch *The Princess Bride* with Yolanda."

"What did Yolanda have to say?"

"He put her on, and she was fascinated by the idea of encouraging Fred to defect. She said anyone who likes cats is a good person in her book, and anyone who would kill Sophie has it coming to them."

"Did you talk about travel arrangements?"

"They want to drive."

"We hackers study our targets, and I bet Humperdinck has checked out any staff reporting to you. Could you call Ray back and suggest he get a rental? Remind me to talk to you later about another idea I had for a decoy. I want you to apply for a job with Homeland Security. There's the perfect opening on the St. Elizabeth's Campus."

"Really?"

"More confusion for the enemy, Fig. Harry and Ron went into *Aragog's* nest so you could go into *Shelob's*. I want you to call Strickland, grovel for a reference, apologize for your behavior when you left, and especially for not including the Asperger's diagnosis in your original job application. Explain that you can now see how your work might have been an embarrassment to many of the institute's sponsors, and you really need a job. I want you to be a turn coat."

"Another false trail?"

"Exactly."

"This sounds awfully complicated. Occam's razor would give it a failing grade."

"We are working on multiple fronts. If only one succeeds we'll be ahead. I just want to stay on the offensive."

"Anything else in that devious mind of yours?"

"Let's say you do get the job at Homeland Security, or an interview. You could put on a white coat, carry a clip board and wander around. It would fool anyone. They'll think you are an inspector and leave you alone, and you might just find the rooms where Fred and Turner work, and maybe Humperdinck and Repo Lady too. I'm sure they'd love to meet you in person."

"I remember a scientist where I worked years ago who did that every day," said Fig. "He never did any work, he just wandered around with a clipboard, chatting to people, especially young women, until someone exposed him for what he was, a parasite mimicking an inspector."

"OK Fig, I know you have strong feelings about science parasites and mimics, but the questions we need to ask ourselves right now are as follows. Will Ray and Yolanda be safe? And can I out-hack Humperdinck?"

"I put my money on you any day, *Mata Hari.*"

"Yes! But *Mata Hari* was mistakenly executed by the French as a spy for the Germans, while she was working to help the French. I don't want to take that analogy too far. By the way, you said you wanted to call Beckie about events at the institute, and I'm keen to hear what Beckie thought of my letter," said Jamie.

Fig got up to go call from a more remote location, when Jamie said, "Fig, you can make the call from here. We now want Humperdinck to know where we are. Make a call or two from Eden Motel, too, when you get a chance."

"Really?" said Fig.

"We need to throw some chum into the water to attract the sharks," said Jamie, with a smile.

Fig reached Beckie on her office phone, at GEPI.

"Hi, Beckie, how are you doing? I guess you noticed that I disappeared?"

"Hi Fig. Yes! Ray told me all about it. Seems you are on an adventure as a fugitive. Right?"

"Exactly! It's interesting but not my chosen pastime."

"I had to sort out all the mess you left behind. It was a real pain in the butt. Where are you?"

"Where I am is not an issue I want to discuss on this phone. Did you see the movie, *The Fugitive?*"

"The one about the killer with one arm, with Harrison Ford? Sure! Years ago."

"Well, I'm living that kind of life right now, though I have no idea how many arms Sophie's killer had."

"Do you think you can come back here, because several of your studies need completing, and you are the only one who can do it."

"Not a chance, in fact I'm thinking of moving to Washington. I'm considering applying for a job I saw with Homeland Security, in relation to biological terrorism, but for now I'm laying low. Someone has it in for me. I think they don't like my research?"

"I've been telling you for a while, Fig, that your website is inflammatory. You seem to be attacking every industry in America. I know our work is based on real damage to plants and animals throughout the world, but they don't want to hear about that."

"That's the whole point of GEPI, to find the problems and then find solutions, in collaboration with industrial, academic and government scientists. I thought we were doing a great job, especially when it came to training young scientists."

"You are forgetting President Miller. He is a complete game changer and I noticed on your site that you called him *The Ecocidal Fool*. Some of our sponsors have CEOs who are on his cabinet. I bet they want to shut you up before you cause them to lose their positions in the new administration."

"Which means they don't give a damn about the environment."

"Fig, the new head of the EPA is an oil and gas guy," said Beckie, "and some other top positions in the EPA have gone to coal lobbyists and big industry types. I bet you are a terrorist in their minds, threatening their profits."

"It is really frustrating to do a good job and get fired for it."

"You are following in the footsteps of your heroine, Rachel Carson."

"And proud of it, Beckie."

"Please be careful, Fig."

"What's going on at the institute? Have things changed. Ray told me he isn't sure what his new boss wants him to do, while she chases down contracts, and that he's working for you."

"Ray is a great help, but he's concerned he may be following you out the door. Did he tell you what happened about our pension money? Strickland and Torres were running around doing damage control. Some mysterious email was circulated showing that they were filching our money to feather their nests, with about a million dollars each after less than a year. I have about $60,000 after nearly twelve years."

"Doesn't surprise me, as those guys are shitheads in my opinion. Does anyone know who exposed them?"

"Did you have anything to do with it?" said Beckie, suspiciously.

"How could I? I can't even get into the institute to read my emails. They locked me out the same day I was fired, and Willie brought my personal stuff from the office the next day, a Sunday morning. They couldn't get rid of me fast enough. I've been worried about you guys. Do you have plenty of work for Ray?"

"I sure do! Several of the new staff have contracts requiring extensive support from our group. In fact, I don't mean to hurt your feelings but the Biological Support Group really struggled with projects based on basic research. You guys were always changing direction, doing things for which there were no GLP guidelines. My job is much easier now, as I can schedule the work way in advance."

"Sounds like Strickland is changing the place into a contract research lab, Beckie."

"You are exactly right, Fig, even said so at the last meeting. At least we have jobs, though Strickland said we will have to raise some of our own money soon, from external grants."

"If I were you, Beckie, I would make a backup plan. There is no way Strickland, who has no background in contract research, will be able to compete with the big contract labs. It's a completely different game to basic research. I did it for five years, but never again."

"The world changes, and we have to change with it, Fig."

"Well, it's changing for the worse."

"Adapt or perish. Sounds like you've chosen to perish, while we have kids to get through college. I do have a backup plan though. I'm working toward my teaching certificate, as it's nearly time for a whole new career. Ted is about to retire and head for his dream of becoming an artist."

"Good for him, Beckie, and you will make a great teacher, in fact you were like a teacher to me. You taught me a lot and worked to keep me in line. We had a good ten years or more together, and I wouldn't have made it without your help. I may be writing to ask you for a letter of reference one day, if I decide not to perish."

"That would be a real compliment, Fig, sorry, got to go, the damn minus eighty deep freeze alarm is going off again. Stay in touch. Bye!"

And she was gone, and Jamie was looking at him, concerned.

"Are you OK Fig? You look sad."

"I am, Jamie. They are destroying the institute, while working to avoid negative press."

"Why can't they just stop funding the place?"

"It would send a message to the public that the sponsoring companies don't care about environmental damage, so they are creating a cover up. First, get rid of the basic researchers by driving them out. I guess I was the last holdout, so they dealt with me. Then they turn the place into a contract lab, resulting in the place gradually becoming less and less visible on the science scene, so no-one will notice."

"And?"

"When they fail to break even on the open market they'll go belly up, while Strickland and Torres will walk away with big retirement accounts, leaving crumbs for the rest of the staff. Your letter will be a road bump, as they have plenty of time to reinstate their robbery."

"You really think this is what they are doing, to an

institute known all over the world, that generated leaders in environmental protection?"

"Sure as eggs are eggs, Jamie. It is all part of President Miller's attack on science in the public interest. I intend to fight back, somehow, until he is out of office and a new administration is ready to rebuild what it took us years to create. Anyway, we have work to do."

———

Mid-afternoon, Fig's burner phone rang.

"Hi Fig, it's Ray. We are here in room 213, and Yolanda can't wait to explore the city. What's the plan?"

"Hi Ray! It's too late to do anything today. You guys go out and have a great meal. I'll cover the cost in the morning. Jamie and I will come by to see you for breakfast. Is eight OK?"

"Perfect, Fig."

"Does that work for you, Jamie?"

"Sure."

When Ray had hung up, Jamie said, "Isn't it dicey to draw attention to that motel, where we plan to set up the honeypot?"

"I thought about that, and decided it's worth taking a chance as Ray and Yolanda may learn something useful, if the honeypot attracts Repo Lady or someone else. I guess Humperdinck never did call?"

"The last time we heard from them was the alert from Lizzy's computer, plus your conversation with Fred on the Metro. Let me think. How about we go out for a nice dinner too, boss, and think about it?"

"Isn't that mixing work and pleasure?"

"It's a business dinner. Anyway, it's too early for dinner. Why don't you work some more on your website for the honeypot, and I'll see if I can catch myself a famous prince."

Fig said, "I've done enough work for the day. It's my turn to read *The Spy Who Came in From the Cold*.

CHAPTER FORTY-ONE

Room 319, Homeland Security, Washington, DC.

"Turner asked me to find dirt on the Bailey woman, as Newton seems to be clean as the driven snow," said Bruce.

"How did they justify firing him from that institute?" said Sally.

"I found that he was diagnosed with mild autism, in high school. They call it Asperger's Syndrome, and it wasn't on his job application when he was hired."

"He was fired for that?"

"They said it caused him to have poor communication skills, which would risk the reputation of the sponsoring companies."

"Pretty sly, if you ask me," said Sally.

"Now I have to find dirt on Bailey. Do you have any thoughts or ideas about the Bailey woman?"

"What kind of thoughts, Humpy?"

"Very funny!"

"It's a compliment, Bruce, and what kind of thoughts?"

"It's odd how these two people, apparent strangers, should meet in Burlington, then stick together like this, working as an efficient team."

"Sex."

"You're probably right, Sally. Newton is divorced, unattached, and not dating, based on his social media profiles. It's just the way he's acting. I can't put my finger on it, but I don't think this is a sex or romance thing."

"When it involves a man and a woman together a lot, sex is always involved, even if it doesn't happen physically. It's just how humans are wired. We are an addictive species, and sex is the biggest addiction of them all."

"Any other ideas that might help us track down dirt for Turner?"

"I'm not tracking them down for Turner, I'm tracking them down for me, because they've pissed me off with this damn wild goose chase."

"The money is good," said Bruce, "so in a way they are doing us a favor, but for me it's more a game of cat and mouse. Can I out-hack Bailey or Newton, whichever one it is? I also admire their guts. They are on their own, fighting President Miller. I'd hesitate to do that myself."

"You're right. I hated the cat being killed. I don't like Turner, but it's a job. I was curious the other day, so I looked at Newton's work on the web. Most of it was over my head, but he's obviously a scientist who likes nature, both animals and plants. He admires Rachel Carson, so I read her book, and it made me wonder if we are on the right team. It isn't like taking down someone who hasn't paid for their car."

"Which one do you think is the hacker?"

"He uses math and computers a lot, but I didn't see him mention computer code on his website. Then I watch you, Bruce, cute hacker that you are, and I can see that code is your life. No! I don't think Newton is the hacker. What about Bailey or a third person? Can you hack from anywhere?"

"You can. Their hacker could be anywhere in the world."

"So what do we know about her?"

"Plenty, except when it comes to hacking."

"See what you can find out, as I need to learn as much as I can about both of them."

"Why?"

"If we come face to face, should I be armed for instance, which might occur during my stake out at Sassy's house for the next few days. Why have I never been introduced to the guy, do you think?"

"Simple! This operation is clearly illegal, and they are using the divide and control approach, just in case the shit hits the fan. I bet even Turner doesn't know everything that's going down. Reminds me of my time in the military, we just followed orders, but never knew what the hell was going to happen next."

"Which branch?"

"USASC."

"And that is?"

"Army Signal Corps, which is where I got to use this stuff, most of which I learned on my own. Did you go to Repo School?" said Bruce, laughing."

"Why do you say that?"

"That's what Newton and Bailey call you, Repo Lady."

"Reaching into her bag Sally said, "Here's my license, RS193 at your service, if you don't pay the fucking bill.""

Bruce was impressed and said so, followed by "Want lunch out, Sally, my treat?"

"It's my turn to pay, so let's get out of this shit-hole before dick head comes back."

As they approached Bruce's car, a Black-on-Black 1979 Ford F-250, Sally said, "Why do you drive this monster?"

"It can't be hacked."

"Are you making the payments on time?"

"I own it outright, I'll have you know. Where do you want to eat?"

"I'm impressed. Is Indian OK?"

Over lunch, Bruce told Sally what he'd gleaned about Jamie Bailey.

"She was born and raised in Mariposa City, Mariposa County, California, as a devout Lutheran. Her parents are Lutherans, and they have posted loads of photos of her on Facebook, mostly at church functions. That seems to be all they do."

"Fucking boring. Go on."

"Hey! Watch your mouth. I might be a fucking Lutheran too," said Bruce.

"Do you remember when you said I look even more beautiful, your words not mine, when I smile? Well, you look even more handsome when you smile, too. Anything else on Bailey?"

"She has a degree in the Arts, music and drawing, from Stanford University."

"Top school."

"How do you know that, Sally?"

"Like you, Bruce the wonder hacker, we also have to study our target before penetration."

More laughter!

"She got a prize for some art project in high school, has raised two kids, a boy and a girl, who are all on the Lutheran goody two shoes program. She was divorced several years ago, from Mathew Brown who is in sales and is gay, but he only came out recently. She took back her maiden name, Bailey, but not her original first name, which was Jayme, with a 'y.'

"Miss perfect has no history of computer science or hacking?"

"Not that I can find, which is really weird, or Newton is doing it, but I can't imagine he has the skills. Math, engineering and computer coding are worlds apart. Any thoughts on how to find out?"

"Is it really important?"

"If she is a black hat, what she is doing is illegal, and can lead to a jail term of ten to twenty years. That would provide Turner with leverage to get at Newton."

"And we could ask for a huge bonus," said Sally, "in exchange for telling him. I bet I can find out. Can I have her ex's phone number, please."

"Sure," said Bruce. "I'll text it to you in a sec, but why?"

"You'll see. I'll call her ex, say I'm an old school friend who lost touch with Jamie, heard through the grapevine that she was married, and I'm trying to get back in touch. I'll ask how they and the kids are doing."

Mathew Brown told Sally they were divorced for a number of reasons, but one was because, "she was always on her damn computer."

CHAPTER FORTY-TWO

The next morning, while walking over to the Honeypot Motel for breakfast with Ray and Yolanda, Jamie caught Fig up to speed on her work the previous evening.

"I eased my way into the GEPI network. My goal, Fig, was to look as though I was being careful, while leaving a payload in the form of a message for Humperdinck that would be invisible to antivirus software."

"Payload?"

"It's a piece of code used to hide messages in the code. I'd previously found some "payload code," and filed it away in my memory banks, just in case. It's a bit like a carpenter going to the hardware store, and spotting a new tool that might come in handy one day."

"I guess I do the same in science at vendor shows," said Fig.

"I reinstalled my backdoor, along with the embedded

payload that contains a message asking Humperdinck to call using the number I left in the dead drops."

Jamie's goal was to bring Humperdinck over to their side, while hiding her physical location. She was up against a professional, but Jamie loved this stuff because it was like a game. Fig had said he was successful in science because he treated it as play, rather than work. Once inside the network, Jamie added some bait that would make Humperdinck's mouth water. She was sure he was checking these servers daily for signs of Fig's hacker. Why was she so sure? Because she would do that in his situation.

The bait was an obvious search for Fig's data files, as if he was trying to extract material he'd forgotten when he was fired. This she linked to the real bait, code that played *The Cliffs of Insanity* music from *The Princess Bride*. She was hoping this would prompt Humperdinck to call, using the burner phone number in the dead drop flash drives. She planned to answer or call him back from a park near the honeypot motel. Jamie knew the network manager of the institute had just resigned, as they were advertising for a replacement. Furthermore, Beckie had mentioned to Fig they were having computer problems. This reduced the chances of Jamie's bait being deleted before Humperdinck found it.

As they approached the motel, Jamie said I'll be with you in about an hour, I just have a little job to do. I'm going to wait in the park for a little while, just in case Humperdinck calls. I have a hunch that he will.

Wishing you luck with it, *Mata Hari,"* said Fig. "See

you when you get back, and Ray can wait for his breakfast."

Then Fig headed into the motel to greet his friends.

———

Half an hour later Jamie was sitting reading on a bench in a nearby park, when her burner phone rang.

"Is that Humperdinck?"

"What the fuck makes you think that?"

"You're the only person who could possibly have the number, other than a wrong number call. I've been looking forward to talking to you, as I've been really impressed by your work, but do you have to use foul language with a complete stranger?"

"I forgot. You're a good Lutheran girl, Jayme with a y, or should I call you Jackie Pritchard?" said Bruce. "Mommy taught you not to swear. Why do you want to talk? Is your lover boy getting nervous?"

"He's not my lover boy, he's my employer and he's a tedious nerd. He offered me a job as a hacker, which was fortuitous, as that is what I want to do as a career. I hope to be a white hat, like you. When I approached companies for employment, they told me to turn myself in to law enforcement. I don't want to go to jail or hacker kiddy school. I'm the best out there, next to only one other person I know, and that's not you."

"Oh really!"

"Yes really!"

"We'll see about that. We are on the way to your location, even as we speak."

"Don't make me laugh. I know where you are, within a room or so, but you have yet to locate me, of that I am quite sure. You don't even know which city I'm in."

"We'll get to you in a few minutes, don't worry, lady."

"Tell them to follow the trash truck, it will save them some time."

"Why do we need to talk?"

"I wanted to see if I could get a better deal. I'm a hacker for hire, but I've had enough of this do-gooder scientist. He is paying me $25 an hour and expenses. Interested in working out a deal? Plus I can give you Newton."

"You've managed to piss me off, so I think I prefer to take you down."

"Wait a minute, Humperdinck, unlike your asshole boss, Turner, the guy I'm working for is at least trying to make the world a better place for our kids and their kids. He's trying to save all the animals and plants on the planet, without which we won't survive. Why help people who are trying to silence him? And why did you guys kill his cat, Sophie? She was just an innocent animal that Newton loved for over ten years. That did upset him and made him more determined to do his work to protect the planet from the crap coming out of the White House. It sure didn't slow him down any."

"I didn't kill his cat, or want to, I'm just doing my job, and they pay me much more than $25 an hour."

"I guess your colleagues killed her. Anyway, apart

from silencing Newton and taking down his website, which you seem unable to do, isn't there more to this than just doing your job? How about being proud of your work, so your partner or wife or whatever will be proud of you?"

"I'll think about it, and my name is not Humperdinck, though I did enjoy the movie." He was thinking of Sally and her lovely smile when Jamie said that.

Bruce Henley, proud hacker, was about to hang up, but thought better of it. "OK! Jayme with a y, let me think about your idea, because the guy I work for is a dick, excuse my French."

"How about we stay in touch? I think we can help each other as fellow hackers trying to earn a living?"

"I'll take the bait, and by the way, in spite of what I said, you really are a fucking great hacker. You pissed me off and impressed me at the same time."

"Thanks, Humperdinck. I need all the encouragement I can get! Come to think of it, maybe you are Farm Boy, with your eye on a Princess Buttercup of your own?"

"No comment!"

"OK! Enjoy your work with that asshole, Turner, and it was a pleasure to meet you. Bye!"

In one phone call, Jamie had established how much Humperdinck knew about her, and how he knew - facial recognition software on security camera video images, she'd bet on it. That was the only way he could have overcome her false ID at the diner. His ego was bruised by her work, and as Jamie knew only too well, "Pride goeth before a fall." But her sweet talk had buttered him up. Social engineering at its best, the most important survival tool for any woman, hacker or not.

"Maybe we can bring him in from the cold," thought *Mata Hari*.

––––––––––

Jamie headed back to the honeypot motel to rejoin Fig, Ray and Yolanda. "Here's my guardian angel and social guide," said Fig, as Jamie entered room 213. This was followed by Fig tactlessly saying, "Ray, you are already a close confidant of Jamie."

Yolanda gave Ray a suspicious look and said, "Have you been flirting with other females again?"

"I'm innocent as the driven snow, aren't I, Jamie?"

"Of course," said Jamie, rolling her eyes, smiling at Yolanda and saying, "Ray waxed lyrical about you. He's a keeper, you are a lucky woman."

Smiles all around, then Fig, who found such conversations confusing, said, "OK! Let's get on with the job. We have work to do. Fred will be on the Metro at 5:15 tomorrow night. He'll get off the train at 6:03, unless there are delays, which are rare. If you," said Fig looking at Ray, "and Yolanda can knock on his door fifteen minutes after he goes inside, he may be all softened up with a drink or two for your cat photos."

"Sounds good to me," said, Ray, "how about you, Yolanda?"

"This is a sweet deal. We get to knock on a door a

few times, and maybe meet some cats and have a free drink, in exchange for a week's free vacation, including a show? Better deal than I ever had in the Jim Crow south."

"That's in play for tomorrow evening. Thanks guys," said Fig. "Next piece of business, did you communicate with Humperdinck, Jamie?"

"I sure did!"

"Was he friendly?"

"Not at first, as he said I'd pissed him off. I made it worse by telling him I am the best hacker of them all, except for one, and that that one is not him."

"And?"

"I think I hurt his feelings," said Jamie. "You men are so susceptible to sweet talk from a woman, don't you think so, Yolanda?"

"Hey! My little finger is exhausted from wrapping Ray around it every day. You need to lose some weight, Ray."

Then Jamie said, "I tried to cut a deal with Humperdinck, and it was no deal at first. Later he said he would think about it. I also learned a lot. He knows who I am, and about my family in Mariposa."

"How did he find that?"

"Facial recognition software, I'm pretty sure. He was curious about us and called Fig my lover boy."

Laughter all round, with an inquisitive look at Fig from Yolanda.

Fig said, "No such luck."

"Boss, that's sexual harassment, I'll have you take the

video course again, if you don't stop" said Jamie. "I told him you were not my lover boy, that you are my employer and that you are a boring nerd."

"That's not nice," said Fig.

"It's spycraft, Fig, and you are the nicest, kindest nerd I ever met, but let's get on with the meeting. You are just like Humperdinck. Too sensitive! So I explained I was working for this nerdy do-gooder scientist, and asked if he could make a better offer?"

Then Ray said, "I hate to interrupt but I'm hungry as hell and I need the money for the trip so far, and to cover the show and meals. Is that OK, Fig?"

"That was the deal, Ray, no problem." Reaching into his coat pocket, Fig pulled out a roll of hundreds and twenties, and said, "It's been sitting here waiting for you guys. Do you want to eat with us or start your romantic adventure?"

Yolanda said, "I want to get to know Jamie better, so let's have breakfast. Afterwards, Fig and Jamie can set up whatever it is they're doing, because I sure don't want to know. I'll plead ignorance at the trial."

After an enjoyable meal, where Jamie and Yolanda got on like a house on fire, Jamie and Fig spent the morning chasing down equipment for the honeypot. On the way out of the motel, Fig reminded the front desk staff not to disturb him in room 301, and that he would not need any room service, towels or bedding. Fig's room on the floor above Ray and Yolanda's was 301, an odd coincidence of which Fig and Jamie were completely unaware.

Fig rejoined Ray and Yolanda for lunch, while Jamie headed back to the hostel to prepare her gear. On going to the hostel late that afternoon, Fig found Jamie testing her electronics for the honeypot, which included an old PC computer, a motion sensor and a tiny camera the size of a large button, that she said had a built-in radio transmitter.

"Jamie?"

"Yes?"

"I read an article recently about a honeypot that was used to capture some Russian spies. Could this one be used to capture us?" said Fig.

"No! Those spies were caught because of a security camera and a skilled white hat employed by a defense contractor. It happened when a well-known hacker, Roger Grimes, was deploying a honeynet in a defense contractor's system. They were all working in the same building. This machine will have no direct physical link to us, except for your reservation in the motel computer. By the way, Fig, which ID did you use?"

"I resurrected Jerome Hanratty."

"Good choice, as it confirms a link they already know. This gear is ready to install. When do you want me to set it up?"

"Sooner the better!"

"I need some quiet time, please, Fig, and it's a bit of a hike this time of night, plus late arrivals tend to attract attention. Could you take the gear back to the honeypot motel, stay the night, then let me in the back in the morning?"

"Sure."

"Could you also recheck the reliability of the power sockets and the hotel Internet, as I may not be able to get a decent phone signal and wifi is not so great on the upper floors of some motels. I would like to capture any photos in real time, before they have a chance to destroy the equipment."

"If Humperdinck is caught on camera, he is going to be even more pissed at you, Jamie, and hopefully, we'll catch both of them."

CHAPTER FORTY-THREE

Room 319, Homeland Security, Washington, DC.

"I sat outside Fred's place last night, Jim, from when he came off the metro, until he turned out the lights. No sign of Newton or Bailey," said Sally.

"I guess it was a waste of time," said Turner.

Sally rolled her eyes, and said, "No Jim! It was the classic boring stakeout, which is the deal ninety-nine percent of the time. The hardest part is not falling asleep or dropping the damn camera."

"Where did you watch from?" said Bruce.

"Across the road in the rental truck, in a line of parked cars."

Turner wanted to know if she was planning to repeat the performance that evening, and she answered in the affirmative, while thinking, "This guy really is a dumbass."

"How about you, Bruce? Any progress on their location and activities?"

"If you consider a phone conversation with Bailey to be progress, the answer is yes. She set up the whole thing."

"How did she do that?"

"She left a message in some payload code at GEPI, asking me to call her at the number she put in the dead drop Sally brought back from Maine. Bailey hid the GEPI message in several places on their servers. It was invisible to the anti-virus software as a cat command buried in image code, an image of *Wesley climbing the Cliffs of Doom*. When I accessed the image it triggered code for the music of that scene. That told me she is a first-class hacker with a sense of humor. The fact that I've never heard of her before confirms it."

"Shit," said Turner.

"Impressive," said Sally, with a big smile, to whom anything that irritated Turner was a plus.

"I already had the number from the dead drop in the Pinto, but I put off calling in case it was a trap. I guess she guessed that I check the GEPI network regularly, which I do every morning, looking for traffic from them. Her message was addressed to *Humperdinck*, which Sally says is a compliment."

"*Humperdinck?*" asked Turner.

"It comes from a movie, *The Princess Bride*, which I enjoyed watching yesterday on Sally's recommendation. It's all about true love, I'm sure you'd enjoy it, Jim," said Bruce.

"Please don't call me Jim, and we have to stop Newton posting that damn website. Maybe Bailey is a better hacker than you?"

"Fuck you, Jim," said Bruce. "In her wildest dreams."

"Maybe you need help from those guys in 301?"

"You mean Ben and Jerry? That's what I call them anyway," said Bruce. "They report to Hotchkiss not Barrett, so I'd be careful about that if I were you, Jim, and I suspect they are spying on us."

"I agree with Bruce, Jim. Hotchkiss strikes me as a classic bully, and I bet he competes with Chariton for President Miller's favor. It's what this whole damn administration is about, currying favor, which is probably why you have us chasing Newton all over the east coast. Is that right?"

"I'm just doing my job, Sally. A job directed by Barrett who reports to Chariton. Hotchkiss made an agreement with Chariton to provide us with resources, and to keep us away from prying eyes at the EPA. For me, it was a chance to work somewhere else and help the current administration. I can't stand these tree-huggers, taking jobs away for some damn butterfly."

"I'd stick with Bruce if I were you, Jim," said Sally. "What else did Bailey have to say?"

"She is fed up working for Newton, who she called a nerdy tree lover. He's paying her $25 an hour and expenses. She wanted to know if we could do better, she even said she could throw in Newton as part of the deal. Her goal is to become a white hat, which is officially what we are, except we are working on an illegal project, as far as I can tell. I mean, if we kill people's cats?"

"This isn't illegal," said Turner, "it's covert, and we didn't kill anyone's cat. It was probably ordered by Hotchkiss after I told him the trouble we were having with Newton."

"Why did you tell Hotchkiss?"

"Not your problem, Sally, but as you know better than anyone, sometimes one has to apply a little pressure to bring people to their senses."

"I don't trust Hotchkiss," said Sally. "He creeps me out, not that I've seen him but a couple of times on TV."

"We didn't kill the damn cat, Sally, but Fred is very unhappy about it. I told him I had no idea who did it, but he was still upset. Anyway, the cat's dead and Newton is still out there causing trouble, and his website is still pissing off President Miller, who does not like being called *The Ecocidal Fool*."

"But he is," thought Bruce and Sally, simultaneously.

"How come Bailey is working for Newton?" said Turner.

"She'd tried to get a job as a white hat, but every attempt led to the recommendation that she turn herself in to the cops. This is common response to self-taught hackers. They are seen as black hats and thus criminals. Hell! How else is anyone going to learn? I had to take some fucking courses and hide my best work. That's the response I would have had too. Kevin Mitnick, the most famous hacker of them all, ended up in jail, until they realized he was a national resource."

Turner decided to let this go. He realized they were taunting him about his name, and resistance was pointless. If he responded they would just dial it up a notch, like his brothers did, but he wouldn't cry this time.

"Did you learn anything else of value in the call?" asked Sally. "Something that would help us catch them. Come to think of it, Jim, why is this guy so important? There are loads of these people, and some of the organizations like Greenpeace are surely a bigger pain in the ass to the president's industrial buddies."

"He's directly targeting President Miller, who then gets pissed at Chariton and Hotchkiss at every cabinet meeting, making them concerned for their own positions, and they like the power that comes with it, so they lean on Barrett who leans on me.

That's why! Furthermore, Strickland just called me to say there was a shit storm going on at that institute in Greensboro, because someone broke into their system and sent an email to all the staff exposing his retirement income. Do you think Newton did it?"

"I would have, if it were me," said Sally.

CHAPTER FORTY-FOUR

Jamie walked from her hotel to the honeypot motel, where Fig had spent the night with the electronics. She'd picked up biscuits and coffee for four and found Fig waiting for her at a door by the rear parking lot. The place was pretty deserted, as traveling truckers were long gone and visitors were still sleeping off the night before. On entering their room, Ray and Yolanda greeted her enthusiastically.

"She comes bearing the nectar of life," said Ray, taking one of the coffees and a biscuit. "Thanks so much, Princess Buttercup."

"You can stop that flirting right now, Ray," said Yolanda with a mock scowl.

Jamie said, "It's my pleasure, Ray, and have you made your plans for your visit to Fred and his cats?"

"We most certainly have," said Yolanda. "First a museum and an art gallery, lunch in The Capital Grille, then the shops. I'm letting Ray take the shopping time off to do whatever. Men hate shopping, and Ray is no exception."

"Me too," said Fig.

"I bet you would go shopping with me," said Jamie, giving him a coy look.

"That's different, but you told me not to mix work and pleasure."

"It's OK if we only buy supplies for work and talk business."

They all laughed at Fig's evident discomfort, while Yolanda gave Jamie a knowing look, and Ray said, "Push back, Fig. It's the only defense against dangerous women."

"OK," said Fig, "let's see your cat paraphernalia, guys. I need to have my money's worth on this jaunt."

Yolanda reached into her bag and pulled out photos of several bedraggled kittens and cats, and a flyer advertising *The Lonely Cat Adoption Agency*.

"Perfect," said Fig.

"This will be the way to Fred's heart," said Jamie.

As they finished off the biscuits and coffee, Fig explained the possible risks. He reminded them that these people made a bomb threat, were persistently tracking them, and they'd killed Sophie. He said that he also suspected that Fred was probably very upset about Sophie."

"OK Fig," said Yolanda. "We know our job is to sweet talk Fred, hopefully to be invited in for a drink to get as much information as we can, and to try to bring him over to your side, and to watch out for anyone following us, right?"

"Correct, except for your last point," said Jamie, "in that we don't want you watching out for spotters, that's our job. If you do, you'll give the game away. These people are clearly professionals."

"Do you really think it is possible for us to bring Fred over to your side, Fig?" said Ray.

"It won't be if we don't try. We are betting a lot on this Fred guy, based on how he looks and behaves. He's no hero and we suspect he has a drinking problem, which could play to our advantage. Let me explain a little more about what is going on."

"Can I interrupt as needed?" said Jamie.

"Of course," said Fig, then he told them the whole story, from beginning to end.

"Quite a saga," said Ray.

"Yes, Ray. My personal website is a thorn in their side. Why Strickland waited a year or so to fire me is a bit of a mystery. Charles Barrett came to my aid. Do you remember that letter?"

"Sure do. It kept you with us for a couple more months. Strickland had you in his sights, isn't that right, boss?"

"Yes, except I'm not your boss anymore because my end finally came, and then harassment, threats and this pursuit began. You need to know this, Yolanda and Ray, because what you are doing with Fred may open you up to harassment, too. My bet is that Humperdinck will work out who you are, pretty quickly."

"Unless we distract them with the other activities we have in the works," said Jamie.

"And the risks are minimal, in my opinion," said Fig, "if all you do is talk to Fred about neglected cats and return to enjoying Washington. Just don't go anywhere alone."

"We are fine with it, Fig," said Yolanda. "Nothing ventured, nothing gained, and you are our friend, and you too Jamie."

"I understand and appreciate it," said Fig, "but it's not too late to back out. If you do, my agreement to cover your expenses stands."

"Forget it, Fig," said Yolanda, "we need an adventure, let's do it. We want to get these creeps as much as you do, since they killed Sophie and threatened the best boss Ray ever had. We are in for keeps."

Ray nodded in agreement.

"Thanks for the vote of confidence. I have to say that none of this would be possible without Jamie."

Jamie said, "This is my first job as a hacker, and I consider it white hat hacking, whatever law enforcement might say, and it is activism in favor of the environment, and I'm not facing water cannons, dogs and batons. This is easy activism, fighting to reduce climate change and protect the environment. I love the work Fig does, even though I can't understand the half of it."

"I can't understand any of what Jamie does," said Fig.

"All for one and one for all," cried Ray, quoting *The Three Musketeers*.

"But there were only three musketeers," said Fig.

"You're forgetting *D'Artagnan,*" said Jamie.

"Trust the Arts major to put me to shame. OK! We have our plan. Go enjoy your day at the museums. Jamie and I have work to do in room 301. By the way, Jamie, I couldn't find any problems with the power outlets, and the wifi is strong and stable, which is surprising on the third floor."

"They probably have a range extender."

As they got up to go, Fig cleared away the paper cups and debris.

"Jamie! This one is house trained, pity he's your boss."

At which Jamie, Yolanda and Ray laughed, while Fig groaned under his breath. Fig was a little slow on the uptake when it came to interpreting the ways and wiles of women, but he sure was falling for Jamie, and she knew it, but had no plans to show it until Fig was no longer her employer.

Fig and Jamie headed upstairs to room 301, where Jamie arranged the computer, camera, and motion detector on the small writing desk, and set to testing her circuits. Once the honeypot was installed, with the camera hidden and pointing toward the door, she had Fig go outside and come back in."

She then showed him the video recording of his reentry on her phone, and said, "If it works that well on the day, whoever opens that door will not be able to kill the system before I get the video."

"I can't wait to watch their expression," said Fig.

"If it's Humperdinck he'll work it out in seconds, groan and then probably stop and have a chat."

"Why would he groan?"

"He'd know I got him yet again. I taunted him about his hacking skills, which pissed him off. Then I told him about your work, and how you were upset about Sophie. I could tell that he did not like her being killed, and he sounded thoughtful about your work. I also said something about his partner, not knowing if he has one, which evinced a response that told me he has a thing for someone."

"Maybe it's Repo Lady," said Fig, "if she's the cute woman who delivered the fake bomb?"

"And maybe Repo Lady didn't kill Sophie. Perhaps something went wrong at their end?"

Fig said, "The plot thickens. I'm starting to think that the three musketeers, or should I say *Les Trois Femmes Musketeers*, are you, Yolanda and Repo Lady, with Repo Lady helping us against her will."

They then double-checked Fig's website on Jamie's honeypot computer, made sure the computer gps was turned on, and that the camera, motion sensor and radio connections were working. They finally put the "Do Not Disturb" sign on the door, and quietly exited the building.

"The die is cast," said Jamie, "so let's hope we reel in a big fish or two, to mix my metaphors."

"Are you sure they will be able to locate the room?"

"Using the *Find my Phone* app or the hacking equivalent," said Jamie.

"Won't leaving the computer gps turned on make them suspicious?"

"Even hackers forget little details from time to time. They probably will be suspicious, for a second, but go ahead anyway. Too big an opportunity to miss. I probably would too, though I'd come with backup."

"Are you sure you don't want to work for the CIA?" said Fig.

"No thanks," said Jamie.

Then Fig groaned.

"What's up?"

"I just remembered that I have yet to grovel to Strickland for a letter of reference, so I can apply for that job on the Homeland Security site, my obligation to the masterplan, *à la Mata Hari*."

A little while later, Fig got off of his phone, and said to Jamie, "Strickland said he'd think about it, though he wasn't sure I was the right material for the job, unless I changed my attitude. He said I needed to be less hostile to the inevitable changes going on in the world and consider people's jobs, rather than some damn seaweed. What a prick! Do you think I groveled enough, Jamie?"

"Top marks. You sounded like a real butt kissing sycophant."

CHAPTER FORTY-FIVE

Sally Smarts was sitting in her hired black SUV on Irving Street, watching toward the Metro station.

It was just after 6:00 p.m. when she spotted Fred coming home. As usual, he was shambling along looking depressed. "This is our co-conspirator? Maybe I need to get out of this before the shit hits the fan," thought Sally.

Fred pushed open the front gate, which was on the opposite side of the road to Sally, and slowly ascended the few steps, while ignoring the general disorder in his front yard. He put a key in the door and disappeared inside. Sally then settled down to watch and she didn't have long to wait. The street was quiet with just a few commuters, like Fred, on their way home from work, though none looking quite so beaten down.

At 6:45 exactly, which made Sally suspicious, a black couple appeared in her rearview mirror, on Fred's side of the street. They were walking in the direction of the station. They approached the front doors of the first few houses before Fred's. At the first no one answered. At the second house a middle-aged lady opened the door on a security chain and promptly closed it again. Clearly nervous of two black strangers on her doorstep.

No answer at the third house, then they went up the steps to Fred's front door and within a minute he appeared in the doorway and listened to their spiel. "What the fuck?" Sally noted he was holding a glass of wine in his hand. "He's a drinker, shit." To her surprise, after examining some papers the black couple handed to him, Fred invited them in.

"Probably Jehovah's Witnesses?" thought Sally.

About ten minutes later, Sally noticed in her rearview mirror a white couple approaching, also heading in the direction of the Metro station. They were walking arm in arm. As they reached Fred's front gate, the guy, about six feet and athletic looking, said something to his partner and headed directly toward Sally. The woman followed him at a distance, and then disappeared behind her SUV, but the doors were locked.

The man looked familiar. He reached into his wallet, pulled out a slip of paper, and knocked on her window. Surprised, she wound it down and greeted the stranger with her best put on smile. He didn't smile. Instead he said, "Excuse me ma'am. I think you dropped this," and he handed her the slip of paper. He then turned and, in no apparent rush, followed the woman behind her truck. In Sally's curbside mirror she saw him rejoin his companion, and then they both vanished into a dark alleyway.

She had to turn on the interior light to read the note, said, "Shit," and got on the phone to Bruce.

"You'll not believe what just happened, Bruce" and she described the events in detail.

"He handed you the note that you put with the fake bomb in his mailbox weeks ago?"

"A copy of it, yes."

"Where did you rent the vehicle and in what name?"

"In my name, at Rent-a-Truck, here in DC. Why? Who cares?"

"Think like a hacker, Sally. The Bailey woman certainly got your plate number and will know all about you within the next hour or so. Furthermore, there is nothing I can do to stop her. If you'd used a fake ID it would be a different matter. Not only will she have your information, but she can employ a handwriting expert that would tie you to the fake bomb, and even the cat, to provide testimony that would stand up in court."

"Damn! What should I do?" Sally was used to frightening other people, but now she was scared for a change.

"It's more what should we do. Do you think I'll leave you to hang out to dry alone, Sally?"

"Oh, Bruce."

"We are going to have to negotiate, and don't tell Turner. I think you and I should team up with these guys, against Turner, who is clearly doing some nasty illegal shit."

"I agree with you, Bruce. In fact I'd already labeled Fred as the backup fall guy."

"You're probably right, Sally, it's how people like Turner and his boss operate."

"Hang on a sec, Bruce. The black couple are leaving Fred's. Let's meet somewhere and talk this over."

"Is this a date?" Sally.

"In your wildest dreams, big boy," she said, with a smile.

An hour later, Bruce and Sally were sitting in a small restaurant having a light meal. "When it comes to negotiating with these people, it's a pity they killed his cat. Newton and Bailey will assume you did it."

"Why me?"

"Because they call you Repo Lady."

Sally, in spite of being nervous, laughed and laughed at that, and said, "These people really know their shit, but I didn't kill Newton's cat. I just delivered a package, as requested by Turner. As I said, it was provided by Hotchkiss. Some guy I didn't know delivered it to my hotel in Greensboro. All he said to me was, "It's with the compliments of Bill Hotchkiss. Please make sure it reaches its destination. Bill asked that you add a persuasive note."

"You certainly did that," said Bruce.

"It was the best I could do at the moment with a scrap of paper and a pen. I guess it was a little harsh."

"Remember that when you meet him. He needs to

know you didn't kill his cat before you do meet him. You might not survive the encounter, otherwise. If I see him first, I'll explain, then let's see if we can work out a deal. I've suspected for a while that our work for Turner is a cover for some really bad shit that the guy he reports to, Barrett, is doing."

"Maybe now is the time to negotiate, Bruce, before the damn stubbornness of Newton, and the hacking skills of Bailey, bring Turner's operation down around our heads."

"Yes, it is time to defect, Sally, if they'll have us and if we can negotiate a truce with Newton, in spite of his dead cat. Do you mind if I say something I've been wondering about for a while?"

"Of course, Humpy."

"You don't seem so angry and hostile as you were when we first met. What's up?"

"I'm starting to trust you, Bruce, making you the first guy in years. My hostile image protects me, especially in repo work. Better they are scared of me than seeing me as a soft target. Maybe we can get ourselves out of this shitty job and move on, if you are interested in someone in the repo business."

"Hell! I'm a certified professional white hat hacker, doing illegal work, who lives in a land of code, and I struggle to understand women. I tend to upset them when I don't mean to."

"I'm a woman and I can't understand them either, Bruce. My anger comes from being treated like shit, first by my dad and then by every man I've been with. I just hope you are the real deal. You seem to be."

"I'll contact Bailey and set up a meeting. You said a black couple came by before the couple who handed you the note. I wonder who those people are. It's starting to look like a clusterfuck. I think Newton and Bailey were playing us to get that note to you, and they succeeded."

They finished their meal, Bruce walked Sally to the Metro and then to her hotel, like a real gentleman. She gave him a peck on the cheek on the hotel doorstep. "Thanks for coming into my life, Bruce," she said, before walking into her hotel.

Bruce returned to his place, floating on air, thinking, "And I thought she was a real bitch. Just another hurt kid, like the rest of us, underneath all that armor."

———

Fig and Jamie made their escape and started walking back to the honeypot motel to meet up with Ray and Yolanda.

"You were right, Fig, they were staking out Fred's place, waiting for us," said Jamie. "Was that Repo Lady's note that you handed to the woman in the SUV?"

"It was a photocopy, and that was the woman who delivered the fake bomb, she's obviously Repo Lady. I recognized her instantly. I had to control myself not to hit her, because she killed Sophie."

"That note was handwritten, Fig. Not a mistake *Mata Hari* would have made. Now we have a lot more information, including the number of her vehicle. It was a rental. The rental company server will take me to her personal information, assuming she didn't use a fake ID."

"We are tightening the noose, Jamie."

"I bet your little visit to Repo Lady's driver's side window was a shock. Let's go find out how things went with Ray and Yolanda. Then we'll wait for Humperdinck to call. We now have them in a bind. Bruce will realize that the note ties Repo Lady to a crime, the fake bomb, and it may incriminate him too."

Later, in room 213 at the honeypot motel, Ray and Yolanda were excitedly telling Fig and Jamie about their first adventure as spies. "It went great," said Ray. "The guy took to us as soon as we showed him our photos of waifs and strays."

"He even invited us in for a drink," said Yolanda, "and he was clearly on his second or third glass. He is a sad, lonely guy who loves cats."

"What did you find out?" said Fig.

"We learned that he doesn't like his job. He did say that he's a certified accountant, working for Homeland Security."

"And?"

"While my beautiful wife had him preoccupied with pussies," replied Ray with a grin, "I spotted something useful on his computer."

"What?" said Jamie.

"Did you watch the movie *Ready Player One?*"

"His ID and password were on a sticky note?"

"Yep! Just like on the bowling ball console of Nolan Sorrento."

"That will save me a bunch of time. Thanks, Ray."

Fig said, "What do you think of the guy as a potential collaborator?"

"I wouldn't trust him an inch," said Yolanda, "he's a drunk who is only just holding it together."

CHAPTER FORTY-SIX

"Please don't talk, Fig, or even make a noise," said Jamie. "It might be best if you step out for a while. I may need up to an hour. We could lose this guy with one slip up."

"No worries, Jamie, you're right. I might cough. Do your *Mata Hari* thing with Humperdinck, and tell me about it when I get back. Coffee?"

"Yes, please."

Fig headed out for coffees and a walk, but something was niggling at his brain.

"Hi, Mr. Hacker extraordinaire?" said Jamie, on her phone.

There was a brief silence, then, "It can wait. I'll call you back in a while. Got to go, sorry."

Bruce was stalling in order to talk elsewhere in private, without raising suspicions in anyone around him.

"He's probably with Turner and Repo Lady talking

about the events on Irving Street last night," thought Jamie, as she waited patiently, hoping Fig would take a while. Thirty minutes later her burner phone rang.

"Good morning, Jayme with a 'y,' what's up? How's hacking hanging today?"

"Could you tell me your name, you have mine, unless you prefer Humperdinck? I'm hoping to get us on the same team. I'm hoping you might be able to help me get a job as a white hat, but first, I have two questions."

"Jerry, and your first question is?"

Jamie thought, "Something has changed. He's more friendly. I bet he realizes we now have some power over Repo Lady, and he wants to protect her."

"How did you get into hacking? I often wonder how it happens, as I never get to talk to other hackers."

"How about you, Jayme with a y? You go first."

"To keep my bank accounts safe, then one thing led to another and before I knew it, I was hooked on the code. It was like a candy box I had to open."

"Video games as a teenager. I hacked them to get a better score and then to make money selling clues and got hooked just like you. I see beauty in the code."

"Me too! Thanks for telling me that, I often wonder if I'm weird?"

"You may be weird, but your second question is?"

"Can we have a meeting with you and Dr. Newton. No tricks. He seems to be in danger, and we are not sure why you people have picked on him."

"Are you recording this, Jayme with a y?"

"No! Why would I do that? I have more to lose than

you do. At least you are covered under the scam of covert ops."

"I'm not recording it either, by the way, and the answer to your question, why Newton, is simple. He's a tree-hugger for sure, but he has targeted President Miller, directly. This has led to pressure from the top down, all the way to Turner, who I work for. But you know all that already, so why ask?"

"Come on, Jerry, Turner is small fry. Someone is using Turner's program to take down hundreds of other environmental scientists. It's just that Newton hasn't given up, and between you and me, he is really good at pissing people off."

"It's in the nature of people with Asperger's, Jayme with a y, but for me it's just a well-paid job."

"So it was you who fingered Newton and got him fired? Nice work, Jerry. Anyway, are you interested in a more fulfilling job, one you would feel good about?"

"Maybe."

"Is Newton the only one being attacked in this way?"

"As far as I can tell, Jayme with a y, he is, but that said, I am interested in your proposition. As you said before, we hackers need to stick together, and furthermore I can't stand Turner."

"So we can meet?"

"Where do you suggest and I promise no tricks, not that you haven't tricked me a few times."

"I was just trying to reach you, in private."

"You both impressed me and pissed me off. We can

talk about that when we meet. I would like to bring along one other person."

"Repo Lady?"

Bruce laughed and said, "Yes!"

"Could you meet us at the Rachel Carson Memorial Panel in the Glover Archbold National Park at noon today?"

"Why there?"

"Because there you will see why Newton does what he does, to save the planet for your kids and grandkids."

"I don't have any kids or grandkids."

"Do you want to settle down and have some when you find the right person?"

"That's none of your damned business, but now you ask, yes. We'll see you at noon."

A few minutes later, Fig walked in the door with coffees, croissants, butter and strawberry jam.

"Humperdinck agreed to meet us at noon, and that looks good. My favorite, strawberry jam."

"Maybe you can bring him in from the cold, *Mata Hari*."

"How did she dress, I wonder?" said Jamie.

"You'd look good in those decorated boob plates she wore, but you would find it hard not to stick out."

"Funny guy. You're my boss, remember, so I don't want any sexual harassment. We have until noon to get there. How about breakfast and a nice leisurely walk to the memorial? It's about four miles."

"Sounds good, how's the coffee?"

Several hours later they arrived at the Park and found

the panel, *Through the Eyes of a Scientist*, which Fig felt compelled to read from beginning to end.

"Her book triggered the creation of the EPA, Jamie, the very thing Miller is trying to destroy."

"I know. I read the book, remember, which is why we went to Maine. Amazing lady," said Jamie, then she noticed a man standing next to them.

"Jerry?"

"Yes, Jayme with a y, and you are Dr. Newton I presume, the elusive tree-hugging fugitive?"

"And you killed my cat, Sophie," said Fig.

"I had nothing to do with killing cats. I like cats, and why do you say that to a complete stranger?"

"Fig, calm down, please," said Jamie.

"Dr. Newton, I wasn't involved in any of that, which occurred without my knowledge. My job was to find you, find more out about you, and pass the information along to my boss," said Bruce, defensively, as Fig loomed over him.

"Then you found my Asperger's diagnosis and had me fired, and if it wasn't for you, Sophie would still be alive, and my apartment wouldn't have been trashed."

Turning to Jamie, Bruce said, "I thought I was here to negotiate a truce or a possible collaboration, not to be attacked in public."

"Fig, Jerry is here to possibly work with us and maybe to catch the people who did kill Sophie, so let's be nice."

"I guess it was Repo Lady who killed her, then," said Fig.

"Dr. Newton," said Bruce, "please follow me and let her explain her innocence for herself. We are not armed or hostile. I, like Jamie, am a hacker doing a job. I suspect that the person you should attack is Turner, or more likely his boss, Barrett."

"If you can't calm down, Fig," said Jamie, "I'll have to do this alone. I know you are upset, but let's have the logical Fig, the Fig I know and trust."

"OK!"

A hundred yards along a gravel path was Sally, sitting on a bench looking nervous. She knew Newton would suspect her of killing his cat, and she just wanted time to explain.

As Fig approached her, Sally stood and said, all in a rush, "Dr. Newton, I did not kill or order the killing of your cat. The thugs who trashed your place had nothing to do with me. That's not my style, and I didn't even know you had a cat, and based on what Bruce says, you are fighting the work of our shithead boss, Turner, so making amends would make me feel much better about something I never did."

"You delivered that bomb threat with that fucking note, that I can use to get you in court. The cops have a record of the whole thing," said Fig.

"I did and I apologize, not that I expect that to go very far with you. All I can do is say I'm sorry."

"Boy, this is a far cry from the cold-hearted but horribly attractive bitch I met a few weeks ago," thought Bruce. It was hard for him to believe the effect a little kindness could have.

"Nice to meet you, Bruce," said Jamie with a knowing smile. "Where from here, guys?"

"I'm sorry I'm so angry. I loved Sophie, and I now can see you had no intention of that happening, Repo Lady."

"I'm Sally Smarts, but I have done work in repo. How did you work that out? But it's a shitty job?"

"Sally," said Jamie, "as usual it seems that the men are clueless, so let's have a little chat. You guys do some male bonding, and we'll meet back here in thirty minutes." Sally grabbed her bag and off they went.

Fig said, "I sure wish women came with an instruction manual. Is it too early for a beer, Bruce?" and they headed off in the opposite direction.

Sitting in a coffee shop, Jamie said, "Sally, do you know that Jerry, I mean Bruce, is in love with you, even with all your rough edges, and you appear to have a few."

Sally frowned, but Jamie continued.

"I'm kind of jealous of your rough edges, Sally. I was raised as a Lutheran goody two shoes and I hate it."

"You're right, Jamie, I can be pretty coarse, but I'm so glad we've met, finally. I hated it when I heard Dr. Newton's cat was killed. We heard it from Turner, after Dr. Newton talked to Fred on the Metro. It was Dr. Newton. Right?"

"Yes, Sally, and I'd call him Fig if I were you. He isn't really into the Dr. thing."

"This is the first job I've had where I've been paid to treat someone badly. Repossession of cars involves dangerous assholes, but Dr. Newton, I mean Fig, seems like a sweet guy. Why do they call him Fig?"

"They call him Fig because that's the nickname his teenage friends gave him. You know? Jeb Newton. Fig Newtons. And it stuck. I know he likes me, Sally, and I like him. But I'm working for him and I don't want to get involved with a fugitive. I think there is someone really bad above Turner who will stop at nothing to silence him."

"I don't think they want a stink and killing someone would make a real stink. I think they just want to shut him up and stop that website popping up over and over again. Even Bruce can't stop it."

"One of my best masterpieces, Sally."

They chatted on, slowly learning to trust and like each other, which reminded Jamie of a line from a famous poem, *The Ladies*, by Rudyard Kipling.

For the Colonel's Lady an' Judy O'Grady, Are sisters under their skins!

CHAPTER FORTY-SEVEN

Charles Barrett's EPA office, Washington, DC. Barrett is on the phone.

"Hi Chaz, what's happening?"

"The usual, Bill. We are fixing things one case at a time."

"I hope the facilities we provided at St. Elizabeth's met with your approval?"

"They are perfect, Bill, and very much appreciated."

"Is Jim getting those tree huggers under control? The president asks me about it every damn cabinet meeting."

"Bill, you know James Turner hates being called Jim. I guess that's why you do it?"

"Sure is," followed by a belly laugh on the other end of the phone. "Well Chaz, is the president going to be happy with what we have to report?"

"Good progress except for one fly in the ointment."

"And that is?"

"Newton. I wondered if you had any ideas. This guy just won't stop."

"Don't say Newton to Miller, he'd bite your head off. I understand from Alec that Newton is growing an army of eco-scientist tree huggers, while Strickland is screwing around at that damn institute he worked in."

"Exactly."

"Believe it or not, Chaz, Newton is mentioned by the president increasingly frequently at our cabinet meetings, and he's pissed. Your friend Newton's name for the president is *The Ecocidal Fool,* which made me laugh, but it's going viral on liberal sites. If Miller finds out you are failing to fix this problem, Chariton will be in hot water, and he'll have you out and back to your food farms in no time flat."

"We've been pretty hard on the guy, including your intervention that James told me about recently."

"He asked for help and he got it, Chaz."

"I wondered if you had any suggestions for actions we could take, now?"

"How about I send a couple of guys around to smash his hands, so he'll never type again? How's that sound? It would slow him down, for sure."

"Be serious, Bill, we can't be doing stuff like that."

"It's been done before by animal rights activists. You know your problem, Chaz?"

"What's that?"

"You are too soft hearted. How about you give him

some of your food products, that might do the trick. He'd die of obesity and diabetes in no time."

"Very funny, Bill, great joke, but what do you suggest, because Alec is starting to press me hard on this one."

"OK! Chaz, I know you don't approve of our methods, but you do like a happy boss. Alec and I have worked together for years. Here's what I suggest. Find a weakness and exploit it."

"Such as?"

"Who or what does Newton care about. Really care about?"

"His cat is dead, thanks for that, Bill. His family is grown, but there is one person I bet he cares about based on what my team have to say."

"And who's that Chaz?"

"The Bailey woman."

"Then threaten to take her out."

CHAPTER FORTY-EIGHT

At the Glover Archbold National Park, after the ladies had returned, they all agreed to have a confab, based on the facts that Sally, Jamie and Bruce were working for pay, Yolanda and Ray were providing friendship and support in exchange for an all-expenses paid trip to DC, though Yolanda said they would do it without that, and Fig was trying to save the environment, in exchange for which it appeared that his life was being threatened. Fig explained who Ray and Yolanda were, and how they fit into the scheme.

"So that's the black couple who were talking to Fred?" said Sally. "You set that up to find me, didn't you?"

"Sure did, Sally, and I don't plan to give up until I find the fucking cat killer," said Fig.

Sally clarified, yet again, that her involvement did not include trashing Fig's apartment or killing Sophie. She said that she was employed as a soft persuader and that there was some other team doing the more aggressive stuff, and who they were she had no idea, but she thought it was probably run by Hotchkiss.

They walked to a local coffee shop, where Jamie said she knew of a quiet corner where they could talk privately.

Over his coffee, black with no sugar, Bruce said, "This is no joke, guys. As Sally told me, hundreds of environmental activists are being killed right now in the Amazon rain forests. By the way, any of you heard of *Climategate?*"

"I have," said Jamie and Fig, simultaneously.

"It was a hacking and climate denier travesty," said Fig. "that occurred about ten years ago. It almost destroyed the life of Michael Mann. Some black hats stole loads of emails from a University Climate Research group in England. Then they worked with climate deniers, probably supported by big oil and gas, and assholes like Turner, Barrett and Chariton, to cherry pick those emails and build a case against climate change science. They quoted everything out of context, the lying turds."

"Fig's right, those climate scientists received threatening letters and death threats. They even threatened to harm their children," said Bruce.

"The bomb delivery from Sally was a similar shock," said Fig. "Fortunately my kids are grown."

"I was just the delivery person, Fig. I had no idea what was in that package. When Fred told us about the death of Sophie even Turner denied knowing about it."

"I believe you, Sally," said Fig. "No sweat."

"Wait a minute," said Jamie, "there must be a serious hit group for difficult customers, like Fig."

"Come to think of it, I think you are the only tough customer," said Bruce, "based on the white boards in room 301."

"Why do you say that?"

"Of the hundreds of names of tree-huggers on those white boards, amassed by Fred by the way, where we work in Homeland Security, yours, Fig, is the only one with a big red circle around it. I think you're right, Jamie. I bet there is more to this than rooms 301 and 319. We owe it to Fig to find out what it is and take it down."

"Then I suggest we keep our little cabal quiet, let Turner keep paying you for as long as possible, while you work as a mole for us," said Jamie.

"Me too," said Sally. "I don't want to work for that turd Turner any longer than I need to, but being paid by him to take him down is perfect."

Fig said, "We need a leader. Who should it be? I suggest Jamie, I mean *Mata Hari*, because she keeps a cool head under fire. What do y'all think?"

"Y'all?" said Bruce. "You really talk like that in the South?"

"Excuse my vernacular" said Fig, "and I sure am glad to have you guys on board, plus you and Jamie won't have to compete anymore."

"What competition?" said Jamie.

Bruce said, "I'm a simple hacker and a man, so I vote

for Jamie too, but the game isn't over 'til it's over, Jayme with a y."

"Women are clearly more intelligent than men," said Sally, "so I vote for Jamie as well. You mentioned your two friends who talked to Fred are here right now? Shouldn't they be included in this growing cabal? It might be helpful to have a beachhead down there in North Carolina."

"Another strategist, great," said Jamie, "and I assume my paychecks will still arrive on time? I'm happy to assume command, with an increase in pay to $30 an hour, if that is acceptable, Fig? Then I suggest we meet at the motel with Ray and Yolanda later this afternoon and make a battle plan."

Bruce said, "Only $30 and hour? That's a bargain, Fig."

"Don't go on about it, Bruce, or she'll put the price up again."

After thinking quietly for a second, while the others waited expectantly, Jamie said, "Bruce and Sally, are you sure you can't be spotted hanging out with us? Is anyone tracking you?"

"You're thinking like a black hat, Jamie, and I doubt it," said Bruce. "Turner isn't that bright and, as far as I can tell, whoever is pulling his strings wants to stay as far from this operation as possible. It would still be best if we assume that we are being watched."

"Meeting is over," said Jamie, "and Bruce, I have something I want to show you at the motel. I think you will find it amusing."

Ray and Yolanda agreed to meet the group at the motel in their room mid-afternoon, as long as they didn't miss their 7:00 p.m. broadway show.

"The four conspirators then took the Metro to the honeypot motel. During the trip, Sally and Jamie talked the whole time, while Fig and Bruce compared notes on their memories of *Climategate* and how they could fight back against *The Ecocidal Fool* in the White House, who had all the power.

Jamie and Fig took Bruce and Sally to room 301 in the honeypot motel. They let a suspicious Bruce Henley go in first, and upon entering, he said, "Fuck!"

"Great expression, Humpy," said Sally, looking at his surprised expression on Jamie's phone as both girls laughed.

"I guess we can close this down?" said Fig.

"No," said Jamie, "I have other plans for this equipment. I'll explain later. In the meantime, let's have the first meeting of the six musketeers in Yolanda and Ray's room, downstairs, if they don't mind."

On arriving in room 213, Fig handed Jamie her glasses, that she'd put down in the honeypot room, then she called the meeting to order. Introductions were made, and again Sally had to apologize for Fig's cat, as both Ray and Yolanda were initially hostile when they found out she was the lady with the fake bomb in the SUV at Fig's apartment, and that she had been spying on them during their visit to Fred."

With a little soothing of sore tempers by Jamie, the

team came together. She said, "First Fig has some things he wants to say. Go ahead, boss."

"We need to find who Turner reports to on his progress. I assume it's Barrett, but you never know. We can probably safely assume that there is a separate attack group, beyond rooms 301 and 319, who make fake bombs, kill cats, and might kill me?"

Bruce said, "The groups in rooms 301, us three hackers and Fred, and 319, now Sally and I, are kept separate as best Turner can. If there is a third group, I don't know anything about it. Do you, Sally?"

"No idea, but I bet it involves Hotchkiss."

"Yes! Fig, but..." said Jamie.

"Wait a minute, Jamie," said Fig. "everyone needs to be brought up to speed on what happened from the beginning."

"OK Fig, carry on," said Jamie, and Fig proceeded to tell the whole story again, for Sally and Bruce's benefit, explaining trophic cascades, EcoWorld, his firing, the harassment, and how he met Jamie

"Your director, Dr. Nicholas Page, was corporate, Fig," said Bruce, "so I was involved in gathering dirt on him. Sorry about that. What else can I say?"

"That's water over the dam, Bruce and Fig," said Jamie, "so let's move on.

"I bet Nick Page is one of the names crossed out on that wall of white boards in the Homeland Security site," said Fig.

"I'll check on that," said Bruce, "as I still have access to 301."

"Thanks Bruce," said Fig. "I've been wondering who really hates my work. Plenty of people in industry don't like my pointing the ecological disaster finger at them, but GEPI is small potatoes, and these industries get a lot of credit for its existence. We dish out advice, that they generally ignore, but they can still pretend that they care about the environment, even though most of them don't give a damn."

"It's all smoke and mirrors with those people," said Sally. "I know the types."

Fig then said, "The firewall between my research and the sponsors came down within weeks of Strickland's arrival, and soon thereafter the best scientists were gone. They were replaced by more manageable contract type scientists."

"There was still one good scientist left," said Jamie. "You, Fig."

"Yes, Jamie. But Strickland soon started his attacks on my research, and I'm sure he was preparing for my ouster sooner, then that weird letter arrived."

"What letter?" said several of the group.

"As Strickland was heating up his attacks on my use of network mathematics, and damage of trophic cascades, ..."

"Trophic what?" said Yolanda.

"Taking out a top predator of one group of plants or animals leading to downstream damage to that food chain, due to over or undergrowth of some population or other, but let's keep going. I can explain all that later."

They settled down, and listened to Fig.

"Anyway, just as Strickland was heating up his attacks on me, behind my back, I received a copy of a letter sent to Strickland, written by Charles Barrett."

"Turner's boss?" said Sally.

"Yep, and this guy clearly has the power of persuasion over the board of directors, or over Strickland at least. It basically said I walk on water and my work was exactly the kind of research envisioned by the founders. Why did he do that, when Turner, who drew that red circle around my name in room 301 at Homeland Security, reports directly to Barrett at the EPA? Jamie thinks it was a set up."

"How come, Jamie?" said Ray.

"I think he was using Fig's work, as it is the most incendiary when it comes to pissing off President Miller, to encourage the board to close the institute. It was a trojan horse, in effect. Evil intent hidden in a message of support for Fig. Back to you, Fig?"

"That's all I wanted to say, Jamie."

Five expectant faces looked Jamie's way, causing her to blush and say, "This is the first time I've run a meeting, so please bear with me. It's clearly time to make a plan and dish out action items."

"Action items?" said Sally.

"Any meeting is a waste of time if action items aren't generated, and then people's feet held to the fire on the ones they accept. I learnt that in the Lutheran school of bake sales. Fig, can you work with Bruce to find out more about Charles Barrett and re-examine everything that led up to your troubles starting, which I imagine was soon after Miller was elected?"

"I'm sure Rachel Carson was rolling over in her grave when he was elected. He's fucking up the planet," said Fig.

"Who is Rachel Carson?" said Yolanda.

"I've got a great book you can read about her," said Jamie, "it's where Fig gets his inspiration."

"Fig, could you also continue to work on your list of environmental activists?"

"No need," said Bruce, "I have access to over a thousand in Fred Sassy's spreadsheet. We've been working on it to find dirt for months. I guess I accepted a shitty job, sorry about that."

"That gets rid of my first job," said Jamie, "hacking into Fred's home computer, so back to action items for the group. Ray and Yolanda, can you be available to do anything we need to set up in Greensboro? Otherwise your work is done."

"Of course," said Yolanda and Ray, simultaneously.

"And what can I do to make up for my part in Fig's troubles?" said Sally.

"Fig's forgiven you and he already promised not to take you to court using a handwriting expert, so we are all friends and that's water over the damn, Sally. I think you and Bruce should continue to work as a team for Turner, as we all work to find *Shelob*, which appears to be Barrett."

"You call him *Shelob*? The spider in *The Lord of the Rings*?" said Bruce.

Jamie said to Sally and Yolanda, who looked confused, "It's just nerd talk, take no notice, they can't help it."

"*Shelob* is our name for the evil genius behind all of this, and the candidates are narrowing down to Barrett, Chariton, Hotchkiss, Miller and a possible unknown," said Fig.

"If we can find *Shelob* we can make them pay for firing Fig, killing Sophie and working to kill the institute. I want them to suffer," said Jamie.

"Spoken like a good Lutheran girl," said Bruce, laughing.

"In that case," said Jamie, "we have work to do. Let's meet back here in two days, so Sally and Bruce won't be missed. Does 6:00 p.m. work for everyone?"

There was general agreement, then Jamie said, "Thanks for your help, and enjoy the show tonight, Yolanda and Ray."

"A final afterthought, guys," said Bruce, "I think I may be able to coax *Shelob's* men into the honeypot room upstairs. It was intended for Sally and me, I guess. Jamie, can you leave your apparatus running, and let's see if we can catch ourselves a hit man or two? I'll let Turner know about it, and then we'll see if he calls in a hit."

"Great idea, Bruce," said Jamie. "Fig, can you remind the front desk again to leave that room alone for a couple more days?"

"Sure."

Then Jamie said, "Are you all OK with everything? It

must be weird for Sally and Bruce, changing sides like this. How can I make it an easy transition for you guys?"

"For me," said Sally, "it is so nice to work with real people who aren't trying to rip me off. How about you, Bruce?"

"The same, Sally, I never thought so much about the environment before, and the future of this planet for my kids and grandkids."

"You have grandkids?" said Sally.

"A man can dream, can't he?" said Bruce.

"On that note," said Fig, "I suggest we take a nice long walk on this lovely day, now the rain has stopped, and get a dinner together, while Yolanda and Ray enjoy the show, and before Bruce returns to his work tracking down dirt on those horrible tree huggers. You don't want to lose that paycheck, Bruce, but could you put in a little sabotage, while you are at it?"

"Yes Fig, I can, and I know just what to do, but I think we should keep an eye on the other two hackers in 301, Ben and Jerry. I don't trust them. Let's have that walk before dinner and learn a little more about each other. I'm pretty curious as to how Fig's brain ticks and how to impress Sally with what a great guy I am."

Jamie said, "Fig's brain doesn't tick, it kind of meanders all over the place, with no apparent plan, which is a deception he uses because he always has a plan. Right, Fig?"

And off they went, the six musketeers scheming away.

CHAPTER FORTY-NINE

While taking a quiet walk in the early morning, while Jamie enjoyed much needed sleep, one of Fig's burner phones rang.

"Is that Dr. Newton?"

"Who is this and how did you get this number?"

"It's your friend, Charles Barrett, known to my friends as Chaz. Do you consider me to be your friend, Fig?"

"How did you get my number?"

"You are not the only one who has access to skilled hackers, like your charming friend or should I say paramour, Jamie Bailey?"

Silence!

"What is it you want?"

"I would like us to meet for a little chat about your friend's activities. We have evidence that she recently penetrated a bank and explored some private accounts.

That was extremely impolite of her. We have enough information to have her arrested and jailed for a considerable period of time, which could be ten, even twenty, years."

"You're bluffing," said Fig as he prepared to hang up.

"I am not bluffing, but I would prefer not to treat such a charming young lady badly."

"I doubt you can prove it."

"Ah! So you admit it, and that's recorded, creating a little more evidence, my friend."

"I'm not your friend."

"You need to realize, Dr. Newton, that our resources far outstrip those of Ms. Bailey, the young Lutheran from Mariposa County. We have the names and addresses of her children, parents and friends."

"So?"

"If you care about her, which we suspect you do, I suggest you consider a negotiation."

Silence.

"I enjoyed speaking with you, Dr. Newton," and the phone went dead.

"Shit!"

Fig headed back toward the hostel, in a bit of a panic, which was unusual for Fig. That call threw him, completely, and the creepy voice of Barrett.

"Jamie. Sorry to wake you, but there is an issue."

He told Jamie about the call from Barrett, which caused her considerable alarm. Then Jamie said, "Do you think he was bluffing?"

"How can we be sure? I'm not going to risk your

future, Jamie. Maybe I should close my site and start a whole new career, like Jeffrey Wigand?"

"I don't see you as teacher of the year, Fig. I don't think you have the necessary social skills, but I really appreciate your desire to protect me, and you owe me $620."

"Really? How can you be thinking about that at a time like this?"

"You are not the only one with overactive logic circuits, Fig. However, as you are paying for our vacation in Heidelberg, before I'm locked up for twenty years, let's call it even Steven."

"Heidelberg, what are you talking about, and aren't you scared of Barrett's threat?"

"I am scared, but we are not beaten yet. The best defense is offense."

"How do you mean?"

"If we can find enough dirt on Barrett in the *Landesbank*, in Heidelberg, it will be a stalemate and we can work from there."

"You are full of Lutheran surprises. OK! Fuck Barrett and the horse he rode in on. Let's take the fight to him. He sounded like a real creep."

CHAPTER FIFTY

Sally and Bruce in room 319. Homeland Security, Washington, DC.

A nervous Fig had called Bruce to tell him about the threat to Jamie from Barrett. They now agreed that Barrett was probably pulling the strings, then Turner walked in and said, "I was just passing by and was wondering how you guys are doing with Newton? I just got a call from Barrett, and he's not amused that Newton is still out there causing trouble with his damned website."

Sally nearly jumped to Fig's defense. She now could see that Fig was many times a better man than this creep. She thought, "He's a parasite living off of the backs of others, while assuming no risks himself."

Bruce noticed her reaction, and said, "We know

where he's staying right now. We even know his room number. Interestingly, the Bailey woman is staying in a hostel a mile away, so maybe they aren't a couple after all."

"Or maybe they just aren't ready to settle down, but I think Newton has a thing for her," said Sally.

"How do you know that Sally, if you've never met them?"

"Just call it a woman's intuition."

Turner said, "You are probably right. They've been working together for weeks. Both single and one thing leads to another."

"It does, Jim, said Sally, looking at Bruce with doe eyes."

Turner ignored her calling him Jim and asked for the address of the motel and the room number.

"What's your plan, Jim, do you want me to pay them a visit?" said Sally.

"No! I'll deal with it, but you've both done great work."

"The pay is great too, boss," said Bruce.

"I'll let you know when I need for you to proceed with further action on Newton. In the meantime there are plenty of other do-gooders to work on in room 301, Bruce."

"I'll get right on it."

"How about me?" said Sally.

"You can do whatever you want for now, on paid leave, until I have another task."

"Can you cover the cost of a show and a fancy dinner, Dr. Turner?"

"Sure Sally, modify your hours accordingly."

On that note, Turner left.

"Sally, why do you think he looked so agitated when I told him we know where he can find Fig?"

"Oh! I've seen that before. The cowards are always nervous before they call in a hit."

———

Meanwhile, Jamie and Fig were at the hostel sitting at the small Formica table covered with coffee cups, crumbs and Fig's computer, scratching their heads about how to deal with Barrett, and how he now appeared as their nemesis, the dreaded *Shelob*.

"At least we know who we are dealing with, finally," said Fig.

"Let's go over the timeline again, Fig. I know we've done it several times already, but we are missing something, and I want all our ducks in a row before we head for Germany. You said you were a thorn in the side of multiple industries due to the nature of your work, right?"

"Mainly because of my personal website and maybe our chlorine research, which seemed to upset Daryl Pickering."

"But they put up with you for nearly a year after Strickland arrived. You must have done something differently that triggered being fired?"

Looking at his phone calendar, Fig said, "I went to an ecology meeting in July, talked about the same old stuff, did a consultancy and attended several meetings with students in August. In September there was that weird meeting where I was invited to talk about my work in relation to reducing the need for animals in safety testing of chemicals, including drugs for human consumption. It was just a one off with a group supported by PETA. I didn't know them very well, many of whom were working at the EPA. The weird thing was how mad they got."

"What caused that?"

"They became really pissed off at my comments on the value of plant-based diets when it came to reducing animal cruelty and offsetting climate change. Some were almost foaming at the mouth. One guy dished out a public insult I know well, 'there goes Newton the philosopher again', said in a sneery voice."

"Really?"

"It started when I refused to eat meat at the official dinner in the evening. These are put on to bring people together and keep the meeting productive. It was laid on in a fancy hotel, at great expense, using grant money allocated for saving animals. But they were all eating beef, chicken, fish, shrimp, cheese, whatever, with that money set aside for saving animals. I couldn't understand it."

"It's not about logic, Fig. They see you as judging them, being holier than thou, plus the dairy industry hates vegans, too."

"Funny you should say that. I mentioned my going vegan in my newsletter a while ago, in response to which I got some really nasty letters from a group of New Zealand dairy farmers."

"In that case, let's go back to your network and assess everyone, even your supporters, for their potential interest in the food industry, animal cruelty and climate change. You pushed a button, somewhere, and it may be in the food industry, which brings Barrett into the picture."

"My savior, Charles Barrett, the CEO of one of the biggest food companies in the world, just threatened you with jail, Jamie. What the hell is he up to?"

"I'll see what I can find out about the guy," said Jamie, and off she went into the world of code, a world in which she felt in control of her life, because it was logical.

Forty minutes later, Jamie said, "Charles Barrett's company, Good Foods, Inc., is the biggest importer of beef from Brazil, where more environmental activists are killed every year than anywhere else in the world."

"So?"

"I know you think of yourself as a scientist, Fig, but in their minds, you are an activist who threatens their business. Furthermore, Good Foods, Inc. is one of the biggest sponsors of your institute."

"How are you handling all this, Jamie? You seem to be putting a brave face on things. I'd rather pull the plug on my work than have you treated badly."

Then Jamie's phone made an odd noise. She looked

down at the screen, and said, "A guy in a suit just broke into the honeypot motel room. Want to see what he looks like?"

"Damn, that's Charles Barrett. Who's that huge bouncer guy standing behind him?"

"No idea," said Jamie.

Fig picked up his phone and called Bruce, "Can you talk freely right now?"

"It's just Sally and me. What's up?"

"We had a visitor in the honeypot room."

"What a coincidence! We told Turner a couple of hours ago that you were staying there."

"She caught him on video, Bruce."

"Hang on, Fig," said Bruce, who went to his computer.

"Turner called Barrett after he left here. I guess Barrett really is your nemesis."

"That's what it looks like."

"I'd like to see that video, Fig. Can we meet up?"

"How about over lunch with Jamie and Sally?"

Jamie nodded agreement and said, "The diner near the Rachel Carson plaque, where we all first met, I liked that place."

Over lunch they compared notes, agreeing that it was Barrett who had entered the honeypot room."

"I checked Barrett's phone log just before coming here," said Bruce, "and he called both Chariton and Hotchkiss before he left for the motel."

"I guess *Shelob* is all three of them?" said Fig.

Sally said, "It's the six musketeers against the gang of three, and fuck them."

"Good name, Sally, but what are we going to do about it?" said Jamie.

"I have an idea," said Fig. "The modern mass food industry ships stuff all over the world, including pigs which spread the flu by the way, which uses lots of energy. They also burn fuels to make fertilizers and pesticides to support their unsustainable monoculture approach to agriculture. This would give Barrett and Hotchkiss a mutual interest in protecting the energy industry."

"Nothing new there," said Jamie. "It's well known that the beef industry in Brazil is causing loss of the Amazon rain forest, and you focused on it in your recent research. That may have gotten up Barrett's nose. Bruce, was that Hotchkiss standing behind Barrett in the doorway?"

"No! No idea who it was."

"Let me take a closer look at that video," said Fig. After a minute, he said, "No idea."

"Why would President Miller care about the food industry?" said Bruce.

"The importation of Brazilian beef has been ramped up in the US since he arrived in the White House. He eliminated the blockade on those imports put in place by the previous administration. He's pandering to his base, as usual."

They waited to see where Fig was going with this.

"What if Barrett of Good Foods, Chariton of World

Wide Oil and Gas, and Hotchkiss, the coal lobbyist thug in charge of Homeland Security, were all read the riot act about my work by President Miller. I'm sure he hates me calling him the now viral name, *The Ecocidal Fool.* I bet Miller told all three to clip my wings or be replaced by other Miller loyalists."

"Why would they care? They are rich men with other careers," said Jamie.

"Because such people love power," said Sally.

"So how do we take them down before I go to jail?" said Jamie.

"I think your idea is a good one," said Bruce. "Social engineering to find dirt on Barrett, which may lie in the vaults of the *Landesbank.* While you two are enjoying a German vacation, Sally and I will find dirt on Chariton and Hotchkiss."

"Then we make a deal," said Jamie. "A deal that closes down Turner's operation and slows down the demise of Fig's institute, while we work with *The Gang of Three* to find a way to make them look good in the eyes of the president."

"Boy," said Bruce, "I bet there were some shenanigans in that church of yours back in Mariposa. All sorts of social fun and games."

"They taught me well," said Jamie, with a smile.

"Could we talk a little more about your thoughts on the *Landesbank* link to Barrett?" said Bruce.

"I hacked into the bank a while ago," said Jamie, "and found Barrett has an account there, plus big bucks are being processed through that very bank for food supplies to US troops in Europe."

"And?"

"Furthermore," said Jamie, "there is a huge DARPA grant being processed through *Landesbank*, which finances Daryl Pickering's research. He's working in a contract research lab in North Carolina, and he was the guy who threatened Fig during that phone call at the institute when all of this started."

"He's the asshole who threatened my salary if I didn't downplay our latest research on chlorine toxicity," said Fig.

"Chlorine?"

"Just details right now, Bruce, but it would appear that all roads lead to Heidelberg."

"And what are your suspicions?"

"That Barrett and Daryl are skimming money from a military food budget as it passes through the *Landesbank*, under the cover of legitimate research."

"You know you are always taking a big chance when you hack into a bank, Jamie."

"I guess you're right, Bruce, but nothing ventured, nothing gained."

"The world of hackers is a close-knit group, Jamie, and I bet you were spotted by a friend of mine, an IT security contractor for several banks, including *Landesbank*. His name is Gerald White. We go way back, and a week ago he asked me about the possible identity of a hacker who recently hacked *Landesbank* in Heidelberg."

"Oh dear," said Jamie, "maybe Barrett wasn't bluffing."

"My friend, who we know as Whitey, said it was the first time he'd spotted such a penetration in that particular bank. He was just asking around because nothing was stolen or exposed, but he found a fairly well disguised backdoor and deleted it, he said."

"Maybe I'm not so clever as I thought," said Jamie.

"No! You are really good at what you do, but it is almost impossible to hide a backdoor from a white hat who knows their business."

"Do you think your friend might work with us, Bruce?"

"Not a chance, he is very risk averse, to the point of paranoia. That makes him a good white hat for the bank and a serious challenge to us."

"Can't we just go public on Turner's illegal scheme of targeting of eco-scientists?" said Fig. "Or I can throw in my chips, and find a new career?"

"No way," said Bruce, Sally and Jamie.

"Forget that, Fig. We owe it to Sophie to take these people down," said Jamie.

"These are powerful people," said Sally, "and one thing I learned from repo work is not to bring a knife to a gun fight. You'll need a damn big gun to bend these people to your will."

"Sally is right," said Bruce, "they would have us locked up in no time, while Barrett, Chariton and Hotchkiss would come out smelling like roses, saying they'd unearthed some terrorists and saved the day."

"Then our best weapon is information with proof that will stand up in court," said Fig.

"Then it is time to risk some social engineering," said Jamie. "I bet that guy in the movie, *Catch Me If You Can,* would be managing the *Landesbank* by now. Let's assume there is a link between Barrett and a scam in that bank and pay them a visit."

"Great idea," said Fig. "I'd like a vacation, now that Bruce isn't recording every time I go the bathroom. How would you like a trip to Germany, Jamie?"

"Only too happy to oblige, boss."

"OK! Let's see what we can dig up in Heidelberg."

"If you find incriminating evidence, how do you plan to expose it to the court of public opinion?" said Bruce.

"If we get what we need, which is still a long shot, I'll call a journalist friend of Ray's, Jason Buno. He said he would be interested in publishing our story in his newspaper."

"Meeting's over," said Jamie, "don't forget your action items."

Fig said, "I'll buy two open return tickets to Heidelberg. I assume you have a current passport, Jamie?"

"Of course, and I've always wanted to see the biggest wine barrel in the world, again. What is your oh so logical plan of action when we get there Fig?"

"I'm taking a leaf out of your book, Jamie. I'm following a hunch. No plan, and if it leads nowhere, we'll at least have a vacation."

"Bruce, can you let Turner know we are going to Heidelberg?" said Fig.

"It might give Barrett and Daryl time to hide all the evidence."

"It might just cause some panic," said Fig, "and there is nothing like panic to cause mistakes."

"In that case, I'll keep tabs on the *Landesbank* when you arrive in Heidelberg to look for signs of panic," said Bruce.

"I thought you said it's risky hacking into banks," said Sally.

"Don't worry. Whitey is good but he's not as good as I am, and in no way is he a match for Jamie, even though he spotted her backdoor."

Jamie smiled at the compliment.

"By the way, Jamie, how did you hide that backdoor?"

"I just disguised it as an equipment accounting program that would normally be running on any bank server."

"I might be able to give you some tips on that, as I specialized in banks for a while."

"Why was that?"

"Money is dangerous," said Bruce, "and when I was black hat I didn't want to become involved with the mob by accident, so I studied banks in order to keep a safe distance. The real power of the Internet lies in information, and knowing which dark alleys not to wander down."

"I never thought about it that way," said Jamie. "I guess it's like an endless city."

"While you are on vacation in Germany, guys, I'll see

if Sally and I can turn Barrett's dirt-digging machine into his worst nightmare," said Bruce.

"But what can I do to help?" said Sally.

"Could you keep an eye on the whereabouts of Barrett, Hotchkiss and Chariton for a few days, to see who meets with whom? They all live in DC and I can send you their home addresses."

"Sure thing, Bruce. Anything to save the planet for your grandkids."

CHAPTER FIFTY-ONE

"Here we go, boss," said Jamie, as the plane taxied toward the runway, "off on another adventure. This is the best job I ever had, and the most frightening, but definitely more fun than working in a bar all night or waiting tables. Do I have to fill out an expense claim for this trip?"

"Sure, and could you submit it to Fred?"

"It's been ages since I had a real vacation," said Jamie, "and whether we find anything useful or not, I plan to enjoy it."

"By the way, I forgot. Bruce called to say he found some interesting dirt on Hotchkiss. He's a real piece of work, like all the people in Miller's cabinet. According to Bruce he is ruthless when it comes to getting his way, which includes supporting any efforts to curry favor with Miller."

"Thus Sophie's demise, I guess," said Jamie.

"Bruce said Hotchkiss and Chariton talk a lot on the phone."

"Looks like Barrett has some feathered friends who flock together. We are up against real criminals, Fig. I know I don't look scared, but I'm actually terrified. I really have no interest in going to jail, or for you to stop your work protecting the environment."

"Wait a minute, Jamie, there's more. Sally told Bruce she'd followed Hotchkiss and Chariton to a restaurant and she overheard Hotchkiss say that they should fire Barrett. He said they should find a replacement if Barrett doesn't shut me down in the next few days. Sounds like Barrett is on probation, Jamie. At least we have real friends. That is one of our strengths, so you are not alone, so don't worry, you'll be fine, Jamie, I'm sure."

"Thanks, Fig. I appreciate it. I guess I knew what I was doing. But I still can't work out how they linked my penetration of the *Landesbank* to me, personally, with sufficient evidence for Barrett to threaten me with legal action."

"They still could be bluffing, Jamie. Don't forget. It's what these people do, spin and lies."

As the plane reached cruising altitude, Fig said, "I thought you were enrolled in a web design program, in Burlington? And how are Edith and John, by the way?"

"One thing at a time, Fig. I put that degree on hold. It was just backup in case I can't make it as a hacker. I called Edith yesterday, and she was relieved to hear from me. I couldn't reach John, but Edith said he's fine. I told her my job was taking me to Germany, and I would call from there. Life is so much easier without Humperdinck on our trail. I feel almost normal, not like a fugitive at all."

"Bruce seems to be in awe of your hacking skills, Jamie, and when it comes to hacking, I don't think he is any kind of pushover."

"What do you think of Sally and Bruce together? They both seem to like each other, but they come from different planets."

"I'm pretty dumb in that respect, but I suspect Bruce may be the best thing that ever happened to Sally, and *vice versa*."

"It's so good to see it when that happens." On which note Jamie blushed and Fig pretended not to notice. They had two uneventful but exhausting flights, including one overnight flight to Frankfurt and a connecting flight to Mannheim, the nearest airport to Heidelberg, which arrived on time, in bright sunshine, at 2:15 p.m.

They shouldered their faithful backpacks and headed for passport control, where they were cleared without incident. However, as they approached the exit Jamie spotted a young man with a sign for Dr. Fig Newton. "It's a limo driver, Fig. I see you know how to impress a girl, I mean your employees."

They approached the guy, who said, "Dr. Newton and Ms. Bailey, I presume?"

"I didn't order a limo," said Fig.

"I was instructed to pick you up, compliments of

Landesbank. I was told they were expecting you on this flight."

Not knowing what to do, Fig and Jamie stared at each other.

"I'm Friedrich, your limo driver, here by special request of Dr. Charles Barrett. You look concerned but you need not be. I'm here to deliver you to your hotel."

"I'm not sure about this," said Jamie, "do you think it's safe, Fig?"

"Most certainly you will be safe and well cared for. Dr. Barrett is one of our oldest and most respected customers. I know him well. He asked us to look after his esteemed visitors. At which hotel are you staying?"

"I don't know," said Jamie.

Handing Jamie a small nicely wrapped package, Friedrich said, "Perhaps this will put your mind at rest. It is a little gift from Dr. Barrett. He warned me that you might be a little hesitant at first, and that this might clear things up. In fact, he said it would clear lots of things up if you know how to interpret it."

Jamie opened the package and started to laugh. She handed a beautifully leather-bound little book to Fig, who just looked confused.

"It's OK, Fig. It's safe to go with Friedrich. Thank you, Friedrich. Which way is the limo?"

"Come on Fig. Trust me," said Jamie, as he stood there, apparently glued to the spot staring at the book, while Jamie and Friedrich headed for the exit.

"We are staying at the MH Heidelberg Hotel."

"I'm sure you are tired from your flights, and it is not

far to Heidelberg. While you are here don't miss the *Großes Fass.* It's the biggest wine barrel in the world. You can see it at the castle, where you can also learn about the long history of our town. How long are you staying, by the way?"

"It depends," said Fig.

Friedrich dropped them off at the hotel with a parting message.

"Herr Dr. Barrett asked me to invite you to join him for dinner at six. This will give you time for a short nap to overcome some of your jet lag."

"Where should we meet him?" said Jamie.

"He asked that I pick you up here, if you accept. I will need to be here fifteen minutes to six to reach the restaurant on time. Do you accept or are you too tired? I'm sure Dr. Barrett would understand and make arrangements to meet you tomorrow."

"Of course we accept, Friedrich," said Jamie. "We would be delighted, and thank you so much for your kindness."

Once installed in their rooms, cleaned up and showered, they had time to walk around before dinner. Fig asked what the meaning of the book was, but all Jamie would say was, "You'll see, so stop worrying. Trust me, Fig. Please!"

"But I haven't read this ancient book, so how am I supposed to know what it means?"

"You've had your head buried in science all your life. Time to widen your horizons, and enjoy the mystery in the meantime. Let's take a walk. We can sleep later."

They strolled along the Neckar river, to the *Bismarck-platz* Park, and all the while Fig was wondering what the hell was going on. He knew it was useless to try to get it out of Jamie, she was clearly enjoying the mystery too much.

"I thought you would be nervous to meet Barrett, and I guess we have plenty of questions for him over dinner, if I can resist killing the bastard," said Fig."

"Fig," said Jamie, giving him one of those unsettling stares, "we need to play dinner carefully. Barrett flew here to meet us after breaking into the honeypot room, in addition to threatening my freedom, based on my *Landesbank* hack."

"Yes!"

"We have to present a confident front, as he doesn't know what we have on him, which right now is nothing, but he doesn't know that."

"Catch me if you can, right?"

"Right."

"Barrett has openly invited us to dinner in a public place, so let's enjoy dinner, while we listen and learn. We may be negotiating my freedom against your love of the Biosphere, Fig, which isn't a deal I like, though I suspect something completely different is going on."

"Why do you say that?"

"The book, Fig, the book."

"Yeh! Right. The book."

"Stay calm and analytical in the way only you know how."

At five forty-five sharp the limo pulled up driven by a

smiling Friedrich, who said, "Dr. Barrett was delighted that you accepted his invitation." They arrived at a classy hotel, the bell hop invited them in and then passed them on to the *maître d*, who escorted them to Dr. Barrett's table in a private room.

"Boy! This is one fancy place," said Jamie. "Enjoy yourself, Fig, you are not alone anymore, you have the other five musketeers on your side, remember, including *Mata Hari*."

Fig just grunted.

They were in a perfect dining room with beautiful hangings, silver tableware, and everything one would require of a delightful German dinner when no expense was spared.

A smiling, immaculately-dressed Charles Barrett stood to greet them.

Fig walked up to him, did not shake his profered hand, and said, "Did you kill my cat?"

Jamie was horrified but said nothing.

"Most certainly not, Dr. Newton, I love cats. Is this how you always introduce yourself at dinner? You accepted. I'm delighted that you did, and I repeat, I did not kill your cat, but I suspect I know who did."

Fig, looking confused, turned and looked at Jamie who had a face-splitting grin.

"Until recently, Dr. Newton, or may I call you Fig, I was unaware that you had a cat. However, I've been an admirer of your research for many years. I'm sorry for your loss, and I know I can help you to get to the bottom of this. But first, I think you should introduce me to your delightful companion, as we've never met. I think dinner, a glass of wine, and some explaining would help to clear things up."

"I loved that cat."

"I understand and no offense taken, but who is this beauty? Good evening! Jamie Bailey, I presume?"

"I'm so pleased to meet you, Sir Percy," at which Barrett burst out laughing, and Fig said, "What did you say?"

"Take care, Dr. Newton, this young lady is dangerous, but I have things I need to tell you and things with which I'm hoping you could help me."

The waitstaff suggested they take their seats, with Fig sitting opposite Barrett. The wine service arrived promptly. After a pregnant silence, Barrett said, "Please call me Charles and let me explain what is going on, though I suspect Jamie, if I may call you that, has already twigged? I'm sure you were both surprised to be greeted by Friedrich at the airport. He is a delightful young man, and I was sure he would manage to put you both at your ease."

"I thought Fig put it on to impress me," said Jamie.

"That would have been an excellent plan, Dr. Newton," said Barrett with a smile. All the while Fig felt awkward, embarrassed and confused.

"Why did Jamie call you Sir Percy?" said Fig.

"I'll come to that, but first I'm sure you remember the letter I sent to Strickland in your defense months ago."

"I appreciated it at the time, but now I don't know

what you are up to, and I did not appreciate you threatening Jamie."

"Please be patient, Dr. Newton, and trust Jamie."

"Just call him Fig, Charles, I'm sure he won't mind when he understands what's going on."

"I learned through the grapevine that Strickland was out to get you fired, and I was sad when I heard you had been fired, in spite of my letter. There are terrible forces at work in America today, and all the evil flows from the White House."

"I thought you were at the back of my firing and the downgrading of the institute," said Fig, "but you aren't?"

"Not at all, but I know who is. First let me explain why we are in Heidelberg. I suspect that in your case you think it is due to a little detective work to find dirt on yours truly, with the help of your black hat companion."

Jamie bowed to Charles, and said, "Employee and I deny everything."

"In that case," said Barrett, "a little bird told me that Fig suspected I am laundering money through the *Landesbank* via connections with my company and food supplies to our troops, possibly with the involvement of a DARPA grant to Daryl Pickering. Is that correct?"

Fig nodded his head in baffled agreement.

Barrett said, "That was an ingenious but incorrect conclusion. It is true that I pass funds through the *Landesbank* and come here frequently, but it is due to a highly confidential matter. I can explain, but I must first have your promise of confidentiality. Perception is everything in my business, as is honesty in yours, Fig."

"Yes!" said Fig. "I promise not so share what you have to say."

"You probably both know that I was in the military about thirty years ago, but you may not know that I was stationed here, in Heidelberg. To cut a long story short, I was young, and I got a young lady pregnant. We knew we were unsuited for marriage, so I agreed to support the child, my son, who you have already met."

"Friedrich?" said Jamie, in surprise. "He's delightful."

"Yes, Jamie."

"Why all the cloak and dagger stuff and what the hell is that book about?" said Fig.

"Fig, your patience will be rewarded, and I am sure you will be happy with my explanation, but please give me time."

"OK," said Fig, taking a gulp of his glass of wine.

"As I said, in my business perception is everything, which includes both Good Foods, Inc. and my recent position at the EPA. If people in my church learned I'd had a child out of wedlock there would be hell to pay. My wife knows all about it, and she loves Friedrich as a stepson. But Friedrich is German speaking and a more remote part of our lives. He has his own family, and my financial support has helped him make his way."

"Why's he driving a limo? Is that his job?" said Fig.

"He agreed to drive the limo as part of our plan to get you here for dinner before you decided to kill me, before I had a chance to explain the truth of my actions, Fig."

"I considered it," said Fig.

"I'm sure you did, but Friedrich is actually on the Faculty of Mathematics and Computer Science in the local university maths department that is respected worldwide."

"Is he really?" said Fig. "He acts like a completely normal person. I wish I could pull that off so well." At which Jamie and Charles Barrett laughed, and the ice was finally broken.

"We shall be discreet, Charles, in fact this conversation never happened, right Fig?" said Jamie.

"Right, but who killed Sophie and who has been hounding us for weeks?"

"All will become clear, Fig," said Charles. "But first we should enjoy our meal and talk of more enjoyable matters. It is important that you trust me, which I can see Jamie already does."

"If Jamie trusts you, Charles, then so do I," said Fig, looking more relaxed.

"It's a long story, which I can tell you both over lunch at the castle tomorrow. First, I think you need a good night's sleep, and Fig needs to become familiar with *The Scarlet Pimpernel*."

"I loved that book as a teenager," said Jamie, "as did all my friends."

"It's very much a book for girls," said Barrett. "I'm sure you will both enjoy a visit to the *Großes Fass*."

Following dinner and a pleasant walk back to their

hotel, Fig and Jamie settled down for a recap of what they had learned.

"Charles is working in disguise, like the main character in that book, Fig. It's the only way he can operate. I'm sure he has to have a solid disguise to fool Chariton and Hotchkiss."

"Okay!"

"Like Sir Percy Blakeney, he has to live the part. No half measures. Let's start by reading it together in the morning, after an early breakfast. I suspect Charles Barrett is a remarkable man, Fig."

"I hope you're right."

"Why not give Bruce a call and see what he has on Barrett, to set your mind at rest?" Fig pulled out his phone, not a burner for a change, and called Bruce's private cell.

"Hi Bruce, we were wondering what you found out about Barrett. He sent a car to meet us from the *Landesbank*, and we are concerned about our safety. It was really weird."

"Not a lot, Fig."

"What's not a lot?"

"He's only worth $23 million, which for a CEO of a major company is par for the course. I couldn't find any offshore accounts. He has a PhD in marine biology, but he built his fortune in the farming industry working for his dad. He became CEO of the company only a few years ago. He was raised in a mid-western family of Methodists, no police record, but to build such a reputation in agribusiness he must be a tough cookie."

"Is there more?"

"He was a deacon in his church before moving to Washington for his current post, which was recommended to Chariton by President Miller. Solid family background, three kids that we know of, and just one odd thing."

"What's that?" said Fig.

"He didn't want to go into the family business. He wanted to be a marine biologist, he even got a doctorate in the subject, but was talked out of it as a career. How, I don't know. He has a clean record, unlike Chariton and Hotchkiss."

"But his company owns some of the worst pig shit lagoons, cattle feedlots and chicken houses in the business," said Fig.

"That's just par for the course in that world," said Bruce, "but there is something odd about that, too."

"Why do you say that?"

"He has been quietly expanding their investment in small family farms, specifically organic farms that sell locally. How weird is that Fig?"

Fig told Jamie everything Bruce had found out, and asked her, "How weird is that for a company built on factory farms, Jamie?"

"Not weird at all for Sir Percy Blakeney," she replied.

CHAPTER FIFTY-TWO

Mid-morning the next day, Friedrich pulled up to a parking spot in the old town with Jamie and Fig, as they planned to take a walk around the shops. This was to be followed by a trip to the castle on the funicular railway. "There is plenty to see," said Friedrich, "including some excellent shops and cafes."

"Let's come back here before we leave, to buy some presents for Bruce, Sally, Ray and Yolanda, and my kids, too," said Jamie. "Come to think of it, Fig, you never talk about your sons. Why is that?"

"I love them, Jamie, I enjoyed raising them, and I'm very proud of all three, but I don't think about people very much. It may be an Asperger thing?"

"Well, you need to work on that, Fig." said Jamie, with a frown.

Then Friedrich said, "We shall meet my father at the funicular and explore the castle, where I'm sure you'll be impressed by the *Großes Fass*. Papa said the castle was similar to the EPA in many ways."

"What does that mean?" said Fig.

"I'm sure he'll explain when he meets us at midday. Could you be back here at 11:45?"

As Fig and Jamie started wandering around the old town, Fig said to Jamie, "I have one advantage over Sir Percy Blakeney."

"And that is?"

"He had to hide his true identity from his wife, and it was agonizing for both of them. At least I don't have that."

"That's the best part of the story, for a girl. All that raw emotion, not your cup of tea, I'm sure."

"It was a great story, Jamie. Except for the constant agonizing of his wife, that went on and on."

"Anyway," said Jamie. "This whole trip has turned into an adventure and a mystery tour. Thank you so much, Fig."

As they approached the limo, after their walk, Friedrich appeared, and Jamie said, "We really appreciate your kind hospitality, Friedrich, and I have a question. Isn't your father a businessman against his wishes?"

"You have been doing some research, I see. That's correct, he wanted to train as a marine biologist, but his sense of responsibility for his family business pulled him away."

On the way to the lower funicular, Friedrich and Fig talked mathematics, to then receive a hearty greeting from Charles Barrett, who was immaculately dressed as usual.

"Friedrich, I know this was a surprise visit, you are welcome to join us, unless you have lectures to attend to?"

"No! Papa, I cleared my desk and schedule for the next few days. This is a special treat for me, to see you for so long. Heinrich is standing in for me on the only lecture I couldn't cancel."

"In that case, Friedrich, could you clarify the role of Daryl in all of this, for Fig? Their relationship didn't get off to a good start."

"You know Daryl Pickering, the guy who threatened my paycheck?" said Fig, in surprise.

"I know him well, Fig. Daryl is a little hot headed, and he is extremely protective of our work together and of Jeff. He thought your work on chlorine was a threat. He has worked on cholera for years and lost several friends to the disease. Chlorine has been a godsend to cholera prevention. That's all that was about, but for you, I understand, it was a difficult moment."

"You can say that again. Strickland used it as one justification for firing me."

"I'm sorry to hear that, but I think you and Daryl would get along fine, Fig. He also has a love of network mathematics. I'll introduce you to each other when the opportunity arises. Under better circumstances."

"I guess we got almost everything wrong," said Fig. "We thought your dad was the evil spider, *Shelob,* at the center of a web designed to entrap and silence environmental scientists."

"Then my disguise is perfect," said Charles. "And it has to be if we are going to fight the edicts of President Miller."

On the way up in the funicular, Charles took Fig aside, and said, "In order to understand what I'm attempting, which included my attempt to protect you, by the way, you have to understand the powers that be and the depth of their corruption. All your problems started with President Miller, who cares nothing for your work. In fact, he cares nothing for the environmental damage that is being done by worldwide human activity."

"So you are fighting a clandestine resistance?"

"Exactly, and it's not easy. That said, this castle has been destroyed multiple times, just like President Miller is destroying the EPA, amongst other government institutions. Some of us are setting up resistance on the inside, but it is a delicate process. If we are spotted, we are replaced overnight. It reminds me of what happened when the Nazis invaded France."

"How come?"

"Wait a minute, Fig. We get off here, but let's you and I meet for a few more minutes to finish this story. It's important."

"OK."

Charles said to Jamie and Friedrich, "Could you start your tour, and we'll catch up in a few minutes."

"Of course," said Jamie.

Friedrich said, "We will see you in the castle."

After finding a quiet alcove, Charles said, "Well, Fig. When the Nazis invaded France, the population broke into four distinct groups, as it has at the EPA in response to Miller's appointment of his lackey, Chariton. The first group tried to stop the Nazis with any weapons they had, even pitchforks. They were dead and gone in a day. The second and largest group just wanted to survive, so they kept their heads down and hoped it would go away."

"And the third group?"

"The collaborators! In the EPA they are the people appointed by and who suck up to Chariton. They are destroying environmental regulations, one after another, at an astonishing rate. In the case of the Nazi collaborators, many of them were killed by the fourth and last group."

"The resistance fighters?"

"Yes Fig! And much of their work had to be done under cover of darkness or with a suitable disguise. It was a life and death situation for those brave men and women. But in our case, in the short-term, it is about the life and death of the EPA. In the long term it concerns the life and death of the Biosphere, the richness of the Biosphere as we know it today."

"And that is why you needed to fool me, for me to understand the lengths to which I would have to go to work with you?"

"Exactly, Fig, and now let's go enjoy the castle."

"Wait a minute," said Fig. "There is more than one

way to work for the resistance, in the case of the EPA. You could leave, if you provide a service that will be needed by the invaders, such as legal. Or you could stay in the hopes of preparing for the storm to pass, rescuing important documents, and such, or maintaining critical research equipment."

"That's true, Fig."

"You can, of course blow up bridges, which in your case, Charles, are your clandestine attacks under cover of the pretense of being a collaborator. Surely a dangerous approach as you will be seen as a collaborator by your friends, maybe for the rest of your life. In fact, that is why *Mata Hari* was executed by the French. They mistook her for a German spy. I'm sure you thought about this before taking the position under Chariton?"

"I did Fig, and I struggle with it every day. We can talk about it some more, later, but first let's go enjoy the castle."

After an interesting tour, including admiring the biggest wine barrel in the world, they returned to the old town for a lunch reservation. Charles Barrett had booked a small separate room again, for privacy. The ambiance was that of an old French bistro crossed with a *bierhalle.*

Fig and Jamie were impressed by the kindness of Charles Barrett and his son. The meal started with stan-dard German fare, including a stein of beer for Fig and a small glass of local red wine for Jamie. Charles and Friedrich confined themselves to water, both exclaiming they had work to do and were, unlike their guests, not on vacation.

As they were enjoying a coffee after the meal, as a "*digestif*," Charles said, "I need to continue my saga, Fig and Jamie, so you know what this is all about."

"Please go on," said Jamie.

Charles said, "President Miller requested that Alec make me his second in command. I've no idea why, because he doesn't even know me. It was probably on the advice of some lobbyist, but it was hard to reject, especially when I saw the ongoing destruction of the EPA by Chariton, a horrible man. You might think, Fig, that I was insane to work for the guy."

"But that was the only way you could see to resist his changes, right?" said Fig.

"Yes!" said Charles. "And, by the way, the money for Friedrich's work with Daryl on the DARPA grant is funneled through the *Landesbank* for historical reasons. It has nothing to do with me, it was just a coincidence. Before the military pulled out, they made extensive use of that bank for work in Germany and saw no reason to change it."

"So when we found that both you and DARPA were involved with *Landesbank*, for reasons of which we were unaware, we assumed you were doing some bad shit, excuse my French," said Jamie. "I guess I'm picking up some bad habits from Fig."

"Yes, but the beauty of it is that it brought us together today. You've probably realized that I hope to recruit you both to my cause."

"I do have two questions," said Fig.

"And they are?"

"Who killed Sophie and why did you break into the honeypot room?"

"Sophie's death was almost certainly carried out under orders from Bill Hotchkiss. I found out that James Turner would occasionally bypass me and make requests of Hotchkiss. They both think me too soft, an impression I attempt to hide, but not always successfully."

"And the honeypot room?"

"I was coming to have this very conversation, and in order to protect you from Hotchkiss, if necessary."

"So you are running a one-man resistance?" said Jamie.

"I do have some support, but I have to take care not to expose my true objectives, which is where I would like to make some suggestions to you Fig."

"OK!"

"You have been tackling this problem through scientific work on trophic cascades, catastrophic damage to food chains, resulting from human activity. You have also demonstrated that these catastrophes, even species extinctions, can be predicted, and thus might be prevented. Right?"

"Exactly, but no-one is listening."

"That's because it's not only a science problem, Fig. It's a people problem, the same problem you have with trying to get people to eat less meat. When you mention you are vegan, they get defensive or angry, right?"

"They sure do."

"Your mathematical modeling is brilliant, but you are applying it to the wrong network. You need to model the behavior of humans, the super predator in the system, in order to find points where effective ameliorative changes can be made."

"My model found you, Charles, putting you at the center of the web, but it was wrong."

"No, Fig." said Jamie. "It was right. It found *The Scarlet Pimpernel*, the real spider at the center of the web. Furthermore, Charles is a classic gateway vertex, he links large disparate groups, such as the EPA, DHS and the environmental activism community, while the information flow through that vertex is relatively low. Your graph theory worked perfectly. And here is your *Shelob*, sitting right in front of you offering you a job, and a chance to really improve things."

"You seem to have another enthusiast for your work, Fig, and you too, Jamie, would be a valuable addition to my company, if you are interested. This is a battle of wits in which the Internet plays a key role. Remember, my goal is to convert Good Foods, Inc., into a purveyor of truly good foods, and to end the horrors of factory farming."

"I'm all for that," said Fig."

"Don't underestimate the magnitude of the task, but let's discuss the matter of your employment a little later, if you don't mind. There is a good reason for that, which will become clear later today. So I would like to know if you both could join Friedrich and I at the *Waldschenke*

Heidelberg Gasthaus later this afternoon. It's less than an hour's walk from your hotel and you could visit the *Stephanskloster* on the way. Once again, Fig will be in for a big surprise."

"I can't wait," said Fig.

"I can accompany you if you like," said Friedrich. "Please remember to dress in warm clothes, because it can be chilly at this time of year, sitting outside."

"Please join us, Friedrich. But only if you don't talk mathematics with Fig all the time," said Jamie with a smile, knowing they would, anyway.

CHAPTER FIFTY-THREE

As Jamie, Fig and Friedrich approached *Waldschenke Heidelberg Gasthaus Biergarten*, a classic German restaurant and beer garden, they found the outdoor facilities to be pretty busy. Then someone called out, "Hi Fig!" He turned and was surprised to find that he knew most of the people there.

"Hi Chris, what are you doing here?"

"Sir Percy will explain, then we can get together, he's over there." The tables were occupied by about twenty scientists Fig knew well.

Then Jamie said, "There's Charles."

Fig sat down opposite Charles, as Friedrich and Jamie joined them, and said, "What the hell is going on, Charles?"

"I think I know," said Jamie. "This is Sir Percy's Army of brave young men, though some aren't men, and some aren't so young."

"Exactly," said Charles. "I need to explain, then you can talk to your friends, Fig. I asked them to leave us alone for a few minutes, while I clarify some things. You look confused, my friend."

"Percy's Army?" said Fig.

"This isn't all of them. They are the ones with both valid passports and who could get away unnoticed."

"Before you explain, I have a few questions, if I may?" said Fig.

"Of course."

"I assume these are people you've already recruited to fight the attacks of President Miller on environmental regulations?"

"Most of them, it's true."

"You explained your threat to Jamie, with exposure as a black hat, but did you really need to frighten her to death?"

Jamie said, "May I take a stab at that one, Charles?"

"Certainly, go ahead, this is fascinating," said Charles.

"Because you were testing the depth of the effectiveness of your disguise. If you could fool both of us, as Turner's team was in pursuit, and be there to protect us if necessary, it was working. It would provide ammunition to convince Chariton and Hotchkiss that you are a dedicated anti-environmentalist?"

Nodding agreement, Charles said, "Next question, Fig, as I answered that one yesterday, and Jamie is correct. This is warfare, not child's play. The planet is at stake."

"How did you find and break into room 301, where Jamie set the honeypot trap?"

"Do you want to see your photo, Charles?" said Jamie, reaching for her phone.

Charles laughed at his own surprised expression, and said, "James called and told me about it, and he sounded nervous. I think he was worried Hotchkiss would find out and he'd have a dead Fig on his hands. The death of Sophie was already causing him trouble enough with Fred Sassy, and in spite of his bluster, James isn't a bad guy. He's just a simple guy who likes to follow orders, an increasingly common type at the EPA right now."

"Who was the guy with you, and what were you hoping to achieve?"

"I went there to protect you, Fig. I was concerned that Hotchkiss would send a couple of his goons, two of whom killed your cat by the way, and do you bodily harm. If I was there, you'd be safe. I called Hotchkiss for suggestions about what to do about your persistence, Fig, and he offered to have your hands smashed so you couldn't work on your website."

Jamie gasped and said, "Do you really think Hotchkiss would do that?"

"Absolutely he would. He's a crook with no conscience. He suggested I threaten you, Fig, by threatening Jamie, so I was forced to follow through. It worked in our favor in the end. Evil is like that, as good generally triumphs, if we don't just stand by, and we do the necessary work to prevent it."

"Damn!" said Fig, nonplussed.

"Fig, you have a lot to learn about us super-predators, and the sooner you learn the better. I can assure you Chariton would also have happily had your hands mutilated to earn brownie points with Miller. The name Chariton is from the Greek, by the way. It means benevolent, which Alec most certainly is not. Most of Miller's cabinet are crooks. I can't stand those people, and if anyone could expose my work it's Hotchkiss. He's sly, mean, selfish and intelligent. Never turn your back on him."

"And the thug standing behind you in the doorway?"

Charles laughed and said, "He's the motel manager. Nice chap, but kind of scary. I told him I was worried about you, as you'd been depressed and that you might take your own life. I got that idea from a movie."

"*The Insider*," said Jamie.

"Not everything is as it seems," said Fig. "My friend is right. If something doesn't make sense, there is something I don't know."

"Any more questions?"

"May I go talk to my colleagues, now?"

"Before you do, I have an important request, Fig."

"Which is?"

"If you want to work for us, and I suspect you would enjoy it a great deal, please take your website down. It is like trying to stop the Nazis with a pitchfork. A nice solid pitchfork, but a garden implement nonetheless."

"Should I do that, Fig?" said Jamie.

"Please do, Jamie. I was getting tired of it because all

it did was piss off Miller, and achieve nothing else, that I could see. I'll use it for gardening in future."

"There you are wrong," said Charles. "It was an inspiration for your friends that played an important role in bringing us all together today. Go talk to them."

With a smile, Fig went around the group shaking hands meeting old friends, who welcomed him into Sir Percy's army. They had loads of questions about his recent adventures, admired Jamie, and told him that Barrett had kept them apprised of his escapades as best he could. They said they were more impressed by Jamie's hacking than by Fig's persistence. One lady scientist, Anne Jarvis, a theoretical physicist, suggested their story would make a great sequel to *The Insider*."

"Quite a woman you have there, Fig. I wouldn't try to keep any secrets from her, on the Internet anyway, if I were you," said a stranger.

"I'm Daryl Pickering, by the way. It's good to meet you, finally. Sorry I was so abrupt on that phone call with Jeff. I was trying to support him, as he was under tremendous pressure to downplay your data, and you were saying bad things about my baby, chlorine."

"No problem Daryl, Friedrich explained it all. It seems we have something in common."

"What's that Fig, may I call you Fig?"

"Of course, and what we have in common is poor social skills." The table agreed with enthusiastic laughter.

"Are you a member of Percy's army, Daryl?"

"No, I collaborate on a research program with

Friedrich, the one Jamie unearthed that's funded by DARPA. We've been working on it for years, and when you get a moment, I've hit an interesting snag with the maths, which you may be able to help with."

"That would be my pleasure. How about we get together back in North Carolina?"

It was a beautiful sunny day, the courtyard was surrounded by lightly wooded countryside, and *steins* of German beer were being delivered to every table, as prearranged by Charles Barrett. Fig was slowly learning to trust Charles, the modern *Scarlet Pimpernel of Eco-Defense*. He wandered back to join him, Jamie and Friedrich, and said, "How have you managed to keep all of these people a secret and what exactly are they trying to do?"

"They are working to slow down and, when possible, block Miller's attacks on environmental regulations and government-funded climate change research. They do this in any legal way they can."

"Such as?"

"Slowing down paperwork, objecting to certain decisions that leads to time-consuming meetings and memo wars. Some of them are remarkably creative. If one is found out by a Miller sycophant, they are gone within a week."

"Off with their heads," said Jamie.

"I've lost several that way," said Charles.

"Shit!" said Fig.

"This is war, Fig. Miller is destroying many agencies and the EPA is at the top of his hit list."

"So you are a modern Sir Percy Blakeney who acts the part of a Miller supporter?"

"Correct!"

"How do you live with your company's horrible feedlots, hog lagoons and chicken gulags?"

"Excellent question, Fig. If you take a careful look at what I've achieved since taking over as CEO of Good Foods, Inc., since my father retired a few years ago, you'll see that I've managed to create fifty-two organic farms, called research units, as a cover. They are all based on the ideas in that remarkable book, *The Omnivore's Dilemma*." I have a team working to convert factory farms to the kind of healthy balanced agriculture described by Michael Pollan. In the process they have to stabilize production, maintain low prices, and keep the board and our investors happy. No easy task, Fig."

"I believe it," said Fig.

"There is a bigger challenge and that is where you come in, my friend."

"How come?"

"If you join us, I want you to change your focus from the biology of intersecting food chains and trophic cascades, to the study of human motivation, and their networks of interaction. Your methods found me at the center of your web. It detected my influence on many groups. I think you called me a gateway vertex. I've been called many names, but never that."

Laughing, Fig said, "So?"

"I want you to find where in the behavior of our customers, the general public, ecologists and, most importantly, politicians, we can make subtle changes to our farming and marketing practices, such that we persuade people to eat less meat, and to eat local meat if they have to eat meat. I also want people to consume fewer dairy products, for a number of reasons of which you are aware, and to be more cognizant of animal cruelty in the farming industry. This would allow my business to slowly get out of the factory farming and dairy businesses for good. I hate it as much as you do, Fig, but once again, I have to be *Sir Percy Blakeney* when I sit in my company board meetings, as much as I have to live that disguise at the EPA, for as long as I manage to survive. No one must suspect that I'm *The Scarlet Pimpernel of Eco-Defense*."

Friedrich was smiling quietly to himself, proud of his American GI dad.

"Please help Papa," said Friedrich, "this whole business is wearing him out."

"And your wife," said Jamie, "is she in on the secret or is she more like Marguerite St. Just?"

"Doris has been in on my plans from the beginning. She is my greatest ally. Doris has told me for a while that I need people like you to help me slow the damage, and to be ready when the rebuilding comes, and most importantly to share the load of this clandestine resistance."

"No wonder Friedrich is worried about you," said Jamie. "It must be wearing you down."

"That's why I need the wonderful people here to pull it off until Miller leaves the White House. If he gets a second term, God forbid, we will have to stay hidden for another six years."

"In the room of requirement?" said Jamie, with a smile.

"And why didn't you follow your dream to become a marine biologist?" said Fig.

"I've always cared about the environment, and I was aware that the family business was built on disgusting feedlots, lagoons of pig excrement, burning of the Amazon rainforest, and millions of chickens kept under horrible conditions. By the way, I work to avoid importing any beef from Brazil that is a product of the Amazon deforestation. Furthermore, we were shipping pigs all over the world, which played a role in the continuing flu epidemics, and I've curtailed much of that. I realized I could do more for the Biosphere from the inside of our huge company, than by becoming a marine biologist, so I let it go, sadly, but I'm so glad I did. Look at what I created," he said, admiring his Percy's Army.

"No one realizes what I'm doing, which is why Chariton offered me the post of second in command at the EPA, where I can obstruct his work quietly, and sometimes effectively, unbeknownst to him."

"*He's nursing a viper in his bosom*," said Jamie. "I'm duly impressed, Charles, and I'm sorry we ever doubted you."

"And that was my greatest Pimpernel success, young lady. I fooled you both. No mean feat."

"Are you both willing to join me? We really need a good hacker, Jamie, and I don't care what color your hat is. Would you like the job?"

"What is the pay scale? Can you beat $30 an hour without benefits?"

"Let's say generous with full benefits and you can work from anywhere in the world. I'm sure we can find a way to give you a legitimate white hat for your cute head."

Jamie smiled, and said, "Thank you, Charles."

"We badly need environmentally conscious scientists to help guide our slow transition. The modern food industry reminds me of the Red Queen in *Alice in Wonderland*, running faster and faster, or in our case selling cheaper and cheaper, but getting nowhere."

"I hate that crap," said Fig.

"You have to understand that this can only be done slowly, Fig. Furthermore, if you join me you will be seen by your colleagues as a turncoat. It's a challenge we all face, as did *The Scarlet Pimpernel*"

Jamie said, "Don't worry about Fig. He doesn't even think about what others think of him, he thinks about science and his precious mathematics."

"But that is the change that needs to come over you, Fig. You need to take your remarkable mathematical modeling and apply it to human behavior. We need help finding areas, or gateway vertices to use your language, in which we can make a difference in the complex human food web, where humans are the problem. There are too many of us human super predators, unlike the trophic cascades being created by the paucity of wolves in Yellowstone and tigers in Sumatra."

"When it comes to trophic cascades, we humans are

the most devastating predators to arrive on planet Earth," said Fig. "and in our case, removal would lead to considerable ecological benefits."

"But are you prepared to join us in our fight for Biospheric health, Fig?" said Charles.

"Sir Percy Blakeney had a team of twenty brave souls, so how can I refuse?" said Fig.

"Then it will be a matter of logistics to bring you two on board," said Charles, with a broad beaming smile.

They started to look at the menus, when Jamie said, "One last thing, Charles, before we eat."

"That is?"

"Would you consider hiring Bruce and Sally, who are now on our team? We called them Humperdinck and Repo Lady until they defected to our side a few days ago. Without them we would never have encountered you or Friedrich. Come to think of it, they are probably a couple by now, who knows?"

"Remarkable" replied Charles. "I had no idea Sally had become a double agent, too." In response to which, Jamie gave him an odd look.

"Come to think of it," said Fig, "why did you hire those creeps, Turner and Strickland?"

"Because they are incompetent," said Charles.

"Any more questions before we enjoy lunch."

Jamie said, "Just one little one. How on Earth do you keep this a secret with all of us hackers out there?"

Then Fig's phone rang and the happy chatter by the whole group stopped.

"Who is this?"

Fig was quiet for a minute.

"Oh! Thanks. Yes, I'll pass it along to the group. I wish you and Sally were here, too."

Fig said, "That was Bruce Henley, who sends his regards, said he was enjoying our conversation, and told me that if I don't turn off my phone, especially the gps and audio, I'll be thrown out of Percy's Army in disgrace."

There was much general laughter and Jamie said, "Good move Sir Percy. You've recruited Bruce and Sally already. What exactly do you see is the use of a couple of hackers in your Army, as you work to keep environmental regulations away from Madame la Guillotine?"

"I think it is time for tit for tat," said Charles. "I want you, Bruce and Sally to replicate Turner's operation, to turn the tables on Chariton and Hotchkiss. My army will provide you with the names of Miller sycophants that are working to reverse the environmental protections of the previous administration. Your job will be to find dirt on them and take them down in the court of public opinion. No killing cats, mind you."

"If we find dirt and use it to manipulate them, won't we be just as bad as they are?" said Jamie. "Furthermore, by working for Chariton, aren't you validating his position as head of the EPA, one for which he is clearly ill-suited?"

"I've struggled with both of those difficult questions," said Charles. "I hate to say the ends justify the means. Maybe we can do it in such a way as to be kind rather than cruel. I think we need to revisit that one, or it won't feel right. For the better good is a dangerous slippery slope. We need an ethicist on the team."

"Bruce and Sally will continue to work as double agents?" said Jamie.

"As long as they can find a way to impair Turner's program, without being caught, otherwise I have plenty of work they can do for my company, as part of your team, Jamie."

"Any more questions? Fig, you look thoughtful." said Charles.

"I want to make a toast. A toast about where this all started."

Charles said, "Quiet everyone, please. Our newest recruit wishes to make a toast."

Fig stood and raised his *stein*, and said, *"To Rachel Louise Carson, and may the birds sing on forever,"* which was met with enthusiastic applause.

Once the applause died down, Daryl stood up and said he wanted to make another toast. This was greeted with enthusiasm, and he said, "I would like to make a toast to Jamie Bailey, for saving Fig's ass," which was met with laughter and applause, for which they all stood and raised their steins, embarrassing Jamie, immensely.

CHAPTER FIFTY-FOUR

Charles Barrett's EPA Office, Washington, DC. Barrett is on the phone.

"Bill?"

"Oh! Hi Chaz, what's up, I was wondering, as I hadn't heard from you in a few days? Any luck with Newton?"

"Your suggestion worked like a charm, Bill. Thanks a million. Newton caved pretty quickly, and the site is down."

"Permanently?"

"I think so, because I sweetened the pot. Carrot and stick, Bill, you should try it sometime."

"You cheeky bugger, but I'll let that go. I can tell you are pleased with your success. What was your approach?"

"I threatened Newton with sending the Bailey

woman to jail for hacking government sites, which could be as much as twenty years. That shocked the bastard."

"Good work, Chaz. And the carrot?"

"Both Newton and his hacker friend are coming to work for us, at Good Foods, with a salary they couldn't refuse."

"Even environmentalist do-gooders have their price it would seem. So much for their holier-than-thou attitude!"

"Don't we all?"

"Speak for yourself, Chaz, but I'm sure the President will be delighted. I'll let him know. Did you tell Alec already?"

"I left word on his answering machine, just before calling you."

"There was no need, Chaz, he's right here and he looks pleased. Good work, we knew you would come through, just don't be so soft on the creeps."

Charles put down the phone, breathed a sigh of relief, and said to himself, "I don't know how you did it, Percy?"

CHAPTER FIFTY-FIVE

Back in Jamie's hotel room in Heidelberg, Fig and Jamie were decompressing and preparing for a few days of real vacation.

"Say, Fig. Now we are about to become employees of Good Foods, is my employment at an end?"

"What?"

"Am I free to go?"

"Of course," said Fig, "but I was hoping we could work together a little while longer."

"Don't look so hangdog, Fig. You are a brilliant scientist and a complete chump. Why don't you kiss me for God's sake, and we'll see where that leads, or would you like to mathematically model it first?"

Later that day, while wandering happily around the town, holding hands, Fig said to Jamie, "Chariton and Hotchkiss still got off scot-free. It's not right. What can I do to avenge Sophie?"

"What would Rachel Carson do?" said Jamie.

"She'd write a book," said Fig.

"Well, there you have it, my friend."

Four months later, during their first real vacation together on the coast of Maine, Jamie said, "Fig, I just received an email from Indira."

"What does it say?"

"If you don't interrupt, I'll read it to you."

"Mum's the word."

"Dear Jamie, thank you so very much for my new car. I love her, and she has brought me lots of luck. She has taken me on some exciting adventures. I decided to sell the motel, and I've moved into a small apartment in Littleton, and guess what? I've met the loveliest man at the local Indian group meeting, and I know Ravi would approve.

By the way, I could tell you were a new couple, you can't fool my old eyes. It was the way you looked at each other.

Love and a million thank yous.

Come visit sometime.

Love,

Indira.

P.S. An important message for Fig. Please pass it on, even if you disagree, Jamie.

Dear Fig, please don't let Jamie push you around. She is a bit bossy with you sometimes. Push back and you'll both do fine.

Love,

Indira.

At which Jamie laughed out loud, and said, "Give me a kiss."

"Only if you ask nicely," said Fig.

"You're learning, my friend," said Jamie.

A moment later she said, "Please!"

ACKNOWLEDGMENTS

I want to thank Eric Wheeldon for saying years ago, "Kevin, I think you have a novel in you," otherwise, I would never have taken on the task. I especially wish to thank my sister, Marian, for a stalwart job of editing, correcting hundreds of grammatical errors, and telling me things like, "A woman wouldn't say that," or "A woman wouldn't say it that way." How was I to know? I'm a guy. Then Vellum for existing, a remarkable writer's tool. I also wish to thank Les Frye for a valuable suggestion concerning my cover design. I also thank Graph Online for their generous permission to use their software for Fig's work to track down "Shelob." Finally, thanks to my intrepid test readers, Sheelagh Anderson, Jessica (Pippa) Young, Nick (Nico) Young, Adelino (Alan) Martins, Donald Joyner, Maya Arnica, Tara (Repo Lady) House and Glen Roddell.

Dr. Kevin Thomas Morgan is a retired veterinary pathologist, research scientist, avid Ironman-distance triathlete and aspiring writer. He works on ways to help older people keep going to enjoy every day they are lucky enough to have. He does this by writing books, creating instructional videos, and giving inspiring talks to groups of seniors. His current interests include reading and learning to write. He enjoys solving problems to help people in pain. Kevin is an enthusiastic vegetable gardener and vegan, with considerable concern for the future health of the Biosphere and the role of climate change. Some of his work is designed to help people who, like himself, have aortic and other vascular diseases. He enjoys friends, family, his companion plants and animals, and not being dead for as long as possible.

ALSO BY KEVIN THOMAS MORGAN

How to Train for Aging

We Can't Eat Grass

The True Story of Plantar Fasciitis

Plantar Fasciitis Has The Wrong Name:

Find Peace of Mind in the Pool

Pain, Good Friend, Bad Master

Autobiography of a Happy Scientist

A Tiny House Fixed My Retirement Cash Flow

Aortic Disease From The Patient's Perspective

ALSO BY KEVIN THOMAS MORGAN

Surgery Recovery Guide

Body Meditation for Optimal Movement

Changing the Way You Move